THE PUPPET-MASTERS

BOOK THREE OF THE CLAN BRUJAH TRILOGY

Based on

VAMPIRE: THE MASQUERADE

By Tim Dedopulos

WORLD OF
DARKNESS

www.worldofdarkness.com

In loving memory of John Hodder and Ken Lacey—

Two truly gentle men who saw something in me long before I ever did. Without their kind and patient encouragement, none of this would ever have begun.

Myself when young did eagerly frequent
Doctor and Saint, and heard great argument
About it and about: but evermore
Came out by the same door as in I went.

With them the seed of Wisdom did I sow
And with mine own hand labor'd it to grow;
And this was all the Harvest that I reap'd—
"I came like Water, and like the Wind I go."
—The Rubaiyat of Omar Khayyam

Previously...

Theo Bell, enforcer for the vampiric sect known as the Camarilla, has been stripped of status and position.

Called to Minneapolis by his old friend Angus Abranson, he discovers a despicable slave ring operated by an alliance of Kindred and mortal criminals. When he rescues neonate Delphine Decourt and her mortal sister Nathalie from the clutches of the slave ring, and refuses to destroy them as threats to the Masquerade, he finds himself facing accusations from the local prince and from his superiors. The more he digs, the worse things become until he uncovers proof that his old friend Angus is an agent of the slave ring. Acting in self-defense, Theo has no choice but to destroy one of the only men on whom he thought he could rely.

Things go from bad to worse for Theo as the hidden puppet-masters of the slave ring reach out to destroy him. The prince and primogen of Minneapolis accuse him of murdering Angus and call a blood hunt, which quickly gets spread across the Midwest as Theo is stripped of his rank in the Camarilla and declared anathema. With only the Decourt twins, the anarch Kristine, and the Malkavian Itio Shima as help, Theo strikes out to clear his name. All the while, a dedicated agent of the slave ring, the Overseer Carnell, is hunting him.

Things come to a head in the industrial wasteland of Detroit, as Carnell lures Theo into a final showdown and uses his own dark powers to drive the former archon mad. Kristine and the twins abandon him to his fate and as the hunter's abilities wear away at Theo's sanity, his fate seems sealed.

At the last moment, Kristine offers Theo her aid, allowing him to gain an edge over Carnell and turn the tide of battle. His sanity eroding, Theo drinks deep of the Overseer's tainted blood until he has swallowed the man's soul entire.

Theo has saved his existence, but plunged himself into a mad fugue state from which there may be no escape....

Prologue

Masterworks

The room was *supposed* to be silent. Deep enough underground to keep the world at bay, it had been designed and redesigned by many different experts over the years. Several layers of protection insulated it from outside influences—noise, smell, vibration, everything. The latest door was constructed from layers of some new polymer or other, the sheets vacuum-separated so that absolutely no sound could get in.

When everything was properly locked down, a pack of rampaging war-ghouls tearing up the rest of the villa could go unnoticed inside. He hadn't even heard their screams as they'd died outside the door—and it had taken his associate over an hour to finish them off, as it turned out. In all, the laboratory had been soundproof for more than four hundred years. After the most recent round of improvements, it was supposedly guaranteed perfect to two hundred and fifty decibels.

The man swallowed his anger, and tried to ignore the small scratching, crumbling noise coming from the walls. Summoning all his concentration, he turned his focus inwards, so that the sound would just wash over him. In theory, anyway.

The grinding shouldn't have been distracting in the slightest—a fact that just aggravated him further, made his emotional balance even harder to hold on to. Whether it was rats gnawing at the insulation, the foundations shifting or even a team of sappers coming through the walls, the noise should have been beneath notice. Instead, it seemed to be inflaming his suddenly traitorous imagination. He imagined he could almost hear voices whispering behind the noise, muttering darkly about death, destruction, the end of everything. Every time he stilled his mind, the voices grew louder in the silence. It was intolerable. He hadn't been this sloppy since that ludicrous debacle in Caesaromagus.

He ignored a sudden urge to grind his teeth in frustration, and tried again to stop his mind from chattering. The whispers started up immediately. He stubbornly refused to translate the sound into words and just stared fixedly out of the blood-traced circle at the stone jars lining the far wall, seething at his own ineptitude.

Eventually, thirty-nine of the longest minutes he could remember came to an end. He permitted his muscles to unlock, stood up smoothly, and turned to look at the right-hand wall. There was no sign of any damage or disruption behind the shelves of tools and manuscripts, and the noise had utterly vanished. He allowed himself the luxury of a small growl—the period of silence was over—and then got back to work.

The cast-bronze altar in front of him was covered in a pure white cloth, woven from the spun fleece of previously unshorn lambs. Three candles dominated the center of it: one made of dog tallow, one colored yellow with sunflower petals, and one purchased on a Thursday by a blond-haired man. Everything else was ready and waiting on a small side bench. He picked up a small metal cigarette lighter, which had been taken from the hand of a week-dead corpse, and flicked the cog.

A surprisingly large flame sprang to life. He looked at it and smiled, amused as always, and lovingly ran the palm of his left hand slowly through the fire, savoring the brief warmth. Then he leaned forward and lit the candles. A vile stench filled the air, and he made a mental note to discipline the idiot who had selected strawberry potpourri for the Thursday candle.

He began an archaic chant. Ancient formulas and invocations rippled off his tongue as he picked a small brass pendulum off the bench. Still chanting, he dipped the pendulum into the candle flames, once into the sun, twice into the hound, and thrice into the thunder, savoring the mounting feeling of power. Then he laid the pendulum down in front of the candles, held his hands out over it, and started reciting an ancient blessing in a long-dead language.

The third word—"*Schempreshkorzash*"—got stuck in his teeth, coming out as a gargled croak. He blinked once, shocked and horrified, as a sudden trembling sensation in the region of his solar plexus warned him that the gathered power was already failing. After so many years, the ancient godling's name should have been no harder to say than his own. He quickly tried again, desperate to save the complicated ritual.

"*Schemprshhhrk—*"

The power drained out of the room like water down a drain. The man screamed in fury and rage, and savagely kicked the altar at the door. The candles and cloth fell to the floor, and the thin bronze cube flew across the room, crumpling as it smashed into the steel. Three months of preparation, and it was all ruined in an instant, fit only for destruction. A second kick scattered the bench and its now worthless contents across the room. He stomped over to the door, leaving the altar cloth burning merrily in the center of the circle of sigils, and wrenched on a plain robe of black cotton. Then he took several long, unneeded breaths and calmed his mind, distancing himself from his emotions. His anger receded to manageable levels. He wrenched the doors open and stepped out into the brightly lit antechamber.

Alexandra was there, sitting idly with an envelope in her hands. The girl looked up as the doors opened and smiled vapidly, full of implanted love. "There is a message for you, Lord. I understand that it is important."

He didn't even growl an acknowledgement, infuriated still further by the intrusion. He snatched the envelope from her, and ripped it open, letting it fall as he read the brief note inside. Fury boiled inside him, hot and sour, at its contents. How had this happened? Why hadn't he been told? There would be an accounting; right now. His vision seemed to swim for a moment, and a low snarl started deep down in his chest, seemingly outside of his control. Alexandra looked around, surprised.

He beckoned to her. "I need your assistance, girl."

She nodded, smiling again. "Oh yes, Lord."

"Remove your clothing, then join me in the laboratory."

"Of course, Lord." She started stripping. He left her to it and went back inside. The wool was still burning, fuelled by the candle wax inside it. The sickly stink was unpleasant, but it would do. Flame, for once, was simply flame. He selected a jar from one of the shelves, opened it, and took out a big handful of the powder inside. He flung it on to the fire, and the reek of brimstone filled the room, mingling with the nauseous stench of the Thursday candle. A moment later, Alexandra walked in, appropriately naked.

He nodded at her. "Close the doors, then come here and lie down inside the circle."

"Yes, Lord." She sounded slightly nervous, but she obeyed.

"Good. Now close your eyes. Do not fear girl, you will not be harmed. I give you my word." She did as she was told, the nervousness replaced with calm. He turned to another shelf and picked up a large, ugly dagger, forged from meteoric iron under starlight during the dark of the moon and quenched in the life's blood of thirteen baby girls. Standing outside the circle, he leaned over and silently hammered the dagger right through Alexandra's heart and into the floor beneath her. The girl convulsed once, then fell still, and the intoxicating scent of hot blood mingled deliciously with the sulfur.

He stood up straight again, hands spread wide.

"Mariel, in the name of our pact, I call thee!" The air shivered. "Mariel, with the blood of the innocent, I invoke thee!" A presence—unseen but not unfelt—gradually grew within the room, making his skin prickle. It was intoxicating. "Mariel, Knife of the Storm's Eye, I summon thee!"

The temperature in the room plummeted, the fresh blood suddenly steaming a little in the icy air. The girl's corpse opened its eyes, stretched languidly, and then sat up. It crossed its legs comfortably and looked round the room. Then it turned to him and spoke in a voice like razors: "Rodrigo? What the fuck do *you* want?"

He nodded in greeting. "Welcome, dread Mariel. I bring you the gift of this woman's soul, bound to her death by the Blade of Worlds."

The corpse grimaced. "Skip the tedious crap, will you? I'm busy. I'll take the girl on my way out. What is it? And what in the name of Lucifer is that disgusting smell?"

Rodrigo glared at the corpse, suddenly a little uncertain. "Oh Mariel, under the terms of our pact, you guaranteed to send me word of our minions."

The corpse sighed and rolled its dead eyes. "Your point being?"

"I should have been told of Carnell's death." He was so irritated that he realized he'd forgotten to be polite.

The corpse's eyes glowed with a flickering flame-light as it stared at him impassively. The moment stretched out. "I haven't had his soul," it mused finally.

"What do you mean?"

"I would have thought that was obvious, even to you. Your puppeteer did not come to me when he died. Someone else has eaten his soul, and I've been trying to find out who. The bastard owes me."

Rodrigo blinked. "Are you telling me Theophilus Bell *diablerized* Carnell?"

"Is that the fucker's name?" The corpse shrugged, the dagger twisting as it cut into the meat of the girl's breast.

"Why did you not tell me of the death at least?" He was having to fight hard to keep the rising anger out of his voice. "Our pact—"

"Shut up, leech." The words were like scalpels, slicing at his mind. Alexandra's corpse grinned nastily, a trickle of blood slipping from the corner of its mouth.

Rodrigo stared at it in amazed fury.

"That's better. Our *pact* ran until the end of days, Rodrigo. In case you hadn't noticed, that time is now upon us. My side of the contract is fulfilled."

"I don't—"

"Listen, vampire. Listen carefully. The dark realms are very, very busy right at the moment. I've got a thousand and one things to organize. The end is here, and I really don't have time to pander to your tedious bullshit any more. Our deal is concluded. If I was hungry enough, I'd shatter this stupid little ward you've got me in, rip your soul out of your withered cadaver, and suck the marrow from your bones for dessert. I can't be bothered, though. You don't have long left, and I can wait for the meager enjoyment your essence will bring me. Deferred gratification is the primary sign of intelligence, you know."

The room seemed to actually tinge with red as rage threatened to overwhelm him. "How dare—"

"Very easily, actually. I've had enough of this pointless shit. I'm off. If you've got *any* sense left in that dickless husk of yours, you'll leave me the fuck alone from now on. I don't have to eat you all at once." Alexandra's corpse started to lie down again. It paused suddenly, and looked round at him again, a mocking smile on its lips. "Oh yeah. Forgot to tell you. Carnell's dead.

Some soon-to-be-fucked asswipe called Bell drank him. See you real soon now, pal. Thanks for dinner."

The corpse slumped to the ground. Mould erupted all over it as the flesh started to liquefy. Alexandra's features slowly melted, and all over her body the skin withered and peeled back. Within moments, she was just a skeleton, a patch of slime, and a rather nasty smell.

Rodrigo howled his fury out at the room. He leapt at the stinking skeleton and smashed the skull into fragments under his fist. The crunch of bone felt pleasant under his skin, and he struck out again and again and again, punishing the girl's remains for the failures of the evening.

Within a minute, Alexandra was reduced to dust and crumbs. He looked around desperately for something else to destroy, before a hint of sanity prevailed, and he finally decided that it was beneath him. He buried his anger deep where it belonged, put the dagger back on the shelf, and headed out of the lab to get dressed.

Rodrigo sat on the balcony and looked out across the lush valley. The full moon was bright, and the forests around the villa rippled in a light breeze, a sea of silvered green. Beyond the valley's edge, the hills fell away to the city beneath. Myriad points of light twinkled in the distance, forming an impossible tapestry. It was a beautiful sight, and one that he usually savored. The modern world did have surprising moments of loveliness mixed in with its blunt ugliness. Even this late, São Paulo would be teeming with mortals going about their little lives, busily creating nightmares and wonders and other bits of tedium to inflict upon each other. It was the ultimate toy — a whimsy, when distraction was needed.

Insects and other creatures chattered noisily throughout the valley. The cicadas were particularly loud tonight, grinding away incessantly. They were the reason that he'd first soundproofed the laboratory—not because they threatened his work, but simply because they were an irritant that he could choose not to endure. He frowned, unhappy with the night's progress all over again.

A melodic female voice caught his attention. "I hear that talking to yourself is the first sign of madness."

He looked around and saw Claudia approaching along the balcony, her fingers trailing along the ornate stone railing, a ruby decanter clasped in her other hand. She was wearing a brilliant red dress tonight, a provocative fancy that might have been suitable for a peasant dancer had it not been made of the finest silks. He looked at her calmly, hiding his alarm at her implication. He hadn't been saying anything, had he? "Good evening."

She stopped by the table, turning to gaze out at the city. "Is it?"

He shrugged. "No. Not really."

"I suspected as much. Tell me."

The urge to gloss over his surprising ineptitude swept over him. He fought it back ruthlessly. This was neither the time nor the place. "I was conducting the ritual of the Soul Forge earlier."

"Yes. I thought it was due tonight."

"I had difficulty concentrating." He spoke to the marble table and its gold inlays, unable to meet her eyes. "On anything. My mind was wandering like a neophyte's. There was a noise too. It seemed to have words behind it, whispers suggesting that the final nights were coming."

She nodded. "The same sort of things that you were mumbling as I approached, then."

He finally looked up at her, seeing no judgment or contempt in her expression, just mild interest. "Was I really talking?"

"Yes," she said simply.

"Strange that I could not hear it myself."

"You said, 'The end is coming, the end; I can hear it; it comes for me.'"

Rodrigo frowned unhappily. "Yes, that's the sort of thing. Anyway, the noise—and the voices—vanished as soon as I no longer needed to be silent. However, when I then started reciting the invocations, I was unable to manage the word '*Schempreshkorzash*.'"

Claudia nodded thoughtfully. "You had no problem then. Do you think that there might have been some sabotage?"

"The demon?" Rodrigo thought about it. "No. It has no idea that I know the ritual. It would have been furious had it realized."

She placed the decanter on the table in front of him, pulled out one of the plush chairs, and sat down. "For you."

He looked at her blandly, hiding his suspicion. "Why?"

"To save you the bother of fetching some yourself," she said, looking at him. "We both know that I wouldn't stoop to crass tricks at this stage."

He nodded reluctantly, poured himself a glass full of the rich blood, and took a sip. It was delicious—unusually thick and spicy, laced through with hints of power. He could feel it sparkling as it slid down his throat and into his veins, invigorating him. "Delightful. Thank you."

"You are welcome." She poured herself a glass, sipping at it daintily, then filled his back up again.

Rodrigo took another long sip, and then continued. "After the failure of the Soul Forge, I discovered that Carnell was destroyed, and invoked Mariel to find out why it had not informed me before. That, at least, was simple."

She looked at him calmly. "And...?"

He sighed. "And it told me that the end of days was upon us, and it would serve me no longer." He was satisfied to notice that his voice stayed perfectly matter-of-fact. "It seems that Bell diablerized Carnell, incidentally."

Claudia arched a perfect eyebrow. "Really? I didn't know the man had it in him. As to the other, that is hardly any surprise. In fact, it's rather the point, don't you think? The demon's timing is likely to be willful—its decision of when the final nights begin is open to interpretation—but that is by the by. This is as good a time as any to move forward to the third stage."

He thought about it for a moment. "I suppose so. Miami could do with another month however."

"Miami will never be totally secure, even if we had another year. It's the nature of the city."

"You're probably right."

"Very well. I'll set things in motion. From this point on, we should both take care to feed well. There can be no other explanation."

Rodrigo nodded reluctantly. "I suppose not. I'll make sure I do not neglect the matter. What about Bell?"

"Carnell's failure is a little disappointing. There must have been something he neglected to take into account. Bell is becoming an irritation. We can afford a little less subtlety in dealing with him now, however. Unless you have any objections?"

He shook his head pleasantly.

Claudia removed a slim cell phone from a well-concealed pocket within the skirts of her dress and dialed a number. A few moments later, he heard the faint electronic beep as the device connected. "Good evening, General. Would you join us, please?" She paused for a moment. "Thank you." The phone snapped shut again and disappeared back inside the red silk.

Rodrigo picked up his glass and swirled it thoughtfully, gazing into the depths of the blood before taking another drink and then refilling his glass again. After a short while, soft footsteps approaching drew him out of his reverie. He looked up to see a lean, powerful man heading toward the table. Long, matted hair hung in tangles around his dark face, almost obscuring the sunglasses he was wearing, and he was dressed in a heavy black leather coat and trousers. He pulled a chair from another table as he got close, and swung it over, sitting down between the two of them.

Claudia smiled indulgently. "Do sit down, General Karsh."

He looked at her impassively. "How can I be of service?"

"We need you to take care of a security matter for us."

"No, really? You mean you're not interested in hearing about the time that I fought a pack of Berbers across the ruins of Carthage, or in seeing me juggle a clutch of flaming chainsaws?"

"Maybe you can play the clown for us later," said Rodrigo ironically. "My thanks for the offer."

Karsh flashed a sour look at him, then turned back to Claudia. "What is it?"

"Bell," she said simply.

Karsh sneered. "I warned you that the lunatic would fail. It'll be a pleasure to take Bell out once and for all. Now that he's persona non grata, it'll be trivial to do."

"I'd advise against overconfidence," said Rodrigo. "Bell is very versatile."

"Oh, I know all about Theo Bell," said Karsh. "I've worked with him several times. I know how he thinks. He won't be a problem."

"Good," said Claudia. "We want this to be as thorough as possible, however. There are several lines of attack that we want you to pursue." Karsh raised an eyebrow, but said nothing, and she continued. "Spread the blood hunt as much as possible. Use your influence to pressure princedoms into adopting it. Keep him isolated."

Karsh nodded perfunctorily. "Naturally."

"There's also the possibility that Bell might have already passed word to some ally or other," said Rodrigo.

Claudia nodded. "Yes. We need to be sure any other leaks are plugged. I want you to coordinate with Lucy in Jacksonville Control. She still has access to Carnell's observation network. Have a full surveillance program activated to watch for signs of Bell. Monitor him and his known allies as much as possible, and if you can identify knowledge spreading to anyone, have that individual eliminated. Whoever it is, General. You may find that information regarding allies is more reliable, as they are unlikely to be on the move as much as Bell himself."

"Alright," Karsh said. "If you want."

"We do," said Rodrigo flatly.

The warlord shrugged. "You're the boss. I'd rather just get out there, summon him to a meeting, and kill the arrogant bastard myself though."

"I'd rather you did it our way," Claudia said archly. "The last thing we want is any suspicion falling on your role."

Rodrigo grimaced. "Besides which, there's no guarantee that Bell would attend such a meeting. Given Carnell's usual thoroughness, I suspect that the former archon may well be something less than his usual self right now."

"He'd come to me." Karsh looked confident. "He wouldn't be able to resist it. He'd want to know what I was after. Particularly if I told him that I had information that could clear him on all charges."

"Maybe," Rodrigo said. "He might also turn up with several assistants and a lot of automatic weaponry. He's suspicious at the best of times, and Carnell's ministrations tend to, ah, bring the worst out in people."

"Don't worry, I'll be a good boy."

Claudia nodded. "We are delighted to hear that, General. Time is becoming critical, and our plans are close to fruition. It would be a shame if something threatened them now."

Karsh turned slowly to look at her full on, his body suddenly tense. "Are you saying what I think you're saying?"

"Indeed so."

"You have proof?"

Rodrigo smiled, a mirthless gesture that did little more than expose his teeth. "Call it strong circumstantial evidence."

Karsh relaxed, slumping a little, and shrugged. "You're welcome to believe whatever you want to believe. I trust you'll forgive me if I wait for some sort of clear sign before I make my mind up?"

"You are entitled to any opinions you wish, General." Claudia sounded completely unruffled. "Just so long as you follow our lead."

Karsh nodded. "Of course. If there's nothing else?"

Claudia inclined her head politely. Karsh rose smoothly to his feet, whipped around, and stalked off without a further word. Rodrigo watched him go and then turned to gaze out at the city beneath, taking occasional sips of his drink.

It was almost an hour later when a thought interrupted his musings. He turned to Claudia, who was watching him dispassionately. "It might be worth setting the Black Hand on Bell."

She shrugged. "I see no harm in it, at the very least."

Rodrigo's mouth twitched in wry amusement. "I suspect that Jalan-Aajav will be on the move. He'll not be expecting to hear from me right now."

"Would you like to use my telephone?" She slid the device across the table.

"Thank you." He picked it up, fiddled with the buttons until the appropriate entry was displayed, and activated the infernal thing. After a period of time, it started ringing.

"What?" The voice was cold—harsh, even—and sounded impatient.

"I do hope this isn't a bad time for you."

"I can talk for a moment."

"Good. I want to engage the Hand against Theophilus Bell."

There was a long pause. "I'm sorry, but that is impossible."

Rodrigo frowned. "Why?"

"The Black Hand will not move against Theo Bell. There are reasons. I'd like to indulge you, but it is not possible."

"Very well," said Rodrigo with a degree of resignation. "I will be in contact shortly."

"Fine. Good evening to you." The line went dead.

Rodrigo glanced at the mobile telephone with some distaste and passed it back to Claudia. "He was unable to help. Apparently Bell is untouchable or something."

Claudia nodded. "They do maintain a list of people that they will not accept contracts for. Even Jalan-Aajav cannot overturn that. It is no matter. I have every faith that our current plans will prove sufficient. The General is as enterprising as he is vicious."

"I hope so," said Rodrigo.

She smiled. "Fear not. Bell will plunge screaming into oblivion, and he will drag his companions down with him."

Chapter One

Upon Reflection

The hallway stretched out into shattered infinity, a dazzling tunnel of shards. There was a familiar man some distance ahead and other people visible at intervals further down. The man was looking right back at Theo, and it took him a few moments to realize that it was his own reflection. He darted a quick look around and staggered as a wave of vertigo swept through him. Every surface was mirrored. Beneath him, the floor seemed to drop away in an eye-bending chain of ever-decreasing bodies. The ceiling was the same above, sweeping him upwards. On every side, countless hordes of his own image stared balefully out. He closed his eyes, a reflex movement to preserve his sanity.

When he opened them again, the mirrors were still there. He could feel millions of eyes boring into him. Every one of them was his own, but that was no comfort. A gnawing sense of panic started to rise inside him, making his skin crawl all the way up his spine. He fought it, telling himself sternly that they were just mirrors, that they could not harm him, that no one was watching. He knew that he was telling himself comforting lies, but after a long moment it started to work, and the panic receded—a little, anyway.

When he was feeling more at ease, he tried taking a step forward. Whole ranks of figures kept up with him smoothly, and the sense of being under ferocious scrutiny snapped back. He ignored it as stoically as possible, and stepped forward again. Looking past the myriad eyes, he glanced around at the glittering tunnel. The surfaces were broken up into panes, and everywhere he looked seemed to be a mish-mash of dividing lines, so that every square foot of glass appeared broken into a crazy grid. It was impossible to see if the tunnel had junctions, or if it was just one solid tube. Only his own figure getting closer ahead confirmed a solid end.

Theo positioned himself in the middle of the corridor and reached for the walls to the left and right. By stretching his fingers, he was just able to touch the mirrors on both sides. They were smooth to the touch, a neutral temperature. He made a quick estimate of the distance to the Theo directly ahead, then closed his eyes, and started walking forward slowly. After about forty feet, he stopped and opened his eyes again.

He flinched before he could stop the movement, and the figure just scant inches from his face cowered back with him in perfect synchronization. He grinned at himself, suddenly amused by his own reaction to something he could have predicted. The change in his reflection's expression killed his amusement though, and he turned right around to see himself once more, standing a couple of hundred feet away. Theo closed his eyes again, and for several moments was able to indulge himself in the reassuring sensation that this was just a normal corridor. He started walking.

He was some distance past his original starting point when his left hand slid off the edge of the glass. He stopped immediately and looked. Crazy reflections and impossible angles danced back at him, and he had to blink a couple of times before they resolved into another corridor running off at a right-angle to the first. He turned into the new corridor and continued feeling his way along. After just a few feet, he came to a side-tunnel. A quick look confirmed that he now had three directions to choose from, all of them indistinguishably confusing. It had to be a maze.

Exploring would only work if he were able to keep track of where he was going. He turned to the mirror on the left hand wall of the tunnel he was in and punched it, hard. The surface remained intact. He tried again, dropping his hip and putting his weight behind it, but again nothing happened. It seemed strange that he couldn't crack the glass. Something elusive nagged at the back of his mind, but he couldn't quite catch it. He tried again, taking a step back and smashing his booted foot into the mirror as hard as he could. Once again, it resisted easily.

Theo decided to change tack. A quick search of his pockets failed to turn up anything sharp, but his jacket had a heavy catch that was easy to tear off. He took firm hold on it, and ground it savagely into the mirror. After a few moments the catch started crumpling, the mirror still unmarked. He stopped, and hefted the catch thoughtfully. Worrying about this place's peculiarities wouldn't get him anywhere. After a bit of thought, he put the catch down in the middle of the pane he was standing on. He was perfectly happy to rip his clothing to shreds, if it got him out.

He started walking forward again, ignoring the side-tunnel, his eyes closed. Some fifty feet later, he felt a gap at his right hand and had a look. Another corridor led off from the one he was in, as bright and featureless as all the others. He glanced down, and his blood turned to ice. There, in the middle of the pane he was standing on, was the catch he had left at the last junction. It was identical, even to the places it had bent. He turned around and looked backwards, but it was impossible to make anything concrete out among the dazzling glitter. He tried to tell himself someone might have moved it while his eyes were closed.

He didn't believe it, but decided to walk back to the previous junction anyway. He twisted the metal of the catch a little further, just enough to change its shape slightly, and then retraced his steps. He kept his eyes open this time, watching carefully for any sign of movement. There was none, and when he got back to the side-tunnel, he was unsurprised to see the catch still in place—freshly twisted into its new shape.

He sighed, and massaged the bridge of his nose wearily. If someone were playing surreal games, then he would play by their rules for the moment. It wasn't like he had a choice. If mapping the maze was impossible, then any direction was as good as any other. He closed his eyes, turned left into the side-tunnel, and started walking. He kept going for more than a quarter of an hour, taking whichever junction came first and then missing one, taking two then missing two, and so on. Every time he looked, the view was the same—thousands upon thousands of Theos staring back at him from all directions.

After a time, he felt the acoustics of the tunnel change, and opened his eyes again. A short distance ahead, the corridor opened up into a larger space. The room was still mirrored, and the change in the pattern of reflection made Theo's head spin a little. A strangely archaic stone fountain—a low, simple pedestal with a circular basin sitting on top of it—dominated the room. The fountain was non-reflective and drew the eye like a beacon. It cast images all around the room, which made him suspect that the walls of the room were not as regular as those of the tunnel had been. He stepped into the room, and a host walked with him, springing up everywhere, sliding in and out of view. There were reflections buried within reflections, all sizes and orientations, so that one mirror might have a tiny Theo stalking back beneath a life-sized one. Trying to block them all out, he concentrated his attention on the fountain, which seemed to be in every mirror, and walked toward it slowly.

The pedestal had been hacked out of a single block of rock. It had a speckled texture that reminded him of granite, but the color was wrong: a reddish gray tinged with flecks of brighter scarlet. The base was simple, a wide circular disk. A tubular column rose out of it, with sharp ridges protruding like spines, evenly spaced. Symbols were carved between the ridges — a mix of peculiar mathematical shapes, vaguely unsettling diagrams, and scrawling, lopsided things that might have been some odd alphabet. There didn't seem to be any pattern or reason to their placement, but they never touched the spines. The column was topped with a deep, curved dish with a small spout in the center, surrounded by little drainage holes, with no markings or other adornments. The whole thing was about four feet high, all told.

He stopped a short distance away from it, suddenly cautious. He'd been walking at random. If this room were the center of the maze, it must have come to him. The conclusion seemed a certainty. He wasn't sure how he knew, but that ignorance didn't bother him at all. This was the heart. There was nothing to do but to play along. He stepped forward and reached out to touch the fountain.

Nothing happened.

He waited a moment, feeling foolish, and then took a step back, uncertain. He slowly became aware of a slow vibration building in the floor of the room. It seemed to be swelling. After a short time, he realized that there was a sound to accompany the vibration, so deep that it was on the threshold of hearing.

Suddenly there was a coughing splutter from the fountain, and a short jet of slime burst up out of the spout. It was a bilious green color, and it stank of rotting flesh and old, stale shit. Theo took another step back, mildly disgusted, as the fetid gunk pooled in the basin. Another gout followed it, and then a third, as if the fountain was vomiting up the collected decay of ages. The whole room reeked. The rumbling noise rose a few octaves to become a buzzing, and suddenly a thin stream of blood spurted out of the fountain. It rose up in an elegant stream, steaming slightly, before falling back into the shallow pool of slime. The smell of it—hot, rich, coppery—cut through the decay like a knife.

Theo stepped forward again, intrigued. Unlike the sputtering glop before it, the blood flowed steadily, and it looked pure. The scent of it made his head swim. He reached out a hand, and let the warm blood wash over him. The red stream filled the mirrors surrounding him, drenching his fingers. He pulled his hand back and lifted it to his mouth. He licked it slowly and grimaced in disappointment. The blood was off somehow, tainted with a flavor that he couldn't quite place. Despite the delicious odor, it was undrinkable. He watched it flow for a long minute. When the basin was almost full, thick streaks of slime swimming around in the tantalizing blood pool, the stream died off.

A moment later, a sharp cracking noise cut off the buzzing whine, and the fountain disintegrated into a heap of bloody, mucus-covered rubble. Theo looked at it, too numb to feel any surprise. The fragments of stone started to vibrate, bouncing around together, and then they were melting and flowing into each other, the blood and slime clinging to them. The whole heap became a whirling cloud of material, which slowly rose into a tubular whirlwind six feet high or more. He could see chunks spinning around madly inside it, glistening with grays and reds and sickly greens. Structure flashed into place, lumps seeming to fly into the correct position just in time to fuse with each other into long, curving lines. Theo barely had time to realize that a skeleton was assembling before the cloud of blood and slime coalesced around the stone bones, and a tall, slender, clean-shaven man stood in front of him, delicate features arranged in a patronizing and unpleasantly sinister smile.

The man flicked a weary look over him and started reciting information. His voice sounded like a whole cacophony of blades scraping over glass—the piercing, sharp edged noises impossibly blending into perfectly intelligible words. Despite everything, he somehow managed to sound thoroughly bored, as if he were reading a dull application form.

"Ehioze Osakwe Kouandete, baptized as, and I quote, 'the slave Theophilus,' known latterly as Theophilus Bell."

Theo blanched. "Ayozi? What the *fuck*?"

The man ignored him utterly, and continued with his delivery. "Born 14th January 1821, at the Bell Plantations of Natchez Trace in the State of Mississippi. Son of Osakwe Glele 'Thomas' Kouandete and Isoke Nourbese 'Mary' Dagbo. Died 9th August 1857, and subsequently reanimated via an infusion of the cursed blood of Caine. Currently of no fixed abode."

Theo stared at him, shocked into speechlessness, a hollow roaring seeming to fill his ears.

The man grimaced. "You're a royal fucking pain in the ass, Bell."

Theo blinked. "Whu…?" He cleared his throat, and pulled himself together. "You'd be surprised how many people have said the same."

The man shook his head. "You know, I really doubt that I would." He looked around the room with amusement. "Nice little place you've got here. Cozy. A little on the egotistical side for my tastes, of course. All those mirrors. Very chic. I suppose you like to watch yourself masturbate." His mood suddenly darkened, blades whirling through his voice. "Thought you could fucking hold out here until I'd lost interest, did you? Very clever. I particularly like the way you blended his essence to yours when you wrapped it up. Put me off the scent for a while, that did."

"I don't know what you're talking about," said Theo dismissively. "Who the fuck are you anyway?"

"I am the Knife of the Storm's Eye," said the man expectantly.

"That explains your throat then," Theo said dryly. "I thought maybe it was the stone vocal chords or something."

The man's eyes narrowed slightly, his voice slicing the air into ribbons. "Give me Carnell's soul back, Bell."

"Fuck you," said Theo automatically. *Carnell?* Bits of memory came swimming up to him reluctantly. A tall, arrogantly handsome man, scuttling headfirst down a wall like a lizard. A hand, wreathed in sickly flame. The odd sensation of drinking down someone else's agony.... Then a big lump of memory fell on him, and it all clicked into place.

"He was a demon worshipper?" Theo laughed, unable to help himself. "That explains a lot. Well, I'd say you just found yourself with a bad debt, fucker. It's not his to give any more."

The demon scowled at him. "It doesn't work that way, Bell. Carnell's soul is mine. The deal is very specific. Ownership of the soul switches from the original consciousness' control to that of the signatory at the point that the deal is struck, and is merely left in its original location until such time as that consciousness is terminated in death—original or final, whichever is the latter. That means you have stolen his immortal essence from me."

Theo put on a bored expression. "Good."

"What do you care for?" The demon sounded like he was trying to be reasonable. "Carnell was a piece of shit. Your enemy. A manipulator, a liar, working for an organization that you have been opposing vigorously for some time now. I can feel your dislike for him burning inside you right now. Take your revenge. Give the soul to me. It won't even hurt you."

"If you get it, you'll make him suffer, right?"

"Oh yes," said the demon eagerly. "Eons of agony and torment. Constant torture and regret, and the burning knowledge through it all that he earned eternal pain in return for a few paltry tricks that lasted for one glittering moment. The ultimate stupidity, paid for with the ultimate price."

"You see, that's the problem," Theo said. "I'm not a big fan of enslavement and torture."

"But Carnell tried to drive you mad and then kill you."

"Yeah, he was a jerk-off, but like I just told you, I *don't* like slavery."

"So you would condemn yourself to eternal agony in your enemy's place, purely for the sake of a moral principle?"

Theo snorted dismissively. "Sweet fucking Christ, no. You're not getting either of us. You've lost Carnell, and I am *not* going to agree to stand in his stead. His deal was with you. You have no claim on me, asshole."

The demon growled threateningly, a noise like a scythe sliding across a whetstone. "Do you really think you can stop me from taking what I want?"

"Yes," said Theo confidently. "If you were able to grab my soul that easily, you would have already done it, instead of standing here bleating on about it."

The demon's face contorted with fury, hints of lightning seeming to play beneath the skin. His eyes lightened, the whites taking on a shiny, metallic tint while the pupils seemed to pulse with gathering clouds. His voice sharpened still further, until Theo was almost prepared to believe that every word would draw blood. "Oh, you smug, arrogant son of a planter's whore. I'm going to tear you into shards and feast on the ashes."

"So come on already," Theo said, choosing his words carefully and keeping his voice laconic. "This is getting really old. Or were you planning to bore me to death? Now that really *is* something I could be scared of."

The demon opened its mouth wide and howled, a ferocious blend of rage, hatred and cold steel. The noise stretched on for an impossibly long time, reflecting back on itself, even intensifying. As the sound grew, the man's flesh started to ripple, the edges and contours drawing out and sharpening. He grew even taller and thinner, his arms and legs elongating. The fingers flowed and hardened, taking on a steely tinge. Within moments, the whole body was firming. The howl stopped.

The creature facing him was over nine feet tall—an insane, glittering confection made of steel, all razor-sharp blades and jagged planes. There was nothing even slightly human left in it. It swept its arms up above its head slowly, a thousand edges shrieking and grinding against each other as it did so. Theo took an involuntary step back when he realized that the tortured scream of metal was still forming clear words. "It's going to be a pleasure killing you, asshole."

Theo glared at it defiantly. "Bring it on, moron."

The demon took a step forward, echoed in a thousand mirrors. It balanced easily on its razor-thin feet and slashed out at him ferociously with its arms. Theo concentrated and threw himself to one side, willing his blood to surge up, expecting to feel it catch fire. Nothing happened. There was no burst of speed, no sensation of the world slowing. The demon's hand sliced down the length of his arm, cutting through his jacket and into the flesh beneath. Theo rolled, came to his feet, and darted backwards, away from the grinning demon.

It took a slow step forward, its movement taunting him. "What's the matter, boy? Not looking so cocky now, huh?"

Theo gritted his teeth, wetness trickling down his arm, and focused on healing the cut. His blood should have responded immediately, knitting his torn flesh to seal the wound. It didn't. He continued backing away, suddenly frightened.

The demon's spine wiggled with an obscene laugh, and it stalked toward him, patiently cutting him off from the exit. "Looks like you forgot to put in your own gifts when you built this place. Who's the moron now?"

Theo circled warily, puzzled. "Fuck y—"

Although it was eight feet away, the demon lunged forward suddenly with a tortured shriek, cutting Theo off. Its arm seemed to stretch out forever. Theo tried to jerk back, but it was too late. Three long, stiletto fingers sank straight into his left thigh, slashing deep. He could feel the blades scoring his bone with blazing white lines of agony. He screamed and fell backwards into a corner, the demon's fingers jerking out painfully through the tattered flesh.

The demon chuckled and strode easily toward him. "Like I said, this place was a nice try, Bell. Shame you're such a shitty imagineer." It stretched its arms out wide, like a threshing machine, cutting off any possible escape. "This is where the fun starts."

Theo scrabbled back as far as he could, his mind whirling. *Imagineer?*

Blades clattering against the glass floor, the demon squatted down at Theo's ankles. He kicked at its head, mildly surprised as the thing turned its face to meet the kick directly. Theo's foot smashed squarely into its nose, and pain shrieked through him as the scalpels that made up its face slashed through the sole of his boot and bit deep into the flesh beneath. He moaned aloud despite himself and jerked his foot back, spattering bright droplets of blood across the demon's shoulders and chest.

The demon grinned nastily and wrapped its arms around itself. "Want to give me another shot, moron?"

Theo's foot blazed with hot pain, cutting through the whirlwind in his mind. The demon leered at him. It was clearly enjoying his discomfort and confusion. The word "imagineer" came back to him, teasing him. The implied meaning was obvious, but there was no suggestion of how to go about imagining something into existence. The demon had changed itself, but it hadn't done anything to the surroundings. Maybe that wa—

The thought evaporated in a blast of anguish as the demon slowly sank its Bowie-knife claws through the bones of Theo's left ankle and flexed. Theo could feel the blades slicing through bone and sinew, and the joint unraveled. A gush of dark blood bubbled up around the demon's hand. Theo realized with a jolt that he was screaming and tried to stop. It was several seconds before his body obeyed.

When he finally subsided, panting for breath he didn't need, the demon looked up into his eyes and smiled.

"This is just the beginning," it said. "Just think, Bell. Eternal agony because you were too proud to return something that you didn't even want. Now that really *is* stupid. Do you understand yet, fucker?"

Theo nodded and desperately imagined himself bounding up fully healed, in control of his powers and impervious to blades. He focused on it so hard that he could actually see it, willing it into existence, closing his eyes and running it through his mind time after time.

He shrieked again as fresh pain erupted. The demon was sinking its other hand through his right ankle, casually destroying that too. Theo's head swam, and he fought not to pass out. Even if the demon suddenly vanished now, he'd never be able to walk again. He'd come so far in the last century and a half, worked so hard. Despair threatened to overwhelm him. It was going to end as it had begun, wrapped in chains.

It was a vivid image, and for a fleeting moment, Theo actually physically felt the cold weight of heavy iron chains wrapped around him. He blinked, fresh hope rising. The demon was gurgling something, but Theo ignored it, and visualized his hands full of heavy bunches of chain. In his mind, they filled his hands, thick enough that he would be able to wrap the demon in them, batter it to pieces even....

He felt a strange sensation in his wrists and glanced down, shocked to see that his hands were melting into blobs of dark muck. Suddenly there was an explosive clattering noise, and long, thick chains of dark iron shot out from his wrists, snaking across the floor. The demon whirled round, astonished, and the chains started wrapping around its legs at incredible speed. The demon hacked down at them ferociously. A cloud of sparks burst from the impact, and then the chains were pinning its arms to its sides.

A moment later, it was entirely cocooned. Theo could hear it trying to say something, but it was too muffled to make out. He imagined the chains tightening, and they responded immediately, slithering over each other to squeeze the demon. A horrific squeal of tortured metal made Theo's head ring a little, and then the resistance faded, and a steady stream of metallic shards poured out of the tube of chains. It made a fair-sized heap on the floor. Theo released the chains, and they came apart, sinking slowly back into his wrists. He felt his arms thickening as they did so, although he hadn't noticed any depletion before.

The metal scraps in front of him wavered slightly. Then they burst, just like a child's balloon, leaving nothing but a faint smell of rotten eggs behind. Theo grinned, and glanced down at his ankles.

They were still fucked.

He tired imagining them whole, but nothing happened. He then tried crutches, fully robotic legs, and even a helper slave, all without any result. He managed to re-invoke chains and even a slave collar easily enough, but couldn't do anything useful with either. The chains wouldn't even crack the glass. He lay back for a bit then, feeling irritable, and thought about it. He was in the heart of the maze. That meant the exit ought to be very near, if only he could see it. It had to be behind a mirror. It was the obvious place to put it. Well, it felt pretty obvious anyway. Neither he nor the demon had so much as scratched one of the damn things though. He thought back idly to a time a hundred and twenty-odd years ago, when his sire Don Cerro and he had toured the capitals of Victorian-era Europe. In Paris, he'd seen a fat opera diva whose voice had shattered a mirror.

He was no singer, though. If anything, he was a Bell. The image—his body stretched out like a gigantic fleshy church bell, with one mighty arm acting as the clapper—was ludicrous, and he laughed.

The sound boomed through the room in gigantic peals, and he froze, astonishment mixing with hope. He took a huge breath and tried again, pitching his voice higher, making it as loud as possible. The wave of ringing sound almost deafened him. He forced it higher still, feeling his throat constrict. The mirrors around him started to vibrate a little, and a wild burst of elation lifted him up. He went higher still, as high as he could, the sound almost liquid in the room. The mirrors were dancing crazily now, glass trying to ripple.

He saw a crack form, and then there was a sudden explosion of tinkling glass and a burst of light so bright it felt like the sun itself. Words of fire hung in the air above him, too distant to read. The glass falling around him sounded like silver rain, and the light, impossibly, seemed to swell. Finally it swallowed up the illegible text, and everything went white.

Chapter Two

The Game

Theo blinked several times, and the white light surrounding him resolved into brightly tiled walls and ceiling and a heavy porcelain bathtub. He stared at the tiles, unsure why they were such a surprise, then shook his head wearily and stretched. Several joints crackled, and he realized that his face and stomach stung painfully. He tried to remember why he hurt and where he was, but his memory wouldn't cooperate. The mortal slaver Liam was dead, and any chance of getting out from under the blood hunt was dead with him. Had he found the gangster's corpse in that biker stronghold he'd trashed? Last night was a dark blur.

A face floated accusingly out of the back of his mind — young, helpless, dead. He groaned, remembering the look in the girl's eyes as he had killed her. Maybe it was for the best that Delphine and Nathalie had taken off. He didn't really want them on his conscience too.

Theo sat up and looked around the bathroom. It was soullessly clean, empty of anything resembling a personal touch. A powerful fluorescent tube-light made the room seem even harsher than it was. It had to be a room in a cheap hotel. He frowned, concerned that he couldn't remember how he'd got there, then shrugged. He could worry about it later. In the mean time, checking the current situation out seemed more important. He clambered out of the bath and went to have a look in the mirror to inspect himself for damage.

A wave of nausea and revulsion flooded through him, and he paused, shocked and confused. Even the thought of his reflection was grossly unpleasant. He puzzled at it for several moments, noticing finally that he'd turned away from the sink area again. Checking for damage suddenly didn't seem that important. He was functional, and if it stung a little to move his mouth, it wasn't the end of the world.

A couple of swift steps brought him to the door. He paused a moment, listening hard. Going through a closed door into totally unknown territory seemed a little foolish. He glanced down at himself, noting with resignation that his clothes were completely fucked again. His T-shirt in particular was little more than black rags.

A soft noise just short of proper audibility caught his attention, and he took a wary step back, treading softly. There was someone in the next room, walking around quietly. He considered the possibilities and fought down a bitter chuckle — it was hardly going to be anyone friendly, because there wasn't anyone friendly left for it to be. He hadn't been staked, restrained or destroyed, so it wasn't going to be an enemy either. Curious mortals? A cleaner, perhaps? His disheveled appearance was likely to cause alarm, raise questions even.

Without knowledge of numbers or inclinations, the best policy appeared to be to bluff it out as an aggrieved customer. He quickly shrugged out of his trashed clothes, moving as silently as possible, and heaped them on the floor. The towels in the room were decidedly small, and after a moment's consideration, he decided to do without. If he could embarrass and unsettle the people in the next room with his nudity, so much the better. Besides which, the thought of the starched, scratchy cotton rubbing against his tender burns was enough to make him wince. He wondered for a moment how he knew that he'd been burned but not how it had happened, but put the question to one side. Then, preparing himself to launch into a furious tirade of injured privacy, he opened the door and stepped out briskly.

The angry words died on his lips. He was in a bland motel bedroom, decked out in a gray color scheme with black and red highlighting. By the state of the carpet and the weak neon filtering through the dark window, the place was cheap. The streetlights visible below put the room on the fourth or fifth floor.

Across the room, Kristine and Itio were sitting at a cheap, plastic-covered table going over some papers or other. Delphine and Nathalie were sitting on a bed, the twins identical apart from Delphine's slight pallor. All four of them were staring at him. Itio looked as calm as always. Kristine seemed irritated, and a little uncertain. Delphine was openly giggling.

Nathalie was staring at his torso and groin, eyes wide and cheeks slightly flushed. "Wow," she managed breathlessly.

Theo fought down the immediate urge to run back into the bathroom for his clothes and decided to save as much face as possible. He put his hands on his hips. Nathalie followed the motion hungrily. He ignored her.

Itio was the first to speak. "I see you, Theophilus. It gladdens me. How are you feeling?"

"Fine thanks," said Theo, determined to hide his curiosity. "How about you?"

"Good," said Itio. "You were magnificent."

"He still is," murmured Nathalie. Delphine nudged her in the ribs. The pair of them shared a look and then burst out laughing.

"Thanks," said Theo impassively.

"Theo," said Kristine nervously. "You do know that you're naked, don't you?"

"Yes," said Theo loftily.

"Oh. Uh, good. Just checking." She looked even more worried now. What was wrong with her? "Your burns are doing well."

"I'm glad you're okay at last," said Delphine, still fighting giggles. "You had us worried for a couple of days there. You look very…" her voice faltered.

"Healthy," said Nathalie. The pair of them collapsed laughing again.

Theo looked at Delphine, slightly startled. "Days?"

"It's the third night since Detroit," said Kristine. "It's not your body I'm curious about though," she added irritably. Theo turned to her, and she shrugged defiantly. "You were babbling like a complete maniac back at the plant, before you collapsed. You can't blame me if I'm a little doubtful about your mental state."

Theo gave in, curiosity and irritation overwhelming his tattered dignity. "Plant? Collapse? What the hell are you talking about? How come you're all sitting around here, anyway?"

"Don't you remember? You collapsed after we took out that creepy freak back at the chemical plant in Detroit."

"Jacobson's?"

Kris nodded. "That's the one."

He frowned. "I don't remember anything happening there."

Itio nodded. "That is to be expected, Theophilus. When I found you in the care of these beautiful ladies, it was obvious that your mind was recovering from the effects of several major attacks. Some loss of memory is a reasonably mild consequence."

"Attack is one way of putting it," said Kris archly. "You sounded like an escaped mental patient, Theo. You were rambling on about witches and spiders and geckos, and kept insisting that you were going to be fried to a crisp or something. Then you just stood there and let that bastard eat you."

A nasty little pain started up in the back of Theo's skull. "Which bastard?"

"I think his name was Carnell. You said he'd been pulling your strings."

Some flashes of memory teased the back of his mind, and he sat down heavily on a nearby bed. "The devil worshipper. I...diablerized him."

"You *what?*" Kristine sounded stunned. Delphine and Nathalie exchanged blank glances.

Theo noticed the twin's confusion. "I consumed his soul," he told them.

Nathalie went almost as pale as Delphine. "That's horrible."

"Yes. It is. He pushed me to it, though. He...." Theo stopped and gathered his thoughts as best he could. "I remember that he had been leading us all by the nose. He killed Liam, and now he's dead too. There's no way to get my name cleared."

"You have stood within the darkness and consumed it in the instant that it would have consumed you," said Itio, his voice suddenly ringing hollow, like church bells. They all looked at him.

"I suppose so," said Theo, bemused.

"You also promised on your sister's name to do nothing to harm Del and Nat, save in direct self-defense," Kris said.

Theo sighed. "I'm sure I did. It seems everyone has been outmaneuvering me recently."

Itio shook his head. "Not so, Theophilus. We are here, after all, and we are all concerned about resolving this situation. I have a significant interest to protect, for example. I do feel a little slighted that you did not mention that Delphine's sire was an ally, but I congratulate you on keeping her a secret from me. That level of secrecy was probably prudent of you. Judging from what she has told me of your Carnell, I think it likely that her obscurity was the main reason that you prevailed."

"Yeah, I had a feeling that I might need to keep some of my hand hidden." He turned to Kris and the girls. "I thought you three had bailed on me though. I figured you had been driven off."

"Oh, we were," said Delphine without any trace of shame. "I was afraid you were going to try to do something to Nat. On top of that, we were being threatened with all sorts of nasty shit unless we ditched you. It made sense to get the hell out of there on the sly, so we did. Doing anything else would have been suspicious. I'm glad I asked Kris to go look out for you afterwards, though. Now that we can be sure you're not going to be forced to turn on us or something, I want to weather this storm with you. We owe you that, at least." Kristine nodded.

"Thanks," said Theo. "I mean it."

"The current situation is pretty odd," said Kris. "I think people are working against you still. That means there should be scope for getting evidence on your behalf. I think there may still be a way to clear you, if we can get to the heart of the organization."

Theo sighed. "Are you talking about your great big conspiracy again?"

"Do not be too doubtful, Theophilus." Itio looked thoughtful. "There is a certain amount of evidence to support Kristine's viewpoint—or, at the very least, to suggest that a person or persons with some sway are still manipulating events against you."

Theo turned to look at him, surprised. "There is?"

Itio nodded. "The blood hunt against you has continued to spread. There is considerable cynicism and confusion regarding what actually transpired in Minneapolis, but despite this, most of the Camarilla territories in the United States have now agreed to uphold the hunt. We have had to be careful when moving you."

"That's hardly conclusive," Theo said defensively. "Paschek is a vindictive bastard, and he'd love the chance to really fuck me over." He wasn't sure he even believed it himself, though.

"Perhaps," said Itio politely. "Even so however, the rapid uptake has been surprising. Hunts of the current magnitude are normally associated with significant betrayals of the Camarilla as a whole, rather than one semi-rural prince complaining about a few dead primogen and ghouls."

"It sounds pretty fishy to me," said Delphine. "Witch-hunts have to be driven."

"It's damned hard work to maintain them, too," Nathalie added. She tore her gaze away from Theo's body for a moment to glance at Delphine. "Wallis."

Delphine grinned back fiercely. "Wasn't it."

"Smooth," said Nathalie.

"Steel."

Theo arched an eyebrow at them. "Girls?"

"Sorry Theo," the twins chorused, and then grinned at each other.

"There are also ramifications to consider," Itio said. "Consider that most of the Kindred population of this country has now heard of your new status, one way or another. The Camarilla princes have had to spread word to invoke the blood hunt upon you. The news has filtered through to the major anarch groups, and to the Sabbat, and has been met with a certain amount of glee."

"I guess that was inevitable," said Theo glumly.

"The peculiar thing is that the Sabbat are not known to have made an offer for your loyalties. When was the last time you heard of a significant player evading blood hunt without the Sabbat offering haven, and even extraction?"

That made Theo pause. The Sabbat were desperate to destroy the Camarilla and were always keen to recruit any ranking vampires that their enemies wanted to kill, partly for tactical knowledge and partly just to rub the blue bloods' noses in it. "I may have too much Sabbat blood on hands," he said, but even he didn't believe it. There should have been half a dozen Sabbat archbishops offering him ranks and honors of all sorts, if only to get an edge over their own rivals.

"They must be under pressure to leave you in the cold," said Kristine unnecessarily.

"I admit it does seem strange," Theo said.

Delphine looked at him mischievously. "Would you go if they invited you?"

Theo scowled at her. "That's a very rude question, childe."

"So I have bad manners," she said impishly. "Are you going to tell me?"

"I am not going to get into a discussion of the relative merits and flaws of the Camarilla and the Sabbat," Theo said stonily.

"Aw," said Nathalie. Theo looked at her. She grinned back, unrepentant, and let her gaze travel slowly down to his crotch. "And I really love naked politics lectures, too."

Kristine shot her a reproachful glance. "The point is that it seems pretty certain that a person or group unknown is working against you, Theo. You don't have to think of them as Meonia if you don't want to, but in the mean time it's as good a name to use as any."

"Names constrict your thinking," said Nathalie, just slightly acid. "They all come with baggage. We don't know jack."

Kris opened her mouth to reply, but Itio cut her off. "Nathalie's observation is a good one. It may prove dangerous to risk even unconscious assumptions. We need untainted information."

Theo nodded. "I agree. If there is some fucker stirring up trouble, I want to find out who and where, and hopefully get some good evidence from him. I would rather like to be able to step foot in *some* cities without being attacked by every vampire in sight."

"There must be people you can still trust," said Delphine.

Theo thought about it for a bit. "Yes. A very few. One of them may have heard enough to get a lead or two from."

"We can do legwork for you," said Nat. "I need to top up my tan anyway."

"I still have contacts too," said Kris. "I can make enquiries."

"I may be able to, ah, pick a brain or two myself," said Itio cheerfully.

Theo smiled at the four of them. "Thank you once again. I seem to be saying that a lot tonight."

Nathalie looked at Delphine. "Rolodex?"

Delphine nodded. "Thief." They smiled in eerie synchronization. "My wordy sister just beat me to suggesting that if we want to keep the other side on their toes, we should take turns at playing chief for the day. Well, you three should anyway. That will stop us getting too predictable."

Theo shrugged. "Sure, why not? I don't see that it can hurt."

"There is wisdom in obscuring patterns of actions and movement," said Itio. "Pretty lady, it is a good idea."

"Talking about obscuring movement, where the hell are we anyway? If it's been three nights, I assume we're not in Romulus any more."

"We're back in Camarilla territory," said Kristine. "Green Bay, to be precise. It's the only place in the area that has not signed on to the blood hunt against you yet. If nothing else, it's safer for the rest of us."

"Yeah, we weren't sure how long you were going to be doing your cabbage impersonation." Delphine grinned.

"That reminds me," Itio said. "I took the liberty, last night, of acquiring some fresh clothing to replace your damaged garments."

Nathalie pouted at him. "Spoilsport."

"Really?" Theo looked at Itio warily. "It's not orange, is it?"

"Of course not," said Itio, unruffled. "I selected items that will help you remain inconspicuous." He got up, crossed to the other side of the room, and picked a plastic bag up off the floor. He handed it over on his way back to the table. Theo took it with a certain sense of misgiving. Itio's fashion sense could be a bit haphazard.

"Why don't you go try them on?" Delphine's eyes were glittering with amusement.

Theo sighed. "What time is it?" He was feeling noticeably hungry.

Kristine checked her watch. "Just after eleven thirty."

"There's still time to hunt, then. Alright."

He opened the bag and pulled out a rolled wad of clothing. He shook it out and had a look. The top was made of some thick, fleecy black material. It had a floppy hood, drawstrings at the neck, and a lurid photo print of some screaming freak with mismatched eyes dominating it. The man—presumably it was a man—looked vaguely familiar. The pants were tan cotton and seemed to be covered in pockets. They appeared to be about a dozen sizes too big. Itio had thoughtfully included a belt, although that was so covered in studs that it would serve better as a wrist guard.

Theo looked up to see Itio beaming at him. "Thanks Itio," he managed.

"A pleasure, Theophilus."

Theo nodded, stood up, and started pulling the clothes on. As he'd suspected, the pants came nowhere near fitting him. He inserted the belt, carefully making sure the spikes didn't rip the thin fabric, and did it up. Nathalie and Delphine started giggling. After a moment, Nathalie came over to him.

"Here Theo, let me." She unbuckled the belt again, running a slow hand over his stomach muscles as she did so. Then she shook the pants out a bit and did the belt back up, several notches too loose. The trousers caught on his hips, but only just, and she tugged one side down slightly. "There. That's much better."

He frowned. "Are you kidding?"

Delphine laughed. "Did you *want* to look subnormal?"

He growled at her. "No."

"Well roll with it then. Only crazies do baggies up around their stomachs like that. Put your top on. It should hide your pubes enough."

Theo shook his head and did as he was told. There wasn't much flesh left visible.

"It suits you," said Itio, smiling. "I knew it would. You look twenty-five again. You can pull your hood over too, if you need to further obscure your face."

"I look like a pathetic teenybopper wannabe," said Theo wearily.

"Exactly," Itio said. "Who would think to look for the renowned Theo Bell behind an outfit like that? No casual observer will notice your face."

"They'll be too busy crossing the street to avoid me," said Theo.

"You look perfectly okay," said Delphine encouragingly. She almost managed to make it sound believable.

A short while later though, out on the street, Theo was prepared to accept that Itio may have been correct. The area was reasonably quiet, but there were still people around. He had his hood up and just walked along casually, minding his own business. Hardly anyone gave him a second glance. Of the few who did, half seemed to find the outfit offensive or intimidating, and the other half seemed to approve. Not just kids, either.

It took about twenty minutes to walk the area and get a feel for it. There were a few bars and restaurants (most catering toward the cheaper end of the market), along with a movie theatre, a smallish mall, and a bunch of miscellaneous stores. It was clean and fairly good-tempered, a pleasant change from the anger and squalor of Detroit. The air was pleasantly fresh, kept clear by a breeze blowing out onto the bay. Theo headed back to a reasonably promising side street and walked along it. After a couple of blocks, he crossed over the road and went back up the street, so as to avoid loitering suspiciously.

He didn't have long to wait. After something like ten minutes, a pair of young women turned into the road and started heading toward him, unconcerned. They were dressed in less than the weather should have demanded, chattering away to each other brightly. Theo prepared himself, still walking toward them casually, and waited for one or the other to look up.

The one on the left made eye contact first, glancing up through a half-screen of glossy black hair. He reached out to her mind and felt the soft warmth of mild intoxication softening out the sharp edges of her smart, dedicated personality. He tightened his mental grip and ripped through her will, plunging down to the soft core of pliant willingness that lay beneath. She slowed, transfixed.

"I need you to come with me quietly," he said pleasantly.

The girl he had just enthralled nodded automatically and murmured her obedience. "Sure."

The other one, a brunette with a mind like a ball of sponge, looked up at him, fear and uncertainty mingling with confusion at her friend's agreement. "Hey...."

He let go of the first girl, confident of the implanted order, and tore straight through the second girl's dizzy psyche as if it were tissue paper. Her eyes glazed even more. "You too," he told her. She nodded.

He led the pair of them down the street a short way, into a quiet, secluded yard he had noticed earlier. When they were out of sight of the road, he looked straight at the girl he still had gripped and strengthened his hold through her mind. "Go stand over there, close your eyes, and stay silent and motionless until I tell you to move again. Everything will be fine, I promise." She nodded again and did as she was told. Then he turned back to the first girl and tore through the alcohol, burying himself back into her unconsciousness.

"Stay where you are, silent and motionless."

She nodded, her eyes full of trust and submission.

Theo stepped closer to her, bared his fangs, and bit into the soft, ebony warmth of her neck. She quivered and then relaxed against him as his mouth filled with hot, salty blood. He sighed luxuriously and started drinking from her slowly, savoring every drop. After a couple of creamily blissful minutes, when he'd taken as much as he could without injuring her, he regretfully pulled back, licking the wound shut and capturing a few last drops of her. Then he gazed into her eyes, feeling her total subservience. He rammed a spike of his will deep into her memories, further scattering her thoughts.

"Go back to the street and wait patiently for your friend. When she arrives, you will go on your way, remembering that you walked down the street, and a man passed you peacefully. You stopped for a moment while your friend tied her shoelace, and then continued. Nothing else happened. Do you understand?"

"Yes." Her voice was barely a whisper. She turned around and walked out of the yard.

As soon as she was on her way, Theo crossed over to the brunette, and tilted her head up to face him directly. "Open your eyes now." She did so immediately, and he looked into them, instantly aware that she was still utterly pliant. He lifted her wrist and bit into it. Her blood spurted into his mouth, spicier than her companion's had been, but without the same depth to it. It was still delicious though, and he lost himself in her heat for a long, timeless moment.

Once he'd corrected the brunette's memory and sent her back to join her companion, he decided to wait where he was for five minutes, to give the girls a chance to get away. No more than fifteen seconds had passed, however, when a small, wet noise just on the edge of hearing caught his attention, and he whipped round to face the direction the sound had come from, taking a step back as he did so.

He looked around the yard carefully. Large portions of it were shadowed, but there was no movement. There was a large tree that might have been hiding someone, but it was in the wrong place. An old dumpster full of rubble across the yard offered more misplaced opportunities. He took another step back, and then noticed the two trench-coated vampires standing patiently in the middle of the yard.

They were an unlikely pair. One was horribly stooped, standing barely five feet high. Its coat did nothing to hide a long, gnarled back twisted into painful-looking knots. It had gray, leathery skin, and tiny, stunted facial features clustered together under big, beetling eyebrows—the only hair on its head. It was impossible to tell its sex.

The other was a little taller and probably male. He was painfully slight, little more than bones wrapped in loose folds. Tight black sportswear—spandex, perhaps—exaggerated his deformity. His head looked enormous, but it was probably just normally sized. An enormous pair of eyes dominated his face; his sockets actually seemed to bulge out of the side of his head, like a pug dog. Dark bristles spread patchily over most of his face and scalp. Along with his eyes, the hair made him look like a hideous, man-sized fly.

Theo looked at them impassively, wishing he had his knife. There was a faint scent in the yard that made the hairs on the back of his neck tingle. They stared back for a long moment, then the fly-faced one scowled. "You were tidy enough with the meat." His voice was shockingly deep and eloquent, rolling out across the yard like an actor's.

His companion nodded. "So the question is, who the hell are you, and what are you doing pissing on this patch?" It sounded as warped as it looked, all dry and spindly, like the scratching of reeds on bark.

They were scourges, probably. Local enforcers. Little more than a minor irritation. Theo shrugged. "I'm just passing through. Sorry if I stepped on any toes."

The twisted one laughed nastily. "This is the ass-end of nowhere, pal. There is no 'through' to pass to."

"Now, we can take you 'through' to the barn to see Martin," said Fly-Face. "Either that, or we just write you up later as another spy left dusting the streets. Eva here likes to play, so she prefers to chalk uninvited guests down as 'threats removed.' I'm feeling idle tonight though, so I'd rather push you on up the food chain."

"I bet you say that to all the girls," Theo said scornfully. The rotten smell of sulfur was getting stronger. "I'm not spying, I'm not setting up shop, I'm not some puny thin-blood, and I *don't* have the time for this crap. Run along like a couple of good little doggies, and your tin-pot prince doesn't have to lose a pair of his…." He paused, opening the gap out into an insult. "Men."

Fly-Face shook his head heavily, pretending regret, and Eva started to say something angry. Theo turned his attention inwards and focused on the power flowing through his blood. He called to it, beckoning it upwards, teasing it out to wash over him. It surged into his aura and ignited, flooding out from him in a tide of authority, demanding respect. The force washed over the scourges, and they both fell still, openly unsettled. The sulfurous stink got much stronger.

"That's better," said Theo. "Now listen. I've done my time on border patrol, so I'm going to be generous. I'm not an interloper. This is none of your business. Fuck off right now, and I won't destroy the pair of you." He flicked a quick look around the yard to see if he could spot the source of the chemical stench. Pollution, perhaps.

The two enforcers shared a long, nervous look.

"Maybe he has a point," said Fly-Face.

Eva studied Theo, nodding absently. "He is rather commanding." She peered up at his face, and her eyes widened. "Oh shit. It's Bell."

Theo cursed bitterly as the pair of them immediately started backing away, fast. He tried to make his voice sound reasonable. "I thought Green Bay was refusing to sign up to the blood hunt."

Fly-Face laughed bitterly. "What's that got to do with it?" The little color there seemed to drain out of the vampire, leaving him just a pattern of gray on black, like the shadows behind him. For a moment the illusion was complete and he was almost indistinguishable from them, and then he vanished entirely. Theo glanced around the yard. There was no sign of Eva, either.

He took several quick steps backwards, until he was up against the wall the brunette had been standing by, and paused. Apart from the general ambient noise of the city, the yard was silent. He looked around, irrationally certain he could feel unfriendly eyes boring into him from all directions. He fought down a sudden urge to cower.

The tiniest ghost of a clink—metal against metal—caught his attention off to the left. Theo reacted immediately, diving forward and to the right. It seemed like the right direction. The blood flashed into life inside him, its heat doubling and redoubling as fresh waves of energy surged through him. His muscles writhed, and the air surrounding him thickened as the world slowed to a crawl. He felt almost giddy with inexplicable relief, even as a series of explosions tore into him—hip, thigh, side of a kneecap. *There.* Over in the direction the sound had come from, Eva was firing a stubby semi-automatic pistol.

Pain surged up his leg, and he walled it off, focusing instead on his blood sealing the wounds over, forcing the torn flesh back together. A nasty crawling sensation writhed its way around the wounds, adding to the pain. It felt like the bullet holes were frothing, but the extra discomfort was a welcome release. He heard a quiet curse coming from straight ahead. Theo pulled his head down toward his chest and swept his arms out wide.

A heavy impact jarred his left forearm, wrenching at his shoulder. He clutched at it reflexively and pulled, swinging round behind the leg. It was Fly-Face. Theo swung against the man's hip, bumping into it. The vampire smashed a heavy blow down toward Theo's head. The punch was ludicrously slow, and he swung away from it, using the extra momentum to get his legs back underneath him. The reek of sulfur was almost overpowering.

He straightened up, smashing his fists repeatedly into Fly-Face's kidneys, the blows flurrying from side to side. The vampire had started a glacial turn, but it was easy to track round with him and keep punching. After half a dozen blows, Theo felt something break, and Fly-Face started to sag.

Theo grabbed him by shoulder and hip, swept him up, and threw him at Eva. The vampire flew across the yard like a rag doll, moaning dully, arms and legs flailing. Theo dashed after him, using him as cover from his companion's pistol. Eva was faster than Fly-Face and managed to duck out of the way of his flailing body.

It didn't do any good. As she came out of her crouch, Theo barreled into her like a freight train. She started folding as soon as he hit her, and it was pathetically simple to pluck the gun from her hands as she tried to bring it down. It was still on auto.

He brought the pistol up to point squarely at her face and gave her a moment or two to register that the barrel was point blank between her eyes. Then he emptied the clip into her forehead, watching grimly as her eyes widened in horror and then puffed outwards further, sagging into a greasy dust.

He threw the gun into her ashes. "Nobody shoots me, bitch." Some of the stench faded out of the air and a nasty suspicion started to gnaw at the back of his mind.

Fly-Face was lying against a wall, coughing weakly. Blood spattered his lips. Theo crouched down in front of him warily and took a firm hold on him so that he couldn't worm out of the way. He shook the vampire a little, until he was sure he had his attention, then looked at him, suddenly tired. "Why?"

Fly-Face spat weakly. "Fuck you, Bell." His voice was a ruin of its former self.

"You didn't have to do that."

"Do you think I had a choice? We tried. That has to be worth something."

The suspicion became a certainty. "The demon, or Carnell. Both, maybe."

Fly-Face coughed again, weaker still. "Fuck you."

Theo shrugged, then brought his fist up and crashed it into Fly-Face's skull like a pile driver. The bone crumpled like wet paper, and then the whole carcass was dissolving. Theo sighed heavily, stood up, and dusted himself down. Suddenly walking around didn't seem like that smart an idea.

He sat down in a patch of shade and focused his mind on his memories and impressions of Itio—his mannerisms, his odd fashion sense, the way his eyebrows crinkled when he did that maddening grin…. Slowly, a painstakingly clear image of the man formed in his mind. When it was solid, almost as if Itio was standing in front of him, Theo forced himself to feel the image falling inwards toward him, concentrating on the impression for all that he was worth. He could feel the summons beating off him in waves. Fatigue slowly stole over him as it drained his energy. He gritted his teeth and sat back, his mind stubbornly focused.

Chapter Three

Old Friends

A small scuffing noise across the yard snatched at Theo's attention, breaking his concentration. He looked toward it cautiously, but there was no sign of anything that might have caused it. He unfolded his legs and came wearily into a ready crouch, just in case. Peering closely, he realized that a worn spot on a patch of brickwork was actually dark cloth. His eye followed the detail out, and then he could see that he was looking at Itio's shirtsleeve. The man was standing there comfortably, looking unperturbed.

"I see you, Itio," Theo said. The man's customary greeting seemed appropriate, for once.

Itio smiled beatifically. "I see you too, Theophilus. I take it there has been some trouble?"

Theo nodded. "A couple of the locals caught me snacking, and took exception to the fact that I hadn't presented myself properly to the prince. They saw sense and were going to let me go, but then they recognized me, and all hell broke loose. I...." He hesitated, unsure how to explain. "At least one of them was a diabolist, like Carnell. Possibly both of them. I'm certain of it."

"That is somewhat alarming," said Itio, looking unruffled. "It may be simple ill-fortune, but it would be imprudent to assume if there is a group active against you, that there are no further representatives in this area."

"Exactly," said Theo grimly. "Which is where you come in, old friend."

"A compliment, Theophilus?" Itio made his voice sound disbelieving and grinned at him impishly.

Theo shrugged, slightly uncomfortable. "Let's just say a realistic understanding of the situation. You're a lot better at moving unseen than I am."

Itio nodded matter-of-factly. "Yes. Yes I am. It will be a pleasure to be of assistance."

A cold, distant feeling crept over Theo. It was reminded him of an afternoon when, as a child, he'd become separated from the others in the thick woods bordering the Bell plantation — the feeling of being all alone, vulnerable, and unpleasantly certain that no help was going to find him. The feeling built until it was nearly overwhelming and then leveled off.

Theo suppressed a shudder. "Thank you."

Itio nodded, and Theo followed him back onto the street. They walked back to the hotel in silence. It seemed appropriate. The town was as quiet as a tomb. Dark windows gaped out at them, resenting their passing. The occasional cars that went past seemed to be wrapped inside little soap bubbles, locking in their reality. They might as well have been a million miles away. Finally, Theo led Itio back into the hotel and up to the corridor that their room was in.

As Theo approached the room, the feeling of isolation vanished, like a balloon bursting. As unpleasant as it had been, he was glad that it had finally vanished but he still found himself feeling horribly exposed, as if hundreds of hostile eyes were boring into him. He thought fleetingly of mirrors, although he was unsure why, and hunched himself up defensively. Resisting the urge to pull his hood round his face more, Theo walked over to the door instead and knocked briskly. A moment later, Kristine opened up and bustled them in to the room.

Delphine looked worried. "What happened, Theo?"

"I was spotted by the opposition—a pair of local enforcers. They didn't recognize me at first, but when they did, they decided to take me out, and they made it perfectly clear that it had nothing to do with the blood hunt. That means they were on Carnell's former team. We fought, and I killed both of them. I decided it was safer to have Itio escort me back—he's a lot better at sneaking around than I am."

Her eyes narrowed. "How did they find you so quickly?"

"I don't know," said Theo, uncomfortable at the admission. "It could just be plain bad luck, it could be there's a hell of a lot of them out there, or it could be they're all concentrated in this region. Or a combination of the three, obviously."

She looked at Theo thoughtfully. "Are you sure that they were the only ones?"

Theo's heart sank, and he shook his head. "Not entirely, no. I suppose there might have been another one who stayed hidden and then went to report in when I was identified. It's unlikely—they were pretty murderous—but not impossible."

Kristine's face hardened. "Then there is no choice. We have to get out of here right away." She turned to Delphine. "I'm not risking your well-being to a maybe, daughter."

Nathalie paled slightly. "She's right, Del. We can't take the risk that they know we're here. They might do anything to you."

Delphine arched an eyebrow. "To me? What about to you?"

Nathalie grinned. "Oh, I'll be fine. I can run off into the dawn, remember?"

"What if they—"

Theo cut Delphine off mid-sentence. "If we're going to get out of here, we should do it right now. There's only five hours of darkness left."

"There are no remaining territories in this area that can be considered safe for you," Itio said.

Theo shrugged. "You want safe, go live in a padded cell underground somewhere. The blood hunt is only against me, remember? The rest of you are not at much risk."

Nathalie looked at Delphine. "How about the warehouse with the snacks? Didn't Theo tell us that it was no-man's land?"

Theo nodded. "You mean the Naperville-Aurora borders? It is—or at least it was last week. I suppose it's a start."

"Better than many," said Itio.

Theo looked at him. "Feel like explaining that one?"

Itio smiled. "There is a house just inside Naperville that I have made use of before, and could call on again in an emergency. The owner is…susceptible to persuasion, and his wife has a wonderful walk-in closet."

Kristine nodded reluctantly. "It is in range, and it has the benefit of being a specific location to aim for. You should be safe there, daughter."

"Any better suggestions? No? Alright, let's get moving," said Theo impatiently.

"There are some people I could make contact with in Chicago," Kristine said. "It might take a couple of nights. I'm willing to do it, but only if I know for sure that Delphine is going to be safe." Theo nodded, resigned. "You have to promise to look after her for me until I come back."

Delphine shot Kristine a piercing look.

"You have to promise to look after both Delphine and Nathalie for me until I come back," Kristine restated, without a trace of embarrassment.

"I expected nothing less," said Theo. "I promise."

"Good," Kristine said. "I'll leave Aurora first thing tomorrow then."

"Not unless we damn well get on with it," said Theo crossly.

Twenty minutes later, Kristine drove across the Green Bay city limits, and the atmosphere in the car eased significantly. Delphine and Nathalie relaxed noticeably, murmuring to each other, and a certain tension seemed to drain out of Kristine's shoulders. Only Itio looked unperturbed, but then very few things seemed to ruffle his feathers.

Delphine mumbled something to Nathalie, then started poring over a large map, nodding in approval as Kristine headed toward Manitowoc. "It's a bit over two hundred miles," she announced finally.

"We'll be there in under three hours," said Kristine confidently, piling on some extra speed. "We should have as much as ninety minutes at the other end to get settled."

"That provides us with plenty of leeway should our primary destination prove troublesome," said Itio.

Theo nodded approvingly. "Good. I don't much like racing tight deadlines."

"Me neither," Kristine said, with a meaningful look back at the twins. "We'll need to make a fuel stop fairly soon, too."

"That's cool," said Nathalie. "Hey Del, would it be okay if I got some food when we stopped?"

Delphine turned round to look at her, puzzled. "What?"

Nathalie smiled. "Ok, no worries, I'll skip."

Delphine shook her head. "What the fuck are you on? Since when did you check in with me? Get whatever you want. I don't want you starving yourself."

"I know things are really hard for you at the moment. I just don't want to make it any more difficult."

Delphine peered at her sister suspiciously. "Is that right? By getting some food?"

"Hey, I love you sis."

"You too," said Delphine.

"That's all that matters," said Nathalie, beaming.

"Yeah," Delphine said. They hugged, but her face was troubled.

Itio noticed Theo's expression in the rear view mirror, and quickly arched an eyebrow at him, the faintest sliver of a grin on his lips.

Theo sighed to himself, tried to get comfortable in his seat, and settled for leaning back with his eyes closed.

The miles rolled past.

They made Aurora a little less than two hours before dawn. The town looked peaceful, and the commercial district on the Naperville border was as tidy and prosperous as Theo remembered. The unit they were heading for was slightly isolated from its nearest neighbors, tucked away where the dumpster, scrap metal and untidy straggling weeds in the concrete yard wouldn't cause offense. The windows and doors were all boarded up securely, and the tall metal shutters that led through to the main warehouse space were chained together. It looked exactly as it had on his last two visits.

A short distance past the unit, a golfing supplies superstore had a large car park that housed several vehicles. Kristine pulled in there, parking the car behind a high-sided white van.

Itio smiled at her. "Beautiful lady, would you feel safer if I examined the unit swiftly?"

She nodded. "Thank you, Mr. Shima. A generous offer."

"I will be but a few moments." He opened the door, and slipped out.

"I can't imagine there's anything going on in there," said Theo. "Michael said that he and the Prince of Naperville were discussing the location's status. I'd be very surprised if they've got round to resolving it yet. Far more likely, they've agreed to leave it alone for a while, pending further talks. In fact, Michael suggested as much last time I spoke to him. He seemed genuinely sympathetic. I'm a little surprised he's signed up to the hunt."

"Maybe he didn't have any choice," said Nathalie sleepily.

"Yes, he may have been pressured into lip-service," agreed Kristine.

"Perhaps," nodded Theo. "I just might risk asking him about it tomorrow evening. I don't have to tell him where I am, after all. We may learn something useful."

"Just so long as you do not endanger the girls, Archon."

Theo winced. "Stick to Theo, would you? Don't worry, I won't do anything rash."

"We'll be fine, Kris," said Delphine with a smile. "Theo's done me proud so far."

"Yeah," said Nathalie, turning round to give Theo a big, tight hug. "He has."

Theo nodded to her uncomfortably. She smiled up at him, snuggled into his shoulder, her breasts pushing into his arm, and pretended to go to sleep. Only her shallow breathing and occasional squirms gave her away. He shot a martyred look at Kristine, who looked back at him in the rear view mirror, amused and utterly unsympathetic.

A minute or two later, Itio's return spared Theo the necessity of peeling Nathalie off. He slipped back into the passenger seat, smiling broadly, and Nat unfolded herself expectantly, looking just a little flushed.

"Most satisfactory. From what you have told me, I would judge that no one has even entered the building. The rooms you stayed in last time look as described." He nodded toward Nathalie. "I even found your chocolate bar wrappers by the television, pretty lady."

Nathalie grinned. "I always knew being messy would turn out useful some day."

They drove back a block to the unit and parked down the side, by a window that Theo had forced open on his first visit. The vehicle was safely out of sight of the road, and within two minutes they had all the stuff inside. Theo decided to spend the day in the same room as he had before, a dusty little office with unpleasantly institutional yellow walls and a green-check floor. He slung his bag down on the floor irritably, grateful that it had been retrieved, but still cross at the loss of his bike and shotgun.

They gathered in the main room, assembling on the couches around the television at Theo's request, rather than at the long meeting table.

Theo waited until they were all back before speaking. "Anyone have any questions or issues?"

"It will serve admirably," said Itio. The others nodded.

"Good," said Theo. "Is there anything else to take care of?"

"I'm slightly concerned about keeping the same car," said Kristine.

"What do you suggest?" Theo ignored the frowns that Delphine and Nathalie wore.

"There's someone in Chicago who'll swap it for a similar but unconnected set of wheels. I know the car is a link back to your family, daughter, but it's also a danger. Even with switched plates."

Theo thought about it. "How trustworthy is this contact?"

"Trustworthy enough, for a villain."

"What will happen to Delphine's car?"

Kristine shrugged. "It'll be sprayed, re-plated, and sold in New York probably."

Theo grinned. "Could it be sold as is?"

"Probably," said Kristine, amused.

"Alright," said Theo. "I say do it."

Delphine nodded reluctantly. "I guess it makes sense."

Kristine smiled, relieved. "Good. Nat, if I leave you my phone and give you instructions, can you deal with it in the morning?"

Nathalie glanced over at her sister, then nodded. "Alright. It'll give me something to do, I guess."

Kristine stood up and headed out across the warehouse floor a bit, the girls following closely. They started talking earnestly.

Theo looked at Itio and sighed. "I don't like any of this shit. Paschek was an asshole, but at least he only sent me up against identifiable challenges."

"I know this has been trying for you, old friend. It may be of some comfort to you to know that it is a critical piece in the puzzle to come."

Theo shrugged. "If you say so."

"Trust me, Theophilus. Things are progressing as well as could be hoped for."

"Really?" Theo laughed hollowly. "Seems like a crock of shit to me."

Itio smiled. "I know. But you survive, you are sane, and the twins are well. The pattern is secure. The other paths are all worse."

"Sometimes, I wish I had your faith," Theo said sourly.

"Mine?" Itio looked surprised. "I am the most secular person imaginable. I take nothing on trust. What seems faith to you is merely access to different knowledge. You, my friend, are the believer."

Theo looked at him doubtfully.

"But you are, Theophilus. You believe in the rightness of your cause. You believe in your abilities and your might. You believe in yourself. You believe in your code, your promises, your strength…. You are rich in belief, old friend."

Theo sat back, troubled. Itio watched him for a while, smiling, and then took himself off to settle down for the night.

A few minutes later, Theo followed suit. Despite his fatigue however, he couldn't get to sleep, and it was nothing to do with Kris and the girls giggling and rustling in the room next to him. It wasn't until the sun crept over the horizon like a sheet of lead that he managed to sink into oblivion.

When Theo awoke the next evening, he allowed himself the luxury of lying in. It was much easier to look at the situation dispassionately when there was some peace and quiet. He thought about old friends and contacts and tried to look at the situation positively, as a series of challenges. There was no way that something this big could be established without leaving traces. Footprint, the intelligence community called it. Someone would know enough to crack a way in. Once he had a solid lead in, he could work his way up the chain. It was just a matter of choosing whom to speak to carefully.

He sighed, irritated that he was being dragged full circle again. Every way he looked at it, the problem came back down to trust—and there was precious little of that to go around Kindred circles at the best of times. He rolled up off the floor, dusted himself down, and headed out to the main warehouse.

Delphine spotted him coming through the door and smiled brightly. "Hi Theo. Sleep well?"

He shrugged. "As usual, thanks. Did the car swap go down okay?"

Nathalie, sitting on the sofas beside her sister, nodded. "Yeah, no problems. I took Dad's car out to that golf store first thing. When I checked back later, it had been changed for a minivan. Kris took the motorcycle a few minutes ago, says she'll catch up in a few days."

Theo looked at her curiously. "What motorcycle?"

"Oh, she had me arrange a bike with them as well."

"Fine," said Theo. "Where's Itio?"

Delphine grinned. "He's over by the table. It looks like he's meditating."

He looked where she was pointing. Itio was sitting erect in a small office chair, his eyes closed and face calm. Theo shrugged, then fished around for his telephone and turned it on, glad to see it still had a fair amount of charge.

"Those things can be traced you know," said Nathalie. "I saw some report on it."

Theo grinned. "Not these ones. I don't know the details, but all our mobile telephones have secure connections."

"Maybe that's why it's so clunky," said Delphine teasingly.

"Hush now, childe," said Theo. "I'm going to telephone the Prince of Aurora, and I don't necessarily want to give anything away."

She poked her tongue out at him, and then the twins settled down to whispering together, low enough that the phone wouldn't pick anything up.

Theo winkled the number out of his memory. It was like pulling a stone from a shoe. Once he had it, he dialed swiftly and waited.

The phone was answered in just a couple of rings. "Michael Aldrich. I advise making this good." Michael had a rich, rolling voice that always made him sound like he was on a stage somewhere. It didn't quite suite his matter-of-fact attitude.

"This is Theo Bell."

There was a momentary pause. "Grief! I suppose I asked for that. Good evening, old chap. What the devil can I do for you?"

"Michael, is your previous offer still open?"

"Naturally." The man sounded amused.

"What about the hunt?"

"What about it? Matter of form. Don't think it's right, myself. Don't think it's right at all. Still, not always wise having an opinion, these nights." Michael sounded rueful.

"Someone's working against me, Michael. This damned hunt is just part of it. It's all bullshit. I intend to blow it open, get my name back. There will be a lot of prestige waiting for anyone prepared to help."

"You certainly have balls, man. I'll be the first to say it. I'm still listening." Michael sounded intrigued.

"Some friends and I took you up on your hospitality last night. If you were to turn up here, alone, you might get the chance to learn a lot more. It's no trap, I promise."

"You do, do you? Alright. Can I bring an interested party?"

Theo thought about it for a moment. "I suppose I can cope with one, yes. I'm feeling a little twitchy, though."

"Don't worry. Best behavior all round. Thirty minutes?"

"Fine," said Theo. "See you then." He hung up.

Itio crossed the warehouse floor, heading toward the sofas. "Am I to assume that some careful surveillance would be prudent?"

Theo nodded. "Please, Itio. I think the best thing is to take the girls with you and go watch from the car. If they send a hit squad down or something, call me, then get the hell out."

To Delphine's credit, she visibly considered and discounted several questions before speaking. "Why don't you wait with us?"

"It would draw attention to the rest of you if I got out of the car when Michael arrived."

"You can at least wait by the gate, so that you're not trapped if something goes wrong."

Theo thought about it for a while. "I'm not sure. Even if Michael is genuine, his people might be a very different story. Staying in view might jeopardize things. I'll be alright here."

"If you say so," she said, clearly unconvinced.

"Look, I'll come check in with you after I've spoken to him, okay?"

"It's dark green," said Nathalie. "Pretty close to where we parked last night."

"Okay. Now get going," said Theo. "I'll come find you afterwards. If I haven't checked in within an hour, take off."

Itio nodded. "Theophilus is right, pretty ladies. We should retire. Fear not, he will be fine."

"See you later," Nathalie said brightly.

Delphine nodded, a little less cheerful. "Yeah. See you later."

"Get out of here, and keep your heads down," said Theo. "Nothing's going to happen to me."

Theo and Itio bustled the twins out of the warehouse. Itio gave him a reassuring wink as he helped Delphine out of the window, and then he was gone. Theo returned to the main warehouse, sat down on one of the sofas, and settled down to wait, phone in hand.

About twenty minutes later, Itio phoned. Theo took the call immediately. "Itio."

Itio cut straight to the point, for once. "Two men in a car approaching you. No attempt at stealth."

"Thanks, Itio."

"A pleasure."

Theo turned the phone off and went over to the main warehouse doors, towering, rust-spotted relics made from folded metal. A person-sized door was set in one of the panels. Theo unbolted and opened it. Moments later an unobtrusive sedan pulled into the lot, drove across the front of the building, and parked behind a large stack of pallets next to a dumpster. The doors opened, and two people got out.

Theo relaxed slightly. Michael was instantly identifiable: a tall, handsome man with large, expressive features and just the tiniest hint of fuzz covering his scalp: his sire's odd sense of humor was a matter of local legend, and Michael had been extensively shaved just before his embrace. The person with him was reassuringly familiar. Doug Siegel—tall, broad, well-dressed—was the Brujah primogen for Aurora, and he had been openly friendly during Theo's previous visit.

Theo nodded pleasantly to them as they approached the door, but no one said a word until they were both inside.

As soon as the door was closed, Theo smiled at them. "Michael, Doug, thank you for coming. I really appreciate it."

Michael nodded, and the group moved a short distance into the warehouse. "That's alright, Bell. Gives me a chance to repay you for sorting me out a couple of weeks ago. What exactly is going on?"

Theo grinned bitterly. "Well, before I answer that, let me ask you a question. How do you feel about the spread of the blood hunt against me?"

"Bloody great overreaction if you ask me," said Michael. "Ludicrous."

Doug nodded. "It's a bit more than just that. I'm hearing all sorts of rumors about you, Archon Bell—from both up and down the chain. Nasty things."

Theo nodded grimly. "Like what?"

"Take your pick: that you torture mortals; that you have embraced a legion of your own family members as a personal army. That you diablerize neonates for fun. At one small Chicago rave two days ago, some space monkey told me that he'd personally seen you taking carnal pleasure from goats."

Michael snorted, grinning. "Well, Bell? Do you fuck animals?"

Theo shook his head wearily, as much at the situation as the charge. "While I was in Minneapolis, I uncovered one cell of a slave ring. It had a lot of influence over the local Kindred. In terms of the charges against me, all I actually did was kill one former friend, and that was in self-defense. That's the truth, I promise. The prince there, Elizabeth, is being leaned on. They might be manipulating Justicar Paschek, too. I suspect that the spread of the blood hunt—and your rumors, Doug—can be tied back to the same source. The people behind the slave ring. One of their agents tried to take me out a few days ago. Damn near succeeded in eating me. I wouldn't be surprised if that Rockton massacre was his doing too. They seem to have a lot of tendrils out all over this area, and getting rid of me appears to be a prime concern."

"That certainly would explain a few things," said Michael thoughtfully. "However, it would seem to suggest that keeping the fuck away from you is a prudent path."

Theo nodded dryly, ignoring Doug's startled glance at his boss. "Probably, yes. They must have a whole stack of people under their thumbs to put this much pressure on me. But there are benefits to coming out to play with me, too. I am going to find these bastards, by hook or by crook, and put them in the ground for good. I wasn't going to bother, but nobody fucks with me like this and gets away with it. Somewhere, they'll have something solid I can use to clear my ass and smoke out some of the fuckers they have in the Camarilla. The Inner Circle is going to be *very* grateful to anyone going out on a limb to help identify a cell of traitors."

"It's a risk, Bell," said Michael bluntly. "Hard to quantify, too."

"That's true. I'll understand if you decide this meeting never happened. All I'm asking for is a little information-digging though, and when I make it back, I'll be in a position to be very grateful."

"You're confident, then?"

Theo grinned. "I haven't been taken down yet, and a hell of a lot of people have tried over the years."

Michael grinned back, his voice booming. "That's the spirit, lad. Not averse to a risk or two myself. Good carrot you've got there; glad to see there's no stick. I'm in. Doug?"

"Miss the chance to help the legendary Theo Bell against a nest of traitors? Are you kidding?"

"Good man," said Michael approvingly.

"Thank you very much," said Theo. "Both of you."

"So what do you need, Bell?"

"At the moment, I need leads more than anything else. Anyone who might be the source of a rumor, who might be putting pressure on princes to sign up to the blood hunt, or those who are otherwise actively working against me. Someone I can…interview a little."

Michael nodded. "I'll get onto it right away. Chicago leaned on me to tow the party line, so I can start by finding out why."

"And I'll find out who that space monkey was," said Doug. "I assume he was lying?"

Theo grinned. "Totally. I never molest anything smaller than a horse. Be subtle though, gentlemen. For your own sakes. Try to stick to people you trust. I don't know how many agents these bastards have, or where they're snooping."

"Don't worry, Bell. Doug and I can look after ourselves. One of us will come back here in a couple of hours, to let you know what we've flushed up on an initial trawl."

"Thank you once again," said Theo. "This means a lot to me."

Michael nodded. "Not a problem. You're a good man, and you were there when we needed you earlier in the month." He strolled back to the door, Doug in tow. "Be in touch soon."

The door opened briefly, and the pair of them slipped out. A few moments later, there was a quiet coughing rumble as the car started up and headed out. Theo locked the door again, then went back to the sofas and sat down, before turning his phone back on.

A few moments later, it rang. He checked and was unsurprised to see that it was Itio. "Hi, Itio."

"I see you, Theophilus. How was the meeting?"

"Good, I think," said Theo uncertainly. "They've agreed to do some careful digging and to report back here in a couple of hours. They seem genuine, and Michael has always been pretty straightforward."

"You sound cautious," said Itio.

"I am a little. We have no idea what we're up against. This might be an almighty mistake."

Itio muttered something unintelligible, then turned back to the phone. "One moment please, Theophilus." One of the girls was talking in the background. A few seconds later, he turned back to the mouthpiece. "Delphine suggests that you join us in the car."

"I don't think Michael is going to do anything stupid," Theo protested.

"Perhaps not, but he might have been observed entering the warehouse, maybe even overheard when talking to you originally."

Theo frowned. "I suppose he might, at that. There's no reason not to join you for a while. Alright, I'll tidy up here and come out to the car."

"See you shortly, then."

"Bye Itio." Theo turned the phone back off and tapped it to his lips thoughtfully. After a few moments, he spun around and headed to the corridor of offices, collecting all the possessions that he and the girls had left. Everything fit comfortably into his gym bag. He missed the weight of his lost shotgun. It would have been a comforting back-up. Even his knife would have been a start.

A couple of minutes later, he was heading out of the side window and across the yard, his bag over his shoulder and his mind full of dusty concrete and old metal. It was just a short walk down to the golf store. The lot was busier than it had been the night before, but not by much. The new ride was easy to spot, a dark green minivan with room for eight that had long ago left behind its soccer mom. Sluggish, probably. Still, it was likely to be unobtrusive, and the station wagon had hardly been a performance vehicle.

Itio spotted him approaching the van and nodded to him pleasantly. Theo let his concentration fade as he reached for the passenger door handle, and the world cramped back in around him again, all brash and jostling. He opened the door and slid in.

"Theo!" The girls sounded identically relieved to see him.

"Hi folks. All okay?"

"Everything is well," Itio said.

"Sorry it's kinda boring and uncomfortable out here," said Theo. "The next couple of hours will be the test."

Delphine looked concerned. "We're not going to stay here today though, are we?"

"No," said Theo. "We'll move on somewhere else. Itio's friend, maybe."

"Perhaps," agreed Itio.

"Good," said Delphine. "I wouldn't feel safe there again."

"So now what?" Nathalie sounded slightly put out. Waiting out in the parking lot all this time would have been hardest on her, of course.

"We sit and wait for a bit more," said Theo sympathetically.

"It may be worth making use of some extra concealment," Itio said.

Theo shrugged. "Thank you, Itio. In for a penny, I guess."

Delphine's eyes narrowed. "Is this going to be like what you did to us at the library?"

Itio smiled gently. "More or less, pretty lady."

She shuddered. "This is going to be a bit icky, Nat. I'll be right here. Don't forget it."

Nathalie nodded, her face tight. "Thanks for the heads up."

Gradually, a sense of dream-like isolation rose up. The others were still in plain sight, but simultaneously seemed to be miles away. Theo had the strangest feeling that if he tried to touch Itio beside him, he'd see his hand stretching out into the distance, but still not actually reaching the guy. The world outside the car was even further away, as if the inside of the vehicle had been removed to some separate dimension. Theo glanced back and saw the twins hugging each other closely. Nathalie was trembling a little.

Theo nodded his thanks to Itio—speech felt about as welcome as a fart in a cathedral, somehow—and settled down to wait.

No more than thirty minutes later, Theo picked up the rumble of motorcycles approaching. The noise was still low when the group came into view approaching from the east, identical black Kawasaki Ninjas with riders in nondescript black leathers. They were riding slowly and quietly, to minimize disturbance. His heart sank.

"Keep still, everyone. That's one of the local scourge packs. I recognize the bikes." He instinctively kept his voice low. Within moments, he spotted another pack heading up from the west. "Okay, this is definitely trouble. There are two loads of them approaching, maybe more. The bastard must have sold me out after all. The good news is that they have absolutely no reason to even glance at this parking lot, let alone examine the van. Crouch down in your seats. I doubt anyone's good enough to spot us, but just in case, let's stay out of direct sight as much as possible."

The girls nodded and slipped to the floor, holding each other nervously. Itio and Theo sank down in their seats, but Theo kept an eye on proceedings, and he noticed that Itio was doing the same.

The first pack cut their engines before they reached the unit and dismounted. They held position until the second pack— four strong—stopped on the other side of the unit. Within moments they had swarmed over the wire, and were zigzagging across the yard. Two remained behind, outside the wire, and Theo could hear still more engines nearby, perhaps ready to launch pursuit if necessary.

"They're going in," he reported quietly.

After several incredibly long minutes, the door set in the warehouse shutters opened, and the black-clad scourges filed out. They had even kept their motorcycle helmets on—presumably, the outfits were designed to allow decent maneuverability. Several of them were openly carrying light automatics. They milled around for a minute or two, then started dispersing.

"They're out now," he said. " They may be coming past soon. Stay down." A little whimpering noise from the back told him that the extra warning was unnecessary.

Within moments, the packs were back on their bikes. Each group continued in the direction they had been facing, so the initial three continued on away from the golf store, and the four approached it. Theo ducked under the dash, flinching as the halogen spots lit up the cab. The engines seemed to hesitate for a heart-stopping moment. Then, miraculously, they were revving up, and the noise was fading into the distance.

He poked his nose above the dash, relieved that the coast looked clear, and then glanced round, to where Delphine was starting to sit up.

"Stay down," he told her sharply. "We'll give it half an hour at least. Never move immediately after evading searchers. If they're any good, they'll have left someone in a strategic position to double-check. It's the oldest trick in the book."

She blanched slightly and cowered down again.

"Just hang tight, kid." Theo made his voice sympathetic. "We're home clear here. We've just got to be patient."

Delphine nodded unhappily and bent back to whisper reassuringly to Nathalie, who looked pale and shaky.

After forty-five nervous minutes, Theo decided that the coast was as clear as it was likely to get. He looked across at Itio. "Do you mind driving while the rest of us stay out of sight?" He kept his voice quiet.

Itio smiled pleasantly. "Of course not, Theophilus. I may not be able to keep you hidden if I withdraw from the group, but if you stay low you should escape any casual detection."

Theo nodded. "Thank you. Did you get that, girls? Keep down, and be prepared to become noticeable again."

Delphine sighed. "That feels really icky too, sis."

"How come?" Nathalie's voice had a bit of welcome spirit to it.

"Exactly."

"Oh."

Theo shushed them gently and sank as far down into the seat well as he could. Itio started the engine up and glanced down at Theo, looking slightly amused.

Theo rolled his eyes back and pitched his voice low, so that only Itio could hear. "I'm getting a bit fucking sick of this."

Itio winked at him and pulled off. The isolated feeling evaporated as soon as the car moved. Suddenly the world was back in force. They were so obvious again. How could anyone possibly fail to notice them? The feeling was horrible, like being targeted with neon spotlights in front of a huge hostile audience. One of the girls moaned quietly. Theo didn't have the heart to remind her to stay silent—he felt the same way himself.

They drove a short distance, turned round a long corner, and started picking up speed.

"One of them is waiting by the roadside," said Itio out of the corner of his mouth. "He is looking this way."

Delphine and Nathalie both stifled small stereo shrieks.

"He is pretending to watch idly. He is now glancing at his bike. He is looking back to us as we pull away.... No, he has gone back to scanning the road. He is now out of sight."

Theo nodded his gratitude to Itio, but he still didn't let the girls get up off the floor until the vehicle was on I-88 out of Aurora.

———

Control pressed a button and waited patiently while a line was established. Eventually, the call was answered.

"What?" It was a man's voice, full of power and barely-checked rage.

"This is Control, General."

"What do you want?"

If Control was in the least bit put out by Karsh's manner, she kept it well hidden. "Bell has been sighted in Aurora. He made contact with the prince there and one of the primogen. Our people on the ground took steps to deal with the problem, but he got away."

"He'll head east or south," Karsh said thoughtfully. "That puts him inside an eight-hour arc. Good. I'll deal with Aurora. Look out for any primaries he may have on the East Coast."

"Of course, General."

"Good."

The line went dead, and Control meticulously wrote up and then filed some notes before turning to a large pin-board map.

Chapter Four

Wheels Within Wheels

The night rushed by outside, raindrops streaking along the front windshield and distorting the streetlights. Buildings loomed close by, like rank after rank of gigantic toy soldiers. The wheels rumbled beneath them, quieter than Theo might have feared. All in all, though, it was starting to get irritatingly similar.

Itio looked at Theo calmly across the front of the auto. "We are currently heading in toward Chicago. I thought you would prefer that than starting out westwards. Did you have a specific destination in mind?"

Theo thought about it for a minute. "I want to get back toward the East Coast. If I'm going to find any answers, I'm going to need access to people, and that means staying firmly within Camarilla territory. That's where my contact base is strongest."

Itio nodded. "I guessed as much."

Delphine stuck her head between the front seats, leaving Nathalie drowsing across the seat. "We want to keep away from Detroit then, right?"

"Yeah," Theo said, with a certain amount of feeling. "Definitely."

"How about Columbus?" Delphine sounded slightly proud of herself.

"I'd rather get clear of Indiana," said Theo. "I'm still not happy about that whole Rockton thing."

"I meant Ohio," said Delphine. "It'll get us a decent chunk of the way east, and it's not as big as Cincinnati. Bigger *is* riskier, right?"

Theo nodded, impressed. "At the moment, yes. I'd guess so, anyway. To be honest, it's hard to be absolutely certain with these idiots. Columbus isn't as far south as Kentucky, either. Good call, kid."

Delphine beamed at him. "So where are we heading from there?"

Theo sighed. "Now you've got me. I don't know what I was expecting, but I'm a bit surprised that Michael grew fangs like that."

"Maybe he didn't," said Delphine.

Theo blinked. "That's a good point. He wasn't there. But where does that leave us?"

"Well, either he put on a really good act with you, they got to him after he started making enquiries and scared the shit out of him, or someone overheard something and took matters into her own hands."

"Yeah. In other words, we know absolutely jack."

She deflated a little. "Only that we have to make sure anyone we talk to is very fucking cautious."

Theo nodded. "Tell me about it. There's not many people I can risk approaching, either. Michael was always a low-probability try, but it was worth it because we were in town, so to speak. There's no more than three or possibly four others I trust to have any degree of personal loyalty in the face of all the shit that's going on around me at the moment."

"I have a fair number of people whom I can contact without personal exposure," said Itio. "I have started speaking to them, and some have already started making discreet enquiries."

"You have?" Delphine sounded surprised. "When?"

"This evening, pretty lady."

"But I've been with you all night so far and you haven't picked up the phone once!"

Itio grinned wolfishly, a strangely sinister expression on his amiable face. "Indeed."

Delphine glanced at Itio once and wisely let the matter drop. "Who's on *your* hit-list, Theo?"

He winced at her poor taste in words. "That's a rather personal question, childe."

She grinned. "We've been over this before. So I'm a little nosier than your average vampire." Her voice took on a serious edge. "Anyway, staying with you is a risk at the moment. I'm happy taking it—I know I owe you—but I figure I deserve to know a little bit to help me have some faith that we're doing more than just floundering about in the darkness."

Theo sighed. "Fair enough, I guess. I have a colleague who dislikes Paschek almost as much as I do. I've saved his life a few times, and he would be prepared to help out. I also have a clanmate down in Virginia who I've known for decades. She's a primogen, now. Finally, there's my sire. I can't believe that he wouldn't at least listen after all this time, and I'm certain he wouldn't work against me." He shot a look at Itio. "Oh yeah, and there's this crazy quester I've worked with a stack of times. Only thing about him is, he's a little unpredictable."

"Thank you, Theophilus," Itio said sincerely. "I do my best."

Theo grinned. "Any time. So does that set your mind at rest at all? Don't forget that your sire is out looking for leads at this very moment, and Itio has been contacting people too."

Delphine flashed a sidelong glance at Itio, then nodded cautiously. "I suppose so. At least there are a few people left. What are you going to do if—"

"Think of something else," said Theo, cutting her off firmly. "Don't worry, Delphine. We'll get to the bottom of this shit."

She sighed. "I hate this."

"Hardly wild on it myself, kid."

"I know, but...." She trailed off.

Theo looked at her, concerned. "What's bothering you, Delphine?"

She grimaced. "Oh, nothing. Everything. You know. I miss my life. Back before I was killed and all that. I'm tired of all this grim dashing around in cars. I want some fun."

"Fear not, pretty lady." Itio sounded earnest. "As soon as we have rectified Theo's little problem, I have a *lot* of fun lined up for you, your sister and your sire. A way of saying thanks for all your assistance."

Delphine looked up at him, uncertain. "Yeah? What sort of fun?"

"That would spoil the surprise, wouldn't it? There is no need to be concerned, however. It's going to start with a massive party and just get better from there."

"A party definitely sounds good," said Delphine. "Not having people trying to kill me would be enough, though." A thought hit her, and she brightened. "Hey Itio, will this party have some sexy guys for me to toy with heartlessly?"

Itio smiled broadly. "Oh my, yes. Very much so."

She grinned. "I like the sound of it already."

Theo glanced back at Nathalie sleeping sprawled across her seat. "Is your sister eating properly? She's looking a little pale, and she's not normally this tired."

A guilty look flashed across Delphine's face. "I guess so. I haven't thought about food much, so it never occurred to me to ask."

"Well, once we're properly on our way, we can hit a gas station and make sure she gets a square meal inside her. She might as well sleep for the moment, though. I'll see if I can sort out reservations for a roadhouse somewhere in the Columbus area, too."

Delphine nodded. "Good one." She sat back again, cuddling up to her sleeping sister, careful not to wake her.

A few minutes later, Itio looked over at him. "Theophilus, do you know what time it is?" His voice was extremely quiet, so much so that it was barely audible.

Theo glanced at him, puzzled, then checked the dashboard clock. "Not even ten. Why?" He kept his voice low too, although he didn't really see the need.

Itio, surprisingly, shook his head. "No, old friend. Not that."

Theo peered at him suspiciously. "You're not getting all apocalyptic on me are you, Itio?"

"Not I, Theophilus. The world itself. This race does not have long to run."

Theo shook his head. "Look, I know these are troubled times, and some of those hokey old prophecies are vague enough that they could apply, but then they're vague enough that they could always fucking apply. I don't think you need to worry about the Final Nights just yet, somehow."

"It may be tomorrow, or a hundred years from now, or a millennium away. That is not the point."

"I'll worry about the end if it comes," said Theo firmly. "At the moment, I'm more concerned about seeing next week."

Itio shook his head gently, the shifting shadows making his face look strangely gaunt. "You will dance the waters that rise up to flood us all, Wave Man." His voice was shockingly hollow, as if coming from some impossibly distant place. "You will skip away from tow and tide on a delicate path of swimmers and sinkers, free at last of the chains that would drag you down. You will deliver that freedom to others before the new dawn finally scours all."

Theo shook his head, perplexed. "That's all I've ever asked for, Itio. I've always been prepared to die helping others join me in freedom. If that's my fate, it sounds pretty good to me. That's what I was trying to do when Don Cerro embraced me, remember?"

Itio smiled, and his face and voice returned to normal. "We'll get onto I-65 as soon as we're through Gary. May I suggest a stop for the ladies to refresh themselves at some convenient time before Indianapolis?"

Theo grinned. "Sure thing. Sounds good to me."

An hour later, Theo turned around to the back of the van, where the girls were curled around each other.

"Sorry to wake you," he said loudly, with a faint smile.

Delphine's eyes flicked open. Sleep wouldn't come at night for the undead. "What's up, Theo?"

Nathalie groaned quietly and stretched.

He looked at her, amused. "We're going to pull in at a service station. I thought you might like to get something to eat."

Nathalie sat up. "Oh, could I? That would be fantastic. I'm starved. Del?"

"I can't, remember? Don't let that stop you though, sis."

"Oh, thank you," said Nathalie, hugging her sister sleepily.

"You might want to go to the toilet too," said Delphine wryly.

"That's a good idea. Thank you so much, sis."

"Yeah, yeah, very funny," Delphine said.

Nathalie just smiled at her.

The vehicle pulled into the parking lot, stopping near the sprawling building that housed the facilities. There were plenty of cars in the lot and a number of motorbikes as well. Theo forced himself to ignore them.

The girls piled out of the vehicle, chatting away merrily arm in arm as they headed into the station mall. Theo watched them go, then turned to Itio. "I'm going to head in too. I want to make some arrangements for somewhere to stay, and I might feed a bit, as well. Those burns are going down, but they're still tender."

"I dislike such places," said Itio loftily. "Utterly new and superficial, all bright lights and empty minds. I will remain here. I can put the time to productive use."

Theo grinned at him. "Sure."

Inside, the service station was much like all the others Theo had ever stopped at. The surfaces were bright and clean with marble-effect floors, white walls and ceilings, loads of strip lights, and chrome metal everywhere. There were several retail outlets, including a shop selling newspapers, candy, books, drinks and several other types of useless crap, another shop selling pre-made plastic-looking sandwiches, a small outlet for trite car accessories, and a large food court with half a dozen familiar concessions. He glanced around the main shop for a few minutes, bemused at the junk that people bought nowadays, then went to look for an information board or something.

As it turned out, the maps and flyers were conveniently near the payphones. Within ten minutes, Theo had reserved a family room at a bland-sounding roadside motel a short distance from Columbus and made arrangements for late arrival and departure. The place sounded reassuringly anonymous, but he'd made a point of avoiding any of his usual aliases when booking. He'd also telephoned Kristine and left a message for her advising her of the change of location.

He then headed to the toilets — one of the few places where a degree of privacy was possible in the mall. The urinals were in a different room from the stalls, so Theo went to the taps and started washing his hands. After a minute or so, a lull in traffic provided a good opportunity. A skinny looking guy was heading for the cubicles, and Theo quietly tagged along behind him. As the man opened the door on his stall of choice, Theo glanced back swiftly to make sure that there was no one approaching and confirmed that the security camera he'd noticed wasn't angled this way, then rushed the guy before he could close the door, clamping a vise-like hand over his mouth. The man's eyes bulged in horror, and he made some feeble gurgling noises.

Theo looked deep into his eyes, and the guy went limp, terrorized into passivity. Theo shrugged to himself and then reached out with his mind. The man's will was almost nonexistent, a tiny shroud of tatters. Theo breezed past it and crushed into his mind. The guy gazed up at him, entranced.

Theo brought his mouth to the guy's ear. "Stay silent and motionless until I tell you otherwise." His voice was a low hiss, just loud enough to be audible.

The guy nodded obediently. Theo dropped his hand, pulled the man close to him, and bit deeply into his throat. Hot blood gushed into his mouth, and he gulped it down hungrily. After a few moments of delicious reverie, Theo judged that the guy had given enough and licked the wound shut. Then he looked into the man's eyes again and smashed into his thoughts, scattering them like droplets of water.

"When the cubicle door closes, you will lock it and remember that you just came in here to do whatever it is you came in here to do. You were distracted for a minute as you entered because you could hear a couple screwing a couple of cubicles down. They stopped, and you remembered you hadn't locked the door. Nothing else happened. Okay?"

The man nodded.

Theo left the cubicle, satisfied to hear the door locking behind him. He got out of the men's room swiftly, glad to be away from the slightly rank smell. The mall area was no more interesting on a second visit, but Theo wandered around it a bit more anyway, to give Itio a little more time. Eventually, he saw the twins coming out of the food court and went over to join them. Nathalie looked a lot more herself.

He nodded to them. "Hi girls. Everything okay?"

"Great, thanks," said Nathalie. "You?"

"Yeah, I'm good. Let's blow this place, shall we?"

An unfamiliar voice cut in, thick with ignorance and contempt. "Fucking whores."

Theo looked up, surprised. A couple of dumb, greasy-looking young guys were standing a couple of feet away, glaring at the three of them.

Delphine beat him to it. "What the fuck do *you* want, pond life?"

"To cut your face up, you filthy, nigger-loving bitch."

Delphine blinked, her eyes going slightly unfocused. Theo sighed to himself. A pair of hicks weren't worth the trouble. He reached over and stretched an arm out to hold her back. "Drop—"

A wild howl from the other side made him whip round. Nathalie was flying into the pair of them, arms flailing, literally shrieking with rage. The guys started laughing, and then she hit them like a steamroller. Theo watched in astonishment as she bashed into the pair of them, staggering them backwards. She then reached up, still wailing like a banshee, took a handful of lank hair in each fist and brutally clubbed their heads together. There was a sickeningly meaty crack, and they both collapsed.

She dropped them, and even as they were landing on the floor, she jumped on top of the speaker's body and started ripping long strips of flesh out of his cheeks and neck with her nails. Hot blood bubbled up from the asshole's face, and Theo's head swam. In the background, someone was starting to scream. He exchange a stunned glance with Delphine, then leapt forward, grabbed Nathalie by the waist and pulled her back.

She fought him, kicking and yelling. She was surprisingly strong, but it was easy to restrain her. "Enough, Nat," he said firmly. "Enough!"

She ignored him.

Delphine came up beside her and put a hand on her shoulder. "He's right, Nat. Enough. They're not worth it."

She subsided finally. "Oh, alright."

Theo looked at Delphine again, then back to where people were starting to gather. "We have to get out of here now," he muttered. He released Nathalie cautiously, ready to grab her again if necessary.

Delphine nodded. "Yeah. Let's go."

The three of them headed quickly for the door, not quite running. People melted out of their way, eager not to get involved. Once they were outside, Theo did start jogging, the girls running to keep up. They piled into the van, glad to see that Itio had already started the engine. As soon as they were inside, he took off, going just slowly enough not to stand out too much.

Theo turned round in his seat and fixed the girls with a fierce stare. "Alright, Nathalie. What the fuck was that about?"

She glared back at him, still seething. "I will *not* have some vile little hick talking about Del like that."

"He wasn't worth the danger," Theo said. "What about sticks and stones?"

"Fuck that," said Nathalie, almost spitting. "The little limp-dick fucker needed to be taught a lesson."

"You ripped his face off, sis." Delphine sounded slightly awed.

"I'd have done a lot worse than that if you'd left me alone," said Nat. "It was kinda fun, actually. He'll think twice before badmouthing anyone again."

"If he survives," said Theo grimly. "Some of those wounds were in very dangerous locations."

"Good," said Nathalie fiercely.

"Look," said Theo, trying hard to be reasonable. "I'm not saying I disagree with the way you feel, but *please* try to remember we need to stay low profile. A run-in with the cops might just be the end of Delphine, Itio and me, if they decide to lock us up for the night."

Nathalie nodded sulkily. "Alright. I'll be careful. He was a fucking piece of shit, though."

"Yes," said Theo simply. "He was. Lots of the population are. If it was up to me, I'd be perfectly happy for you to tear them all into ribbons. Sadly, it's not—the police tend to want the last say."

"He's right," said Delphine. "I wanted to take him out too, but it wouldn't have done any good."

"Okay, I get the message," said Nathalie. "I'll keep a lid on it, okay?"

"Thanks," said Delphine.

Theo turned back to Itio, who was heading patiently down the Interstate. "We had a little encounter in the service station. Some subnormal hick took offense at Nat and Del going off with someone of a different skin tone and got all personal about it. Nathalie was unimpressed, so she clubbed the guy out cold and then tore his face up before I could stop her."

"Impressive," said Itio laconically. His eyes were distant however, and his lips were pursed.

―――――

They were settled in the Columbus Faithouse motel by four a.m. The room was perfectly adequate—the bathroom was large enough to easily accommodate the three vampires and had no windows. Theo still had a few wedges, some aluminum foil and a couple of traps, and felt secure. The place was just over the road from a large out-of-town strip mall too, which cheered Nathalie up somewhat.

Theo had been pondering the question of where to head next while Itio drove and the girls retreated into their own little world. Once Nathalie had pillaged the vending machines and Delphine had finished unpacking her various knickknacks, Theo joined them and Itio in the main room.

"I think we should head to Maryland tomorrow," he said. "Hagerstown, specifically."

Itio arched an eyebrow. "I assume that this opinion is not just whim?"

"It's Don Cerro's neck of the woods," said Theo. "He's in Gettysburg. Claims he likes the sense of history. It's also handy for Washington, Philly, and Baltimore, and both Richmond and New York are in range. I don't know anything about the political climate there at the moment—I don't much care if they're hunting me or not—but I do remember hearing that the local principality is weak. There aren't that many of us in the town and the whole area's still a mess after the big dust up with the Sabbat a few years back." Itio had stayed well clear of the sect war that had raged up and down the Eastern Seaboard in 1999, but Theo had been in the thick of it and knew some of the territory pretty damn well.

"Sounds reasonable," said Itio approvingly. "I see no reason to propose anywhere else."

"It doesn't sound much fun," said Delphine. "Then again, that's probably a good thing at the moment. Let's go for it. It would be cool to meet Papa Bell, too." She grinned mischievously.

"My sire would undoubtedly find you delightful," said Theo, grinning at the thought. "He always had an eye for pretty young things. You might want to keep Nathalie at arm's length, though. He can get a little impulsive at times."

Delphine frowned at him disapprovingly, and he beamed back at her.

"Anyway, we might end up spending a few days there. I'm kinda sick of moving around so much. Nathalie, would you mind setting up a place for us to stay for a week or so?"

"No problem," said Nathalie cheerfully. "It'd be good to be able to do something useful. You want a short-term apartment, yeah?"

"Yes," said Theo, a little impressed. "They're much better."

"Okay, no problem. I'll sort it out one way or another. I'll arrange a motel for tomorrow night too, because no leasing agent is going to hand over keys at four in the morning. While I'm thinking about it, I noticed a gardening place over at that mall. Give me a bit more cash, and I'll get a bunch of rubble sacks or something, too."

"Great," Theo said. "Quick thinking. Thanks."

She smiled. "No problem. I don't want anything happening to any of you. I'll pick up some basic supplies for myself, too. Anyone else want anything?"

Delphine grinned wryly. "Just bricks and mortar."

"Covered. Itio?"

Itio shook his head, slightly bemused. "Thank you pretty lady, but no. I have all I need."

"'Kay. How about that cash, Theo?"

He fished in his pocket for a hundred and passed it over, keeping his expression serious. "Will that be enough?"

"Great. Thanks, big guy." She beamed at him.

Theo had a momentary vision of her tearing that asshole's face up earlier and felt a sudden wave of disorientation. The slavers had done some terrible things to Nathalie, which might have influenced her more than he'd initially thought. He smiled back at her, suddenly feeling old and tired.

———

As it turned out, Nathalie was as good as her word. The next evening, they woke up to find that she had print-outs confirming reservations for a short-rental house a little way outside the center of Hagerstown, along with a booking reference number for a motel on the town's outskirts for late that night. She'd also managed to find a bunch of five-foot gardening sacks—they'd be a tight fit, but the plastic was thick, jet black and totally opaque—along with a couple of bags of groceries and a bunch of make-up.

Delphine almost screamed in delight at that, grabbed the pouch and the pair of them vanished into the bathroom for twenty minutes. When she came back, Theo was forced to admit that although she looked overdone, it was nearly impossible to see her true pallor. Then Nathalie came out similarly prepared, and they really did look truly identical, the first time that Theo had seen them so.

They set out for Hagerstown shortly after dark, leaving a message of the new destination for Kristine. Nat seemed to be as chirpy as ever throughout the trip, even bossing them all around a little when it came to check in to the motel she'd found. There was no repeat of her attack of sudden fury. The next evening, they visited the house that Nathalie had signed for during the afternoon. It was perfect, in a fairly anonymous neighborhood called Wood Point, neither too quiet nor too busy. They'd be able to come and go without attracting much interest. The house had an upstairs bathroom that was easily light-proofed, a big walk-in closet, and a basement that had no windows at all. It also had a back door that led out onto a small park—named Hellane, Theo noted with some amusement—in case an escape route were required.

Once he'd inspected the house, ensured that the bathroom and closet were totally secure against sunlight and prepared a few tricks to leave around just in case, Theo tried a call to Don

Cerro. His sire was out of town though, and Theo was not about to leave a message.

Stymied for anything more constructive to do, Theo took the car out for a drive around town, figuring that it had to be safer than just walking aimlessly—particularly in a little place where street punks of the type he was dressed like were difficult to find. He spent an hour or so just meandering around within the city limits, getting a feel for the place.

Itio, who said that his sources had researched the town for him, confirmed what Theo remembered from tactical briefings during the summer and fall of 1999. The place was low-profile in Kindred terms, even for its size. It did have a prince who held sway over the whole of Washington County and then some—a crusty old German aristo who had been a resident since the town's incorporation in 1752 and claimed to be related to the original founder. There were only three other Kindred resident in the town however, all well settled, so the title was little more than a joke. They'd gone to ground during the Sabbat offensive and apparently weathered the storm by being not worth the trouble. According to Itio, the territory had signed up to the blood hunt, but that didn't seem to pose any threat. Visitors were welcomed grudgingly and encouraged to move on quickly. As there was nothing for Kindred to either visit for or to stay for, though, the prince didn't seem to ruffle anyone's feathers.

The place seemed to live up to its reputation. It looked like a nice little town. It was quite picturesque in places, with plenty of space given over to parks and greenery. The houses were prosperous in a small-town way, the restaurants and cafes pitched to match. The place had theatres, cinemas, late-night shopping, a baseball stadium—for the Suns, no less—and even a museum of fine art, according to several road signs. The nightlife was bustling, in a well-behaved kind of way. It looked like the kind of town that probably had a mandatory lawn code.

One that was enforced. Theo wasn't entirely surprised to see that a disproportionate percentage of the population appeared to be white.

It wasn't *all* Norman Rockwell, though. The community college looked sedate enough, but the Hagerstown Speedway, a few miles west of town, seemed to offer a potential source of rowdier entertainment. The fact that people would undoubtedly come to the track from out of town increased its utility as a possible hunting ground. It certainly wouldn't be to the prince's taste.

Satisfied, Theo headed back to the house. There didn't seem to be any prospect of the locals going after his blood, of being in league with Carnell's group, or even, frankly, of having ever heard of him. He grinned, savoring the sense of obscurity, and turned into Wabash Avenue. A motorcycle was parked in the drive of the house they were renting.

He parked quickly and hurried into the house. Sure enough, it was Kristine. The ladies were gathered in the kitchen, so Theo went in to join them, calling for Itio as well.

He sat down opposite the twins and nodded to Kristine. "How was your trip?"

"Tolerable," she said, smiling slightly.

Nathalie sneered. "It's certainly taken you long enough. You do know this stuff is serious, right?"

Theo blinked, surprised at her reaction. Delphine looked concerned, too.

"It was a little further than I expected to have to come," said Kristine apologetically. "That bike wasn't really designed for a long haul."

"A bad workman blames his tools," said Nathalie unpleasantly.

"Nat!" Delphine sounded shocked.

Itio came into the room. "Welcome back, beautiful lady. Apologies on my tardy entrance. I was checking on an interesting rumor. I trust all is well?"

Kris nodded gratefully. "Yes, Mr. Shima. Thank you."

"Did you manage to find anything out, Kristine?" Theo cut in briskly, to head off any further bickering.

"Well, background information regarding your case is pretty easy to come by. Everyone seems to be going on about it. The general assumption is that you've gone rogue following some disastrous attempts at summoning demons. The common story is that you've embraced a whole string of pretty young white girls as your personal toys, slaughtered half of the Minneapolis primogen, and now embarked on a ludicrous quest to gain power by diablerizing every elder you can lay your fangs on. Plenty of people don't buy it, and a few even seem to respect you for it, but for the most part, opinion is pretty negative. I tried Paschek's office, but his aides would only confirm that you have been suspended for gross dereliction of duty pending further investigation."

Theo sighed. "I suppose it could have been worse."

Kristine nodded. "I suppose so. There's more, though."

"About me?"

"No. At least, not directly. Several of my contacts are hearing rumors about disappearances. Kindred, mostly young. No one seems entirely sure where they are going to. Some are simply not returning from trips, others are just dropping out of sight. I know that's nothing particularly new, but it's happening in suspicious numbers and not just to flakes—people who were considered trustworthy have been vanishing, too. Some territories are worse than others. Miami is acquiring a particularly nasty reputation, even for Sabbat turf."

Theo frowned unhappily. "That could be the operation shifting up a gear, I suppose."

Kristine nodded. "Finally, I have an interesting statistic for you. Even counting your hunt as one item, there have been more blood hunts, assassinations and purges in the last three weeks than there have been in the previous six months. Again, Miami seems particularly vicious."

"Miami's not exactly a peaceful place at the best of times," Theo pointed out.

Kristine nodded. "I know. It is unusually bad at the moment though. Significantly so."

"Is that it?" Nathalie sounded unimpressed. "It's a bit pathetic, don't you think?"

"Hey," said Kristine, sounding hurt. "That's not exactly fair. I have a load of people looking for information. That was just the surface level stuff."

Theo frowned at Nathalie disapprovingly. "Quite. It's a complicated business, child."

"Maybe it is, but it's not rocket science to see when someone's not pulling their weight." Nathalie sounded defiant.

"Nat. Word." Delphine sounded strangled. She got up and left the room, her sister sulkily in tow.

"I don't know what's got in to her," Theo said.

"It's okay," said Kristine mildly. "She's just jealous."

Itio nodded. "I wanted to pick up on one of your points, pretty lady."

"Sure."

"One of my contacts reported that she was hunting with a friend in Miami when they were ambushed by a sizeable group. The friend was overpowered, staked, blindfolded and carted off. He has not reappeared since."

"That's pretty cut and dried," she said.

Theo nodded. "It does suggest something is going on in that direction. Miami is a big territory, though. Let's see if we can narrow it down rather than go haring off looking for needles in haystacks. Don Cerro may be able to uncover something. He still has a lot of political influence."

Delphine came back into the room, Nathalie in tow. They both looked relaxed again.

Kristine shot them a glance. "Sure, let's try Cerro. One of my contacts might turn something up in a night or two, as well."

Nathalie just nodded amiably.

An unpleasant wave of suspicion began to nag at the back of Theo's mind. He stood up and headed for the door. "Delphine, could I have a quick word with you please?" The twins started to get up. "Alone?"

Nathalie shrugged and sat back down. Delphine looked at her quickly, then turned to Theo. "Alright."

He waited until she joined him at the doorway and then ushered her across the hallway and into the living room.

"It's high time you and I had a talk," he said.

"What about?" Her expression was defiant.

Theo looked her square in the eyes. "What the hell is up with Nathalie?"

Delphine flinched slightly, but her expression was defiant. "It's no good getting pissed now. You didn't leave me any damn choice, Theo."

A sinking feeling started in the pit of Theo's stomach. "What do you mean?"

"You kept pushing and pushing, trying to fucking brain-wipe her, talking about having to kill her, about how much of a threat your entire fucking Camarilla would consider her. I mean Jesus, what was I supposed to do? I didn't want to lose her, and I certainly wasn't about to start reaming her fucking head. There weren't any options."

"What did you do, Delphine?" Theo's voice was low and threatening.

"I've started feeding her little bits of my blood. Kris told me about it."

Theo stared at her, horrified. "You fucking *ghouled* your own sister?"

"Is that what you call it? Look, I know you've got this whole slave hang up thing, but it's not like that."

"Oh, really?" Theo knew his voice was a lethal murmur, but he couldn't seem to raise it. "We use the term for a reason, childe. Ghouls are strange. The dead blood inside them gives them vile urges—grossly perverted, disgusting, murderous even. The temper becomes a terrible thing, coiled through and around with all-consuming envies and jealousies. Only one thing matters—the mistress. The rest of the world drops away. The personality, too. You're left with a twisted, evil creature—pathetically eager to please when you are there, consumed with longing and hatred when you are not. How dare you do that to someone you claim to love? How dare you?"

Delphine had gone pale. "No. I think you're exaggerating. That's not how Kristine described it at all. Have you ever had a... a ghoul yourself?"

Theo spat on the floor. "Of course not."

"Then you don't know," said Delphine eagerly. "You're just guessing, going on what you've seen and heard—and on your problem with slavery."

Theo shook his head in disbelief. "Two weeks and you know it all, eh kid? Maybe it is my fault. I should have warned you."

"Fuck off, you sanctimonious prick."

Theo looked at her coldly. "Keep her under control, Delphine. If you're going to enslave your own sister, I guess I can't stop you. She's your responsibility though. Give her orders to behave like her old self with us, to make sure she takes care of her physical needs, and to do whatever it takes not to draw attention to us."

"I'm not going to order Nat around!" Delphine looked offended.

"Yes you fucking are, childe. Otherwise she's going to get herself killed—by flying off at the wrong person, by pushing Kristine too far, or by not drinking for three days because she's not sure it's what you want. If you train her carefully, you can have someone with you who looks, sounds and mostly behaves like your sister. Just pray you never learn how to look into her mind, because I think the horror would finish you off."

"You're just trying to make me feel guilty," said Delphine rebelliously.

"Guilty? Christ, childe, you should be howling to the heavens for mercy. Don't take *my* word for it, though. After all, what do I know? You'll see for yourself."

He walked out, leaving her to think it over in peace.

Chapter Five

Overexposed

Two nights later, Theo was sitting in the kitchen with Kristine and Itio, going over even the most fragmentary leads and trying to pull some sort of firm information out of them. The general consensus seemed to be that anyone who knew anything was keeping quiet about it.

Theo rested his head in his hands, frustrated. "How about whispers or rumors? Isn't there anything related to these disappearances?"

Itio shrugged. "Discounting the more fantastical stories, I was passed a rumor of a small facility, hidden behind what looks to be a commercial unit in a quiet street. Inside it, there are tanks in which victims are placed, and somehow prepared before being shipped on. There was no suggestion of a location, of course. There never is."

"The Way Station," said Kristine, perking up a little.

Theo looked at her. "Excuse me?"

"One of my contacts said that the Kindred who disappear are taken to a central place called the Way Station, where they are held for transfer in batches to their end destination."

"No location," said Theo. It wasn't a question.

Kristine shook her head.

"Well, I'll bear the name in mind I guess. It doesn't exactly give us anything to work on, though." Theo sighed. "How about the girls? Have they come up with anything on the Internet?"

"Not so far," said Kristine. "They're down at the library right now, trying to sift through some batch of data or other. Something to do with unusual missing persons by area. If we adjust it to approximate Kindred population, we might find something useful. It'll be another night, though."

"Maybe I should use myself as bait," said Theo.

"That seems a high-risk proposition," Itio said mildly.

Theo nodded. "Maybe. But it's bound to flush *someone* out, and then maybe we can use them to start working our way back up the chain."

"Or maybe they'll just whack you from a mile away with a high-powered sniper rifle," Kristine pointed out.

Theo shrugged. "It could be worth the risk if nothing else flushes out over the next few nights."

Kristine shook her head doubtfully. "Let's see if we can get hold of Don Cerro again first, shall we? You could also try your other contacts too. Dangle yourself as a carrot once you have no other options left. You're not really on a deadline, after all."

"Of course," said Theo, nodding. "He was supposed to be back yesterday apparently, so maybe he'll be around tonight."

"Is it my turn to call him again?"

"Nope. It's Itio's." Theo tossed him the telephone.

Itio deftly snatched the phone out of the air, opened it with a mocking flourish, and made the call. A few seconds later, the line was answered. "Ah, good evening. May I speak with the inestimable Don Cerro?" He paused. "An old friend." He flashed a tentative thumbs-up at Theo and Kristine. "Thank you." Another long moment passed. "I have a call for you, sir. May I be impertinent enough to ask whether this line is secure? Excellent. Will you hold for one moment? Thank you."

Itio passed the phone back to Theo carefully, grinning.

Theo took it. "Good evening."

"Good evening, Theophilus." The rich voice sounded relaxed and cheerful. "I rather thought that you might be in contact. Your timing is exquisite, as always. Tell me, pray, was that Itio Shima a few moments ago? The voice sounded familiar."

"It was."

"Convey to him my regards, if you would be so kind." Don Cerro sounded amused.

"Of course. Sir, I need your help."

"Yes, Theophilus. I assumed that would be the case. I was planning on indulging myself with a rather well-known local candlelight ghost tour tomorrow evening. It departs from Baltimore Street at seven o'clock. No one will notice two gentlemen conversing quietly in the crowd, I think."

"I'll be there," Theo said, amused.

"Excellent, Theophilus. It will be a pleasure to talk to you in person. In addition, the walk will sharpen your memory of Civil War history, and who knows, you may even spot a ghost. Some are said to, on these tours." Don Cerro sounded positively mischievous.

"I'll look forward to it," said Theo with a smile.

"Until tomorrow."

"Bye."

Theo hung up. Kristine and Itio were looking at him expectantly. He grinned at them, suddenly cheerful. "Don Cerro will meet with me tomorrow. It seems he wants to take me ghost hunting."

Little slate-effect signposts along Baltimore Street, pretending to be tombstones, pointed the way to the beginning of the ghost tour. The tour offices were in a low, white building that looked authentically period, but the rest of the area seemed mostly tidy brick structures. Still, there were plenty of people around. Theo purchased a surprisingly cheap ticket from a tall, white-mustachioed man dressed as a nineteenth-century country gentleman and then hung back near the street, out of the way.

There were a number of people assembling for the tour. Several elderly couples had bought tickets, as had a smattering of younger folk and a handful of families. One of the families in particular promised to take up a lot of attention. The parents looked bored to begin with, and the mother—a large, selfish-looking woman—only stopped droning on at her oblivious husband long enough to cuff one of her brats every now and again. There were three children, somewhere between eight and twelve, and they seemed to largely ignore their mother's scolding. They were running around the yard, playing some irritating game that may or may not have involved impersonating a jet fighter. Everyone else was eyeing the five with greater or lesser degrees of resignation.

As seven o'clock approached, Theo tried to guess whether his sire would try to meet up with the tour, or whether he would just come to the office. It was difficult to tell. Knowing Don Cerro's sense of humor, it was possible that he would leap out at Theo from around some dramatic corner or tree trunk. The other possibility—that the phone line had been less secure than Don Cerro believed—was unlikely, and Theo tried not to dwell on it too much.

He braced himself for action just in case, loosening his new knife in its sheaf. Nathalie had purchased it for him the day before. It wasn't as good as his old Bowie, but it was sturdy, as several thick branches in the park behind the house had attested.

A deep, rolling voice jerked Theo back to reality. "Good evening, ladies and gentlemen, and welcome to...."

Theo tuned the guide out and glanced around the crowd. To his relief, Don Cerro had joined the group and was standing beside a couple of tourists—Southerners, if the piles of coats and scarves they were wearing were any guide. He noticed Theo's look and nodded to him pleasantly. For his part Cerro was his usual dapper self, wearing a casual tan suit and a cravat just flamboyant enough to brand him as a European tourist. His pronounced nose and eyebrows added to the Old World air.

The guide started off from the courtyard, already holding forth with a stream of nonsense about how incredibly haunted Gettysburg was. Theo held back for a moment, then fell in beside his sire.

"Thank you for coming," said Theo, talking quietly enough not to disturb the tourists in front of them.

"Yeeeeeeeeeeeeeee!" screamed one of the jet-fighter children as it ran past.

"You're very welcome, Theophilus," said Don Cerro, after a suitable pause. "Tell me one thing truly. It will not affect my decision to aid you."

"Of course," said Theo.

"Did you do these things that they are saying of you?"

"No," said Theo simply. "I swear. I did have to kill Angus Abranson, but that was entirely in self-defense."

Don Cerro nodded. "I am glad. I am sorry for Angus's loss, but I understand these things. It would have saddened me to think that you had lost your sense of perspective. Regardless of what I may say to that nasty, puffed up little adder Paschek, I have always been and still am proud of you."

Theo just nodded at his sire, not quite trusting himself to speak.

"Which brings us rather nicely to your current predicament," Don Cerro said, with a sympathetic smile. "I..."

"Dakka-dakka-dakka-dakka-wheeeeeeeeBOOM!"

"... could probably dance the rumba naked right now and no one would notice," he continued wryly. "However, I have no wish to disgust these good people. I will do whatever I can to be of assistance, Theophilus. I have heard the stories, of course. Maybe you could tell me the facts?"

Theo nodded and launched into a detailed summary of the previous three weeks or so, from his arrival in Aurora right through to that evening. He included as much as he could remember of Carnell, along with Kristine's theories and even the rumors that Doug Siegel had heard. Don Cerro let him talk, and by the time he had finished, the group was standing around a singularly un-spooky oak tree. The rest of the group looked somewhat awed however, so presumably the guide was spinning a good story.

Don Cerro mulled things over for several moments before speaking again, keeping his voice quiet. "And what do *you* think, Theophilus? What do your instincts tell you?"

Theo sighed. "I have a nasty feeling that Kristine is right, and the disappearances—and even some of these hunts and purges—are related. If this operation really is big enough to hound me so relentlessly, it must have had more than one slave base, and I can't be the only person to have stumbled across them. They must have support at the highest quarters."

"Or hired help," Don Cerro mused. "If duties and support are occasional, and the pay-off is significant, even the most powerful may acquiesce."

"Coercion could be involved too," said Theo. "I certainly get the feeling that Minneapolis was being squeezed rather than bought."

"Money, power, continued existence, suppression of embarrassing material—it is all but different types of reward," said Don Cerro.

"I suppose so," said Theo thoughtfully.

"You need a link in the chain, am I correct?"

Theo nodded. "Yes. Somewhere to start working upwards."

"The higher the better, then."

"Of course. But I'd imagine that each step further up is that much riskier to investigate."

"I shall be cautious, Theophilus."

"Please do," Theo said. "Really. These bastards seem to be getting everywhere. Don't mention anything to anyone who isn't absolutely trustworthy, and be careful about telephone lines, too. Look at how quickly they got to me in Aurora."

Don Cerro smiled calmly. "I understand. I shall keep your name out of it, avoid home meetings and even make sure that paperwork is delivered to my tree. Will that suffice?"

"Your tree?"

Don Cerro grinned. "There's a lightning-split oak in the park across from my residence. I occasionally have packages delivered there, if they are discreet or the carrier distasteful."

"I see," said Theo, amused by the image.

"Come to visit me at home tomorrow evening, Theophilus. It is a tall, blue building on East Sixth Street, in modest grounds. Hopefully I will have some information for you. In the meantime, my son, I urge patience and prudence. Do not do anything rash."

"I'll be careful," Theo said.

"Excellent. I will take my leave, until tomorrow." Don Cerro flashed an amused eye at the jet children, now brawling noisily off to one side. "Enjoy the rest of the tour."

Theo looked at the little bastards and sighed. Behind him, Don Cerro slipped off into the night.

Back at home, Cerro settled into his favorite leather armchair and considered the evening's revelations. It was an uncomfortable matter, however it was sliced. He tried it from several different angles—coincidence, minor competing groups, paranoia on Theophilus's part, and so on—but there was no getting away from it. The notion of a singular group with reasonable amounts of influence over the Kindred fit the evidence better than anything else and left the fewest loose ends. He thought for a moment about what kind of group could possibly have influence over the Camarilla and also desire a stream of enslaved vampires. He shook his head stubbornly, disliking the direction that his mind was trying to take him. The 'why' was not so important, anyway.

He gazed across the room, not really seeing the books he usually cherished. It was an evil thing, this octopus. Still, there was no one better suited to its dispersal than his childe. He smiled, thinking of Bell's pathological determination. All it would take would be one little crack in the group's armor, and Theophilus would find a way to widen it up into an entrance. Someone had to know something. Someone who knew things….

Milton was a nasty little man with unpleasant personal habits. He was probably a paranoid schizophrenic, and he was most definitely obsessive-compulsive. He produced a strange newsletter that he distributed by post, among other means, in which he declaimed all sorts of plots and evils, usually perpetrated by the government, space aliens or space aliens in government. He was excellent at ferreting out unlikely pieces of information however, and Cerro had used his services twice in the last three years. If anyone would know about mysterious kidnappings, he would.

He called loudly to his servant. "Emma! Please find me a copy of a small newsletter named…." What was the damn thing called? "*A Closer Luke*. It should be in last year's files somewhere."

"Yes, sir." The girl was somewhere off in the house, her voice muffled by distance.

He didn't have long to wait. After a few minutes, Emma brought him the pamphlet. He smiled at her, enjoying the sparkle in her dark eyes, and then turned his attention to the paper.

It was a cheap production, a photocopy by the looks of it. The masthead was a digitally altered version of the Last Supper of Christ, with little alien heads superimposed over several of the diners. The numbers "8:17" were prominent below the magazine title, presumably a biblical reference.

Cerro turned to the back page. Milton's contact details were there, so he grabbed the phone and dialed the number that was listed. After a few seconds, the line was picked up.

"Closer Luke, good evening." It was a whiny voice, made worse by the way that the man sounded like he was breathing into a shallow tube.

"Mr. Milton?"

"Yes?"

"Ah, good evening Mr. Milton. This is Corleone." That particular alias had always amused him when dealing with conspirologists.

"Good evening, Mr. C. Long time, no hear. I trust all is well?"

"In a superficial sense, Mr. Milton, yes. Thank you. Yourself?"

"They haven't got me yet. What can I do for you?"

"There seems to be an unusual wave of disappearances and abductions going on at the moment. I have heard the term 'Way Station' linked to these vanishings. Some sort of staging post. Do you know anything about it?"

Milton thought about that for a moment. "It rings some bells, Mr. C. A very black operation, I think. Targeting foreign infiltrators and spies, maybe."

"Perhaps," said Cerro agreeably.

"When did you want information?"

"As soon as possible, please."

Milton coughed nervously. "Alright. I'll need five K though. More if the material is risky."

"That is acceptable, Mr. Milton." As if a few thousand dollars mattered either way.

The man could barely contain his glee. "Always a pleasure doing business with you, Mr. C. I'll get a report to you by tomorrow lunchtime. Same address?" That was the split oak.

"Yes thank you," said Cerro. "You will be able to collect your first payment then."

"Perfect," said Milton. "Was there anything else?"

"No thank you," Cerro said.

"Good night then, Mr. C."

Cerro hung up thoughtfully, already considering other avenues. Anderson was trustworthy, but unreliable, and not really in a position to know much. Durocher was brilliant, but he simply couldn't be sure about the man. Besides, he was French, and he would insist on sniping about the Basque. Van Looy and Blacker? Cerro shuddered. Not until all other options had been investigated. Havelock, however…. Perfect. The man's integrity was beyond reproach. He'd been a special liaison to the Council of Justicars for decades, fronting a supposed lobbyist group cum information gathering operation in Washington. Cerro flicked through his notebook until he found the correct number and dialed.

Some sort of blandly polite secretary answered the phone. "American Medical Associated. Good evening."

"Good evening," said Cerro pleasantly. "James Havelock's office, please."

"May I say who's calling?"

"Dr. Cerro." Havelock didn't deal with any real doctors, so standard practice was for Kindred to use the title.

"I'll just put you through, Doctor."

The line cut to some inoffensive holding music and then to a ring tone, which was answered swiftly. "Don Cerro, how pleasant to hear from you." Havelock's voice was mellow and welcoming, a very welcome change from Milton's nasal whine.

"Good evening, Mr. Havelock. I take it you are well."

"Yes, thank you. How has Gettysburg been treating you?"

"It has been lovely to relax for a while and simply enjoy myself. I have had a lot of reading and traveling to catch up on."

"I'm glad you've had the chance, Don Cerro. Is there something I can do for you?"

"There may be," Cerro said mildly. "This is in the strictest confidence, you understand."

"Of course," murmured Havelock.

"It has come to my attention that there may be an organized group behind a current rash of disappearances and assassinations in our community. I find the notion displeasing and intend to put an end to it. I was wondering if you had noticed anything out of the ordinary—patterns, suspicious behaviors, that sort of thing."

There was a long silence. "Don Cerro, I believe I know what you are referring to. This is an incredibly delicate subject, however. We must not discuss it further over the telephone. I can be outside the National Military Park's Visitor Center in four hours." The man sounded extremely concerned.

"Thank you," Cerro said. "That would be very generous of you."

"Not at all. You haven't spoken to anyone else, have you?"

"Of course not."

"Thank god. Please don't, Cerro. You are in terrible danger. I'll explain everything when I see you later."

"Very well," said Cerro, slightly bemused by the vehemence of Havelock's reaction.

"Good man," Havelock said breathlessly. "I will see you shortly. Until then, keep tight, and trust no one. No one, do you hear?"

"It shall be as you say. Until later, Havelock."

"Later, Cerro." The man hung up.

Cerro put the phone down and decided to hold off making any more calls until he'd spoken to Havelock. He called out to Emma to fetch him five-thousand dollars from the safe and then crossed to the bookcase and cast his eye over it. The pride of the collection was a mint first edition of Cervantes' *Don Quixote*. He carefully removed the second volume, settled back down in his chair, and immersed himself in a charming world of windmills and madmen.

At midnight, Cerro reluctantly extricated himself from his book and carefully returned it to its shelf. Emma had delivered the money he'd asked for, which he slipped inside a jacket pocket, and he headed for the door, pausing only to grab a coat and his favorite swordstick cane. How many times had Theophilus shook his head at that particular Old World affectation? Cerro smiled.

Before heading out to the visitor center, he crossed to the park opposite. It was as empty as usual this time of night, the assorted dog-walkers having mostly gone to bed already. The split oak was off to the left. The trunk was severed all the way down to head-height, the two halves pulling apart. The tree still lived on however—battered and scarred, but enduring. Cerro had always admired it. He fished around in the top of the cleft and pulled out the small plastic sack that served as his unofficial post office box. He popped Milton's money in there and dropped it back inside. Once he was content that is was secure, he strolled back to his car and made his way to the Visitor Center.

The parking lot was empty, but he was a few minutes early. He left his coat in the Mercedes and sauntered idly over to the Visitor Center information board, mildly curious to see what they were up to this season.

A prickling sensation at the back of his neck, as if he were being watched, made him turn around. A tall, powerfully broad man was striding toward him across the lot, moving almost silently. Karsh. He had a thick mane of black hair, and his dark skin was slashed by a lacework of scars. Cerro watched him approach, suddenly uncertain. The man was an animal at the best of times. During his service as a justicar, Cerro had dealt with Karsh—the Inner Circle's so-called warlord—several times, but he had not seen the man in over a decade.

"Karsh? What are you doing here?"

The Camarilla's warlord ignored him completely.

Cerro took a step back despite himself. "Did you come here with James Havelock?"

Karsh sneered nastily, raised his hands and flexed them. Long, razor-sharp claws glittered in the moonlight. He was almost across the parking lot and showed no sign of slowing down.

"Havelock's dead then," Cerro said, unlocking the catch on his swordstick and bracing himself.

Karsh did pause then, just a few yards away, and laughed nastily. "He sent me."

The revelation cut like a razor, but Cerro smiled, drew himself up to his full height, and flicked the body of the cane off the blade, bringing it up to a salute in point. He recalled the thousands he had fought over the years, flashing through them in an instant, drawing strength and confidence from centuries of battle. The poise flashed through his entire being, magnified instantly by the power in his blood. He felt himself wrapped in a cloak of splendor and knew then that this animal before him would yield or die, as had all the others. He gazed down at Karsh dismissively. "And I send you back, dog. As you are or in pieces. It matters not."

Cerro had seen Karsh in battle only once and it had been terrible indeed. The man was said to have been walking the night since the Mongols threatened Europe. But the warlord was a physical warrior and Cerro knew that victory often came in the mind, before it did in blows and strikes. And indeed, the warlord paled and took half a step backwards.

"Dare you think you can prevail?" Cerro's voice rang out across the night. "I give you this one chance to save your miserable existence." He pointed the sword out toward the road. "Run, now, and never return."

Karsh took another half-step back, hypnotized by Cerro's majesty. He clenched his teeth and took a slow step forward, then another. His face cleared. "Nice try." Suddenly he was rushing forward, claws extended.

A whirlwind began in the center of Cerro's stomach, a blast of speed and strength that exploded out to snatch him up in its power. It took over, moving him with the speed of his thought. The whirlwind whipped his limbs around into a guard, swayed his body out of the way of Karsh's clumsy lunge and drove his sword viciously through the warlord's lower back as he lumbered past.

Cerro gasped. It was like stabbing a sandstone cliff. The blade went in a short way, but even with all his strength and leverage, it was impossible to drive it further. Karsh whipped round, nothing but a dark blur, and then Cerro was flying through the air, his chest blazing with pain. His back howled as he landed, but he ignored it, scrambling upright. The blood seethed through him, little jags of agony in his chest showing where it was forcing bone back together.

Karsh was bearing down on him again, smiling horribly. He reached round behind himself, pulled the sword out of his back, and tossed it casually back to Cerro even as he closed. Cerro barely had a surprised moment to get the blade ready before Karsh was on him in a maelstrom of flashing claws. Cerro parried desperately, all the speed of the whirlwind barely enough to let him do more than fend off the warlord's flickering talons. The man was almost unimaginably fast—faster than

Cerro, even. He tried to cut at the hands behind the deadly claws, but somehow the flesh was never quite there.

A tiny excess of pressure on one feint gave Karsh an opening, and a claw raked agonizingly down the inside of Cerro's arm. The wound shrieked, the cut too razor-sharp for his blood to get a grip on. He fell back a step desperately, and another. Karsh followed slowly, enjoying himself. It was time to take a risk before the bastard sliced him to ribbons. Cerro quickly fell back a third and fourth step, then as Karsh was taking a confident step forward, he dove at the man's legs.

Karsh kicked at him, but Cerro managed to twist out of the way. He slid between Karsh's legs, his blade held up. It whipped through the warlord's groin, slashing deep into the flesh. Karsh screamed, staggering for an instant, and Cerro snapped his blade round, cutting a deep, quick slash across the back of Karsh's knees, aiming for the tendons. The stagger got worse, and Cerro stabbed the blade upwards, behind the groin, into the man's abdomen.

Karsh howled again, jerking forward and carrying the sword out of Cerro's grip. It was a long scream of agony that went on and on, modulating into...laughter?

Cerro's blood went cold, and he started scrambling to get up from the ground.

Karsh turned around, still staggering slightly, a broad, evil grin across his flat face. "Not bad, peacock. My turn."

He reached round behind himself and pulled the blade out, grunting a little as he did so. Cerro backed away as quickly as possible, reluctant to take his eyes off the man. Karsh shook the blade down a little, then contemptuously bent it into a mangled knot.

Cerro turned to run, the whirlwind inside him snatching him up to almost fly across the lot. A moment later, agony bloomed throughout his torso, and he ground to a halt. It felt like he had been stuck through with a dozen red-hot pokers.

Dull pain erupted in the back of his head—barely noticeable next to the volcanic fire in this back—and he fell forward onto the ground.

Karsh flipped him over and held him down despite his struggles. Cerro was weakening, his energy almost exhausted, the pain so bad he could hardly force a muscle to move. Karsh grinned down at him, flexed his fingers menacingly, then opened his arms wide and drove the claws through either side of his neck.

White fire tore through every nerve in Cerro's body. There was a momentary rush of air, a sudden sensation of flying, and then everything ceased.

Chapter Six

The Web

Theo was preparing to head back to Gettysburg the next night when Kristine's telephone rang. He decided to wait until after she'd taken the call. He glanced at a local paper that Nathalie must have brought in—corruption in the town hall, a butchered girl in a park—and wandered idly into the lounge. Itio was sitting in there, eyes closed. Theo looked at him uncertainly and settled for sitting down in a soft armchair.

"I see you Theophilus," said Itio pleasantly. His eyes were still closed.

"Good evening, Itio. How are things going?"

"Well enough, thank you. The pattern is holding, and events are slotting into place around it. It will be a grand prank, one to set before a king." Itio's eyes flicked open. "But perhaps you were enquiring about the hunt for information?"

Theo smiled. "Actually, I meant it in a general sense. If you do have any information though, that would be useful."

"Fragments still," said Itio. "There is a lock that can only be opened by sliding a catch on a different wall. The third tank is broken. Eight died screaming their innocence last night. Items of that nature. I am still trying to juggle them all into one coherent image, but it is proving difficult. I remain confident that some useful material will be obtained, however. The pattern demands it."

"You never know," said Theo, keeping his face straight. "Are the girls in the library again?"

"So I believe," Itio said.

"They must have a lot of data by now."

"I understand that they hope to finish this evening. I have not pointed out to them that without accurate census data for the Kindred, the process is largely pointless. I think that Delphine knows it deep down, but the pair of them strongly feel the need to be useful."

"I sympathize," said Theo.

"As do I," Itio murmured.

Kristine came into the living room, looking worn. "I think we have a problem, boys."

Theo looked around, immediately concerned. "What's up?"

Her voice was disturbingly flat. "I've just been speaking to one of my contacts in Chicago. He's an antiquarian and gossipmonger. Does a lot of business with the sewer rats. He's one of the people I visited last week. I must have idly mentioned Aurora in passing, because he thought of me straight away. Justicar Cock Robin executed the entire Aurora city council last night, with the assistance of a pack of his archons."

Itio was looking strangely intent. "Eight died screaming, Theophilus. Eight died screaming."

Theo tried to ignore Itio's words and stared at Kristine, astonished. "What? Why?"

She shook her head. "Diabolic corruption, apparently. The word is that they were caught during a demonic ritual. The justicar destroyed Michael, his entire circle of primogen, and two of his chief aides. The Ventrue are particularly furious, because it's left them with no one strong enough to retain the territory, and the Toreador are going to claim it instead."

Theo frowned, worried. "Michael was no diabolist. I guarantee it. I'd have smelt it on him." He looked at Kristine's worried expression, and Itio's curious one and sighed. "Look, I don't know exactly what happened, but those idiots who jumped me back in Green Bay stank of sulfur, and the smell faded as they died. I know it meant they were diabolists. I can't explain it any further. I just know. And I know that I'd have smelt it on Michael and Doug."

"Then it must be something to do with our visit," said Itio, surprisingly matter of fact.

Theo suppressed a shudder. "I suppose so."

Kristine's face hardened. "We've been here too long."

Theo glanced at her curiously. "Hagerstown?"

"Yes. We'll be leaving traces by now. The girls are quite distinctive. I think we should move on as soon as possible."

"Hang on, let's not panic. There's no one here to have noticed them. No reason why anyone would dream that we might be in this area. Isn't it safer to stay where we are for a little while longer? At least we have a fairly secure base here."

Kristine shook her head. "There is one reason why they might look for us in this area. Don Cerro."

Theo sighed. "Alright, I guess you have a point. But if we stay out of sight, we should be fine. At the very least, let's hear what he has to say before we decide."

"I believe that to be wise," Itio said.

"Alright then." Kristine nodded reluctantly. "I'm going to go and find the girls, though. I don't want them out of my sight until we're safely on the move again."

Theo shook his head. "You have a strange definition of safe."

"We can talk about it later," she said. "I'm off to the library. Are you going to be here?"

"It depends," Theo said. "I've got to get over to Don Cerro's now. I'm not sure how long it'll take. I shouldn't be too late back, though."

"I see. How about you, Itio?"

"Actually, lovely lady, I was about to ask Theophilus if I could join him this evening."

Theo looked at him. "You were?"

"Indeed," Itio said.

He thought about it for a moment. "I don't see why not. You've known him longer than you've known me. I can't imagine he'd object."

Kristine smiled grimly. "Actually, I'd rather the two of you were together anyway. There's safety in numbers." Theo arched an eyebrow at her. "You are welcome to think me as paranoid as you wish, Archon. Personally, given this evening's news, I feel that a bit of elementary caution is highly overdue."

Theo tried to make his voice conciliatory. "You're probably right, Kristine. It certainly can't hurt to be a little more careful, for a while at least."

She nodded, slightly mollified. "Okay then. I'm going to go look over the girls. I'll take the bike. Be careful tonight."

"We will," Theo said encouragingly.

Once they were en route to Gettysburg, Theo glanced over at his companion. "Tell me, Itio. Do you think she's mad?"

Itio considered the question for some moments, his face almost comically thoughtful. "I'm not really an expert in madness you understand," he said finally.

Theo nodded, careful not to smile. "I understand."

"Well, with that said, I do not believe her to be mad in any conventional sense. I think that she has had some harsh experiences recently, and that maybe she is somewhat less rational than usual, but that is a long way from madness. Regarding her fear of the actions of this group, I regret to say that her seemingly overzealous approach to caution may well prove sensible. If I may say so old friend, I am beginning to think that maybe you are not taking the threat as seriously as you should."

That shut Theo up for a bit. He tried to consider Itio's point objectively. At length, he shrugged reluctantly. "Well, I suppose it's possible. To be honest, I find it difficult to believe that anyone would go to such bother over me. It's not as if I know anything."

Itio laughed. "Modesty, Theophilus?"

"Not that," Theo said uncomfortably. "It's just...." He trailed off.

"You have been pursuing this matter relentlessly and making yourself a difficult target in the process."

"It wasn't my idea," Theo protested. "If Angus hadn't kept trying to kill Delphine, I'd have moved on immediately. Then it became a matter of trying to regain my status and get this blood hunt lifted. I never wanted to get involved in any of this shit."

"Do you think that they know that?"

"I suppose not," he said grudgingly.

"From their point of view, you have appeared out of nowhere, infiltrated and destroyed a secure installation, evaded every attempt to have you killed—destroying several of their agents in the process—only to vanish into thin air. Worse still, you have a reputation for zeal and for an unswerving hatred of slavery. Can there be any doubt that they must consider you a serious problem?"

"Well.... I suppose not."

Itio beamed at him encouragingly. "Well, then. If we are agreed that you must seem to present a clear threat, real or imagined, then surely we must also agree that they will act to rectify that threat directly."

"Alright, yes," said Theo cautiously.

"We do not know the full extent of their capabilities, save that they would appear to include a network of agents, either plentiful or lucky, and the ability to frame a minor prince and his council as diabolists. Do you again agree?"

"Unfortunately," muttered Theo.

"So, given that an aggressive organization of unknown—but apparently significant—resources has decided that you personally are a serious threat, would a degree of paranoia not seem perfectly reasonable?"

"Since you put it that way," Theo said, trying to keep the irritation out of his voice.

"I'm glad we're agreed," said Itio pleasantly.

Theo stifled a martyred sigh and concentrated on the road. Traffic was light, and they made good time on the way to Gettysburg. It took a little while to navigate through the town, but in the end, Theo was only a few minutes late by the time he tracked down Don Cerro's residence. It was an attractive period building, undoubtedly original, set in extensive, well-tended gardens. Theo pulled up a short way down the road, and the pair of them headed back to the house and up the path.

Theo raised his hand to knock on the door and paused, suddenly wary. He gave the door a slight push instead, and it swung open. Concerned, he shared a long glance with Itio. After a moment's thought, Itio raised one hand in a gesture that quite clearly told Theo to stay put. He then swung the door slightly wider open, slipped inside and vanished.

A few minutes later, Itio reappeared in the doorway, coalescing out of a patch of plaid shadow. He beckoned Theo inside and pushed the door shut behind him. The hall looked like a bull had rampaged through it. Theo's misgivings seemed to solidify into a ball of lead in the pit of his stomach. Itio's expression was strangely still. "Persons unknown have searched the house thoroughly, and there are two dead mortals upstairs. Attractive young women. I am sorry, Theo. There is no sign of your sire."

Theo sighed heavily. "He might...."

Itio shook his head, and Theo trailed off. "He would not have let this happen. If he had gone into hiding or been led off on a wild goose chase, he would have found a way to contact you."

"Damn." Theo felt wood splinter under his fist and was moderately surprised when he looked down and found that he'd punched a hole in a table. Anger bubbled up inside him, hot and resentful. "The stupid bastard. I fucking told him to be careful who he spoke to."

"We should leave this place, Theophilus." Itio's voice was carefully neutral.

"Don't you think...."

Itio was shaking his head again. "This house is dangerous for us, my friend. There is no reward here. They have thoroughly ripped everything to shreds. In the study, there is hardly one sheet of paper intact. Anything that remains here will be a trap."

"There must be something," Theo said desperately. "Some way to justify...."

"Do you think you and I would be able to find something in here in a few minutes that several people may not have found in the course of hours?"

"Fuckers." Theo smashed his hand down again, boiling fury surging inside him. The table cracked and slowly toppled apart. "I'm going to fucking get whoever did this. *That* is a promise." He leaned down absentmindedly, still looking around the hall, and idly picked up a piece of wood, shaking bits off it. Itio looked at him nervously, and he realized that he'd ripped a leg out of the ruins of the table. He glanced at it, slightly surprised, and then shrugged. "It may come in useful." He tucked it in the back of his pants.

Itio let the comment pass. "Come, Theophilus. There are snakes arising to encircle us. I can feel them."

Theo nodded numbly and let himself be led out of the house. Halfway down the block toward the car, he remembered something that his sire had said the night before and grabbed at Itio's arm. "The tree."

Itio turned around and looked at him sympathetically.

"Back in the house, you asked me if we could find something in minutes that they had missed in hours. The tree."

"Which tree?" Itio's expression was a complex blend of concern, confusion and surprise.

"Follow me."

Theo led Itio over the road and into the parkland beyond. "Somewhere over here, there's an oak tree that's been split by lightning. Don Cerro told me last night that he sometimes uses it as a drop site for items—or couriers—that he doesn't want coming to his home. He said he'd make use of it, to humor me as much as anything else, I suspect. It's here somewhere."

"Let us hope that it is near the road. This appears to be part of the National Military Park."

"He made it sound close to the house. 'Across from my residence' was how he put it." Theo coughed, trying to ignore the lump that had just appeared at the back of his throat.

"Very well," said Itio. "Let us start by walking directly away from the house for a short distance."

Ten minutes later, after doubling back several times, Theo spotted what had to be it, off to the left. He made a beeline for the tree, Itio following a moment behind. It was certainly impressive. The trunk had been split right down the middle to shoulder height, the two halves pulling apart to sag close to the ground. Amazingly, it appeared to still be thriving. There was a dark crevasse in the trunk where the split began. It had to be the place.

Theo reached his hand in and felt around the crevasse. It was unpleasantly wet, but all he picked up was a crop of splinters. He cursed, and punched the trunk in frustration. "Nothing."

"Wait," Itio said. "Did you hear that?"

"No? What?"

"When you punched the tree, I perceived a crinkling noise."

Theo looked at him doubtfully. "Are you sure?" He fumbled around again. "I can't feel anything in here but damp wood," he said disgustedly. A thin ridge brushed one of his fingertips. "Wait a second." He felt over it again. The texture wasn't quite the same. He pried at it, surprised when it moved easily. "String." A few frustrating seconds later, he managed to snag it with a fingertip and pulled gently. A moment later, he could feel plastic. He took a firm hold and lifted it out of the crevasse.

They could both see that it was a clear plastic bag. Inside it was a plain cardboard folder, with the words "Way Station" written across the front.

———

Theo let Itio drive on the way out of Gettysburg. The man looked concerned, muttering quietly to himself from time to time. Once they were outside the town, Theo felt a surprisingly familiar wave of itchy vulnerability, and it took him several moments to figure out that Itio must have been making him less obvious.

"Thanks for that Itio," he said vaguely. His mind felt like it was swaddled in cloth.

"We have exposed ourselves dangerously," said Itio.

"Have we?"

"It would be insanity not to have someone watching the house. If we have any grace, it lies in the fact that you parked some distance from the building, and thus the watchers may still think us inside."

Theo looked at him blankly.

Itio arched an eyebrow. "I have been obscuring our visibility since before we left the house. With hindsight, I am not entirely surprised that you did not notice. Provided that the observers did not overhear us on the street, they may think that we are quietly searching the building, if we are lucky. It may even be possible that they first observed us approaching the house and thus did not make special note of this vehicle, but that seems like a little much to hope for."

"I see," Theo said. "I hadn't really thought about watchers, just…." *Just finding the fucker that murdered my sire and ripping his heart out of his chest while he watches.* A hard knot of fury settled in behind his breastbone, a very welcome spot of warmth. The rest of his body felt like ice. He cradled the anger, feeding off it. It was possible Cerro still survived, or had gone into hiding, but some deep, dark instinct told Theo things wouldn't end that happily. Some said there was an unbreakable bond of blood between sire and childe, and Theo thought he could feel that now—in its sudden absence.

"I understand," said Itio. "We have to get out of this area, however. Tonight, I think."

"Alright," Theo said. "I don't see any point in staying here now anyway. Where are we going to go?"

"The answer to your question may be in that folder on your lap," Itio said gently.

Theo nodded. "Alright, I'll have a look through it in a second. I want to phone Kristine first." He fished around in his baggy trouser pockets, eventually coming up with the telephone. He keyed her number and waited. She picked up the phone almost instantly.

"Kri—," he began.

"Hold a sec," she hissed urgently. He ground his teeth together and waited. About a minute later, she came back to the telephone. "Sorry about that, Theo. I was in the library."

He growled, irritated. "You made me wait for some fucking librarian? This is important."

"I didn't want to draw attention," she snapped. "We have to be careful."

His anger receded as quickly as it had come up. "We have to leave. They got to Don Cerro. I think he's dead. Itio thinks we're okay for an hour or two."

"Oh, fuck." Kristine sounded stunned. After a pause, she continued briskly. "Don't come back to the house. It might not be safe for you. I'll get our stuff and a new vehicle and meet you at the Speedway with the girls. Where are we heading?"

"I'm not sure yet. I might have a lead. I'll send you a text message in a moment. Maybe the girls can sort out a motel or something in the right direction while you're still in the library."

"Alright, Theo. Make it as quick as possible, though. I want to get moving."

"Talk to you later." He hung up. "She's going to meet us at the speedway." Itio nodded approvingly. Theo opened the plastic sack on his knees and took out the cheap card folder. Inside it were several photos and a short handwritten note. He read it first.

> Marietta, NC is the most recent Way Station I can find. It might still be current, but more likely they've moved on again. It's a little flyspeck in the middle of nowhere. My guy insists that they have mainly been bringing woodsy types through in the last few months—some sort of cell devoted to mapping and observation, perhaps. Please be careful with this information. The operation is double-black. NSA probably. I'd hate to lose a customer.

—M.

It wasn't much, but it was better than anything else they had. Theo grinned savagely and sent Kristine a short text message containing the name of the town. Then he put the letter back in the folder and had a look at the photos. There were three of them, eight by six, grainy black and white. One was just some pathetic little half-dead village scene, all dust and corncobs. A road ran through the middle of the photo, fringed by a few tumbledown houses and several sprawling barns.

The next picture was a frontal of one of the barns from the previous image. The focus was better, and three areas had been ringed in red pen. The barn still looked like a pointless piece of shit, but Theo looked closely at the ringed areas and then blinked in surprise. One of the rings was at the bottom corner of the barn. It looked like there was a small set of LEDs or sensors in a neat column in the middle of the corner frame, at ground level. Another ring was next to it and appeared to show a glimpse of a reflective surface behind a split knot in a plank. The final one was around a small bump at the top of the door. The bump was a bit regular, but it was difficult to make anything out.

The final picture was an enlargement of the bump. Underneath a thick layer of dust and cobwebs, it was quite clearly an alarm system of some sort, and wires snaked out of it in all directions. Theo studied it for a bit, then slipped the photographs back in with the letter and closed the folder.

"The staging post is in North Carolina," he said grimly. "Some tiny little shit-hole. It looks like a barn, but they've done all sorts of crap to it. Sensors, metal plating, alarms, stuff like that."

"Deep, dark vaults await, strewn mockingly with petals. Their walls run red with the tears of the stolen and the damned. Then the laughing strangers come and pluck the children from the floor." Itio was staring through the windscreen, and his voice was like the slamming of a tomb door.

"That certainly sounds like the right place," Theo said, just a hint of resignation in his voice.

Itio blinked and then grinned out at the road. "Or the wrong one, depending on your point of view."

"Yeah," said Theo, too worn to quibble.

A while later, they pulled in to the Speedway. There was obviously an event of some sort scheduled that evening, because the lot was nearly full. Itio parked, and after a quick look around the vehicle to make sure that they had removed all possibly useful or identifying items, they left it to go mingle with the crowd near the entrance.

Theo was still dressed in urban clothing and quickly became aware that a lot of the patrons—almost exclusively white— were eyeing him with various degrees of disapproval. Whenever he could, he made eye contact, challenging them to do or say something. He was mildly irritated than none had the balls.

After a few minutes, the crowd had thinned to a trickle, and he decided to check on Kristine' progress and fished out his mobile phone. He started dialing, and a heavy elbow smacked into his arm. He only just managed to keep hold of the phone. A meaty-looking middle-aged guy sauntered past, looking pleased with himself.

Theo ground his teeth together, and tried to control the sudden burning fury in his chest. "You're fucking welcome, asshole." He made it loud, so that the man could hear it over the roar of the speedway cars.

The meaty guy turned around, his face thick with anger. "Say what?"

"What," said Theo, slowly and precisely; the desperate need to hurt something billowing inside him. Itio glanced over at him calmly.

The asshole's brow furrowed. "Think you can be funny with me do you, boy?"

"I wouldn't bother," Theo drawled laconically, trying to rein in the red clouds threatening to engulf him. "I doubt you'd understand a word of it, you dumb son of a bitch."

The man's face reddened. "You call my momma a bitch?"

Theo chose to take it as an order and pulled his face into an infuriating smirk. "If you want. Your momma is a bitch. Hell, for all I know she's an ancient crack-whore who stinks of rotten syphilis and old goats. How's that do you, hero?"

The man shook his head furiously, little bits of spittle flying, and cocked back a ham-like fist to punch Theo in the face. Theo ignored Itio's raised eyebrow and allowed the man to hit him. He was so pissed that he barely even felt it.

The guy was looking at him dumbly, so Theo took a half-step forward and brought his knee up hard into the man's saggy gut. He folded like a deck chair. As he went down, Theo grabbed him by the shoulders, flipped and threw. The asshole spun into the air and flew twenty feet to land heavily on a car hood, face first.

The half-dozen or so people nearby were all staring, and one man was rushing over to check on the asshole.

Theo shrugged, fighting hard to keep himself under control. "He threw the first punch."

"What are you, a fucking lawyer?" The speaker was a tall, scrawny man. "I know Ted, nigger. I ain't never seen you before, though."

Further back, another voice cut in, loud and urgent. The other guy at the car. "Hey, he's fucking dead!"

Itio melted to one side and vanished. There was a click, and then a gunshot rang out. A sudden lance of pain tore into Theo's shoulder. The white agony of it ripped the shards of his self-control apart, and a red hurricane whirled up to consume him.

...a flowing dance of destruction... bone splintering... screams, prey fleeing... delicious hot blood spurting into his mouth... a stinging spray of bullets... flesh crumbling under his fingertips... the world blurring... mocking streaks of wailing light... tinkling glass and metal tearing... pouring fury into the strain...

Theo slowly came back to his senses, his fury spent. It took him several seconds to work out that he was looking at a twisted bar of metal and plastic, crumpled in his hands. He blinked. It was the siren bar of a police cruiser, partly ripped from the torn roof. His hands were drenched in blood, but he wasn't aware of any pain. It was then that he realized he was standing with his feet through the cruiser windshield. Through the holes he had torn in the roof, he could see the mangled corpses of two police officers inside. Two more innocents weighing on his soul.

He looked around, slightly stunned. The parking lot was empty of people. There were several impressive patches of blood, but no corpses to be seen. Itio was standing by the side of the car. "Theophilus, are you back?"

Theo nodded, suddenly feeling empty. The anger in his chest had vanished, leaving just hollow coldness "I am." He hesitated. "How many?"

Itio looked sympathetic. "Three others. I have removed the corpses, and hidden them with two witnesses and the speedway gate guard. Our pursuers will surely have heard about this incident and cannot be far away. We must leave immediately. Kristine arrived during your display and is parked a short way down the road. Go to her quickly. Get out of plain sight. I will follow as soon as these two are removed. It may buy some minutes of confusion."

"Itio...." Theo changed what he was going to say. "See if there is a shotgun in the cruiser, please. A flashlight would be useful, too." He pulled himself out of the torn vehicle, and headed off in the direction that Itio had indicated.

Itio caught up with him, as he was just starting to head down the road away from the speedway, and passed Theo a slightly bloody pump-action. Sirens were audible in the distance. Theo nodded his thanks, and they picked up the pace a little. Itio turned into the mouth of a small lane. A large, clunky black sedan was idling there. Through the tinted windows, Theo could make out Kristine in the driving seat and was surprised to see that she had her hair pulled back in a tight ponytail. Itio got in next to her. Theo paused for a moment, then ripped off the fetid, blood-soaked top he was wearing and used it to clean his pants up a bit. Then he wadded it into a ball, threw it into the bushes and got into the back, slipping in next to the twins and putting the gun on the floor.

Kristine immediately took off, accelerating hard to a reasonable speed, then eased right off. Itio said something quiet to her, and she nodded. Almost immediately, Theo started to feel cut adrift, a small piece of flotsam cast into the night. He glanced round to see the girls hugging each other unhappily. Kristine flashed a quick look around the vehicle, her eyes slightly wild, then nodded once, curtly. "You're good, Mr. Shima. Hush now, people."

Itio smiled encouragingly at Theo and the girls.

The blaring sirens grew louder, and an ambulance tore round a bend ahead of them, charging past toward the speedway. A pair of slightly ratty squad cars were just behind it, holding a couple of grim-faced men each. None of them so much as glanced at the sedan.

A few moments later, Theo noticed lights approaching on the road behind them. He turned to look, and a small pack of sleek black motorcycles came into view. There were three of them, Hondas at a guess, traveling fast. He reached over and pushed Delphine and Nathalie down in their seats, then huddled with them, the table-leg digging into his back. Kristine ignored the bikes, and they caught up in moments. They slowed, and through the window Theo could see the lead rider looking into the sedan. Kristine looked back at him, her face pulled into an expression of slack-jawed surprise that made her look about twenty years older. The lead rider looked away, and then the bikes were zooming off.

"They may return," Kristine said pointedly. Delphine took a breath to say something, but Theo laid a finger over her lips, cutting her off.

Ten minutes later, as the sedan was about to get onto the highway, the bikes rushed by again. This time they discounted the sedan at a glance.

Once they were on I-70, Kristine looked around the vehicle fiercely. She fixed her eyes approximately where Delphine would have been, had they not still been huddled on the floor. "I don't want to hear so much as a whisper until I give you permission, and it won't be before Washington, I tell you that. Until then, this car has to appear to have just one passenger." She turned back to the road.

Theo nodded his agreement at the girls and then helped them slide back into their seats quietly, fishing out the table-leg and dropping into the seat well as he did so. Nathalie curled up with Delphine, then glanced at him. She eyed his torso with an appreciative grin and then draped her legs across his lap.

Theo stifled a weary sigh, put his arms round her knees to stop her slipping off him, and watched the night roll past.

Chapter Seven

Eyes

Once Kristine relaxed enough to allow Itio drop his concealment—somewhere short of Richmond—everyone settled down a bit. No one mentioned the speedway or the motorcycles; there didn't seem to be any need. The sedan was surprisingly comfortable—ten years out of fashion perhaps, but roomy, and with decent seats.

Theo patted the upholstery appreciatively. "Nice car."

"Thanks," Delphine said with a grin.

He looked at her flatly.

She poked her tongue out. "Alright, so Kris actually got it. I was the one who suggested airport long-term parking."

"Good thinking," he said approvingly.

"Yeah, well, if it's good enough for BP…."

He shot her a blank glance.

She giggled. "Doesn't matter." She sobered up abruptly. "Hey, I'm really sorry about your sire."

Theo sighed. "Yeah. Thanks. At least he managed to leave a lead for us. Which reminds me, where are we actually heading? Surely not to the town itself."

"I booked us a room in a roadhouse just the other side of Lafayette," said Nathalie.

"Do not worry too much about your current state of undress," Itio said, smirking slightly. "I do not have your build, but I do possess a spare shirt-like garment made of some super-extendable substance that you should be able to squeeze into."

Nathalie giggled. "A muscle-boy top? Cute!"

Theo sighed. "Thanks, Itio. I didn't really think about that side of it. I just didn't want to...." He checked himself with a quick glance at the twins. "Uh, get the car dirty."

Kristine nodded. "Well, it's not as if you're going to be on parade anywhere, Archon. The accommodation should be fairly private, and we can look into finding somewhere in the town for the following night, if appropriate."

"It's a bit on the small side," Theo said wryly.

"Then it might have some usefully abandoned places," Kristine said. "How strong is this lead, anyway?"

"I don't know, to be honest. Stronger than anything else we've got. The place sounds like it's probably been abandoned, but it may have something we can use in there."

Kristine grimaced. "I hope so. I'd hate to be back at square one again."

Theo couldn't think of anything much to say to that, and the car lapsed back into silence. After a while, he grabbed the table leg, pulled out his knife, and started whittling it down. It seemed appropriate somehow.

After an uneventful night in another dull motel bathroom, they got on the move quickly. Nathalie was a little waspish, but Theo put that down to the rather isolated location she'd been stuck in during the day. It was only about an hour from the motel to the South Carolina border. A short way before it, just before a town called McDonald, they turned off the interstate and headed onto a small country lane that appeared to be called Chicken Road. The countryside spread out in front of them, a seemingly endless stretch of black tobacco fields broken only by occasional pinpricks of light.

"Christ, I thought this afternoon was boring." Nathalie sounded disgusted.

Delphine half-shook her head. "I don't know. I don't much like it. It's…kinda barren."

Theo shared a quick glance with Itio. "It's not really our natural territory, kid. It's kinda difficult to blend in when everyone knows the moles on each other's faces by name. Proper cover can be tricky to come by, too."

"Yeah. The thought of all that space is making me feel kinda claustrophobic. Hemmed in. Does that make sense?"

Kristine looked around quickly. "It affects us all in similar ways, daughter. Try not to worry about it. We'll stay here no longer than we have to."

"It doesn't bother *me*," Nathalie said. "It just looks fucking dull."

"Of course," said Kristine mildly.

Theo stepped in quickly. "How far is the town?"

Itio glanced at the map. "I would expect it to be no more than seven miles."

"Good," Theo said. "I want to get this done swiftly if possible."

They rattled around the country lanes for ten minutes or so, heading into what looked like total darkness. A long stretch of thick woodland made all of them uncomfortable, even Nathalie and Delphine. They finally came through it and saw lights a mile or so ahead. Delphine cracked some joke to Nat, but Theo didn't quite catch it.

Itio looked at the map again, and said, "This is it." The twins fell silent.

The town showed more evidence of construction than Theo had expected. Between the wan streetlights and the half-moon rising, there was enough light to get a good idea of the place.

There were maybe a couple hundred buildings clustered together around four or five roads. No more than two or three dozen actually showed any sign of light, however. Either the residents of Marietta used very heavy curtains, or the place was largely unoccupied. Many of the roofs were sagging with age, and a good percentage of the chimneystacks were crumbling unhealthily. There were a couple of church spires, one of which appeared to end in a broken scar.

As they got closer, they began to drive past long-deserted farmyards and barns, all in various stages of collapse. One or two showed signs of possible inhabitation—rusted-looking vans in yards, broken windowpanes stuffed with rags, and so on. The ramshackle structures appeared with increasing frequency, and then a filthy town sign flashed passed. No one spoke.

Things did pick up a bit inside the town limits, but not much. The unsteady houses grew thicker on both sides of the road, which narrowed a little, and showed signs of actually having had a sidewalk once. Most of the houses looked as if they'd been abandoned for twenty years of more. Every now and again, a rubble-strewn gap in between buildings indicated where a structure had given up the fight.

A few junctions began to appear, little alleys networking the larger roads together. Along with them came indications of some genuine occupation—the houses looked fit to live in, with curtains in some windows and presumably functional cars parked at the now-solid sidewalk or pulled into battered driveways. Some streetlights were still functioning, and they gave the air a thin, yellow tint that Theo found somehow depressing.

A small row of stores sprang up on the left side of the road. There was a combined hardware and grocery store, a small drug store, a newsstand, and a meat-and-potatoes restaurant—which was actually open and even appeared to boast an aging customer or two. The shops soon gave way to housing once again, which got steadily crummier. Within another mile, they were back among the tobacco fields.

Delphine and Nathalie exchanged a long look, but said nothing.

Kristine pulled up on the side of the road. "No sense going any further out. Did you see anything that looked right, Theo?"

Theo shook his head. "We're going to stick out if we just cruise town, though."

Itio looked up from the map thoughtfully. "I believe I can take us through most of the town without traveling the same stretch twice."

"I guess that will have to do," said Theo. "We need to find the site. In a place this size, if anyone wants to keep an eye out for strangers, they'll already have seen us. We can assess the situation once we've tracked the place down."

Kristine grinned at Itio. "Lay on, MacDuff."

He directed her onward for a mile or two of decrepit countryside, before a left turn brought them alongside a large, ivy-drowned cemetery. Theo shook his head. They turned left again a short while later and took another road into Marietta. This one fed them across the bottom of the strip of shops and out past a couple of small commercial units which may or may not have been in use. A sharp left turn just on the town outskirts took them past an abandoned church—the one with the broken tower that Theo had seen earlier. A block or so down, one row of slightly larger houses looked almost pleasant, before they gave way to the worm-eaten decay of the rest of the town. Another left took them down the back of a row of what might once have been farm laborers' accommodations and on to a stretch of obviously derelict village named Alligator Branch Road.

Theo recognized it immediately. They were looking at it head on, rather than along the length, but the cruddy house immediately in front of them was in the photo. The barns were off to the right, where the road started to fade into a dirt track.

"That's the place," he said quietly. "The one on the far right."

Kristine backed up a little way and stopped the car under the overhanging branches of an old tree. They could see the barn clearly still across the road junction, partly illuminated by a street light.

"What are we going to do now?" Nathalie was obviously trying to make the question sound practical rather than just fright-driven.

"If they're here, there's no way they could have missed our presence," Kristine said. "I say we get out of here now before they know for certain we're interested in them, then come back tomorrow, maybe head in across the fields or something."

Itio shook his head gravely. "Sometimes, there is a time as well as a place. I would like twenty minutes to observe. From here will do."

"I didn't enjoy my stay in that motel so much that I'm desperate to repeat it," Theo said. "We should at least have a look now we're here."

Nathalie pouted, but kept quiet.

Kristine shrugged. "Alright. But I'm keeping my eyes open, and if I see anything suspicious, I'm taking off."

"Of course," Theo said.

They sat in silence for the most part. Itio was staring at the barn so intently he might have been in a trance. By contrast, Kristine had twisted round in her seat and was looking around constantly, trying to watch all directions at once for any sign of a threat. If Itio even noticed her fidgeting, he hid it very well. The girls were restless, but Theo did his best to ignore them and studied the barn.

It was some fifty feet long and about twenty feet high at the top of its sagging roof and seemed to be made out of cheap wooden planks. Areas of it had been weatherproofed with black plastic sheets, and there was a rusted padlock securing a clasp so rickety that it would probably fall out of the wood if anyone so much as breathed on it. Weeds grew up all around it, but there were several tire ruts in the ground in front of the doors.

If there were any surveillance cameras, they were very well concealed. They were too far away to make out the sensors he had seen ringed, but he could see the shadowy hump of the alarm system above the door, and occasionally he thought he saw a glint of moonlight reflecting between wooden slats. It was a most unlikely place. The unwelcome thought occurred to him that maybe it was just some yahoo's illegal still. He forced himself not to dwell on the prospect. This was the only lead they had.

Somewhere off across the fields, an owl hooted—a low, mournful sound that seemed to sum up the desolation of this little forgotten corner. It hooted again, and as the noise died down, Itio spoke, his voice so distant that it was difficult to tell the two apart.

"The worms feed, and care not what it is they feast upon. It is pulp now, soft and bloated with years. The trees rustle their disdain. They have seen much and will see still more. The beast's back is broken. The burdens that it carried wore it out, and it was left behind to die. It is the way of things. The moon does not turn its face, for there is nowhere to turn from, to turn to. This is a place of toad and rat and wolf, my friends, not of man."

Nathalie was staring at Itio, her eyes wide and her skin pale. Delphine nudged her, looking slightly wild-eyed herself, and started whispering to her. Kristine was eying the man skeptically, but looked composed.

Itio pulled himself upright in his seat and looked around the car, his face mild. "The building is deserted."

"What did you mean by 'wolf?'" Theo looked at Itio suspiciously.

"Oh, I'm sure it was nothing, Theophilus," he said breezily. "Come, let us go and investigate."

They piled out of the car, Kristine carrying the flashlight that Itio had found the night before. Nathalie seemed nervous, but she was even more reluctant to stay behind. Delphine stayed close to her sister, talking reassuringly. Theo led the way over to the barn, with Kristine hanging back to keep a watchful eye on the twins.

When they reached the barn, Theo glanced up at the alarm box and then down to Itio. "Are you absolutely certain this place is abandoned?"

"Yes," Itio said simply. "There is no one here. However, that device may have remote reporting functions. I should be able to bypass it simply enough."

"Great," Theo said. "Thanks."

Itio gestured at his midriff. "If you would be so kind…?"

Theo looked at him, puzzled.

Itio smiled and laced his fingers together. "It would be easier if I could get a small lift up."

"Sure." Theo stifled a sigh and bent down, his hands enmeshed.

Itio put a foot into the cradle and took hold of Theo's shoulders. Theo straightened back up slowly, so as not to jog him too much, and tried to ignore Delphine and Nathalie's giggling.

Itio placed his other foot on Theo's forearm and stood up straight. "If you could just hold still now, Theophilus." He fished around in a pocket for several moments and pulled out something that Theo couldn't quite see.

"Children of the Night," Delphine intoned gravely. "What music they make." She started giggling again.

Theo shot her an irritated glance. "Did you want to do this?"

She snorted. "Of course not, oh mighty assassin. I'm sure you have many dread and fell powers that I can't even begin to imagine."

"Nice top, by the way," Nathalie choked out between fits of quiet laughter. Even Kristine was grinning.

Theo growled at the twins. "Look," he began.

Itio tapped him on the forehead with what felt like a drill bit or screwdriver. "Gently please, Theophilus."

Del and Nat burst into a fresh round of quiet hysterics.

Theo shot them a sour look and then closed his eyes loftily.

A minute or two later, Itio rested a hand on top of Theo's head and twisted around slightly, presumably so that he could look out. "It is done. We may enter with impunity."

Theo lowered Itio to the floor again. "Thanks."

"Not at all, Theophilus. You were…." He paused, his eyes sparkling mischievously. "Outstanding."

The padlock was considerably stronger than it looked, and the clasp was nowhere near as loose either. Although the lock had a standard keyhole in the bottom, it also had a small dial set in the back, where it would be out of sight. The rust was all on the front and sides. Theo gave it an experimental tug. It felt secure, but not insurmountable.

He spread his legs wide to brace himself, got a firm grip on the padlock, and pulled. The doors rattled slightly, and there was a slow squeal of tortured metal. He threw his weight behind it, aware that the padlock was trying to cut into his fingers. There was another grating noise and then a sharp metallic shriek. He staggered back a pace, the padlock and clasp in his hands. Long, thick metal bolts protruded from either end of the clasp, gleaming brightly. They were around six inches long and terminated in jagged shears.

"Here," he said, tossing it to Nathalie without even a hint of a grin. "Stow it somewhere, will you? We'll slot it back in when we leave."

She caught the piece and fingered the ends of the bolts silently, and he was gratified to note that she looked slightly awed.

The doors were a lot heavier than they looked. The reason why quickly became obvious—as they opened, it was possible to see the thick metal shutters attached to them. Once the gap was wide enough to get through, they slipped inside and pulled the doors to again, using Kristine's flashlight to see by.

The room was considerably smaller than the barn around it, the concrete walls and roof presumably thick enough to deaden any sound. It had two levels, that of the ground outside and a deeper area that had been hollowed out, a little like an empty swimming pool. Metal steps led down to the lower section, which was crisscrossed with mesh walkways and workspaces and took up about half the area of the room. Tall, featureless metal lockers lined the walls of the upper section, one after another. There was an empty space at the back of the room, behind the lower section.

Theo headed toward the back, stopping to occasionally flip open a locker. They were all absolutely empty inside, flush with the floor, but surprisingly sturdy, with heavy locks. Each was nearly seven feet high and two feet wide. He looked at one, struck by its similarity to a rectangular coffin. A chill ran down his spine. A staked vampire didn't need a cell. Just a box.

He walked along the row of what had to be holding pens, praying that they'd built so many purely to make sure, and came to the dark space at the back. His spine immediately started tingling, and he paused, wary. Peering at the ground ahead, he spotted traces of chalk, maybe a slightly darker stain further in. Recognition hit and left him cold. It was some sort of ritual circle. He stepped backwards, repulsed by a very faint tang in the air.

He decided to leave it alone and walked back to the edge of the lower level. The wire mesh balcony looked sturdy enough, so he stepped out onto it cautiously. Kristine was down there with the girls, investigating a small roofed unit that he couldn't see into.

She spotted him and waved. "Find anything interesting, Archon?"

"Just Theo, please." She gestured an apology, and he continued. "The lockers are storage racks for staked Kindred. There's some evidence of ritual work in the space at the back. How about you?"

"This looks like some sort of compact morgue facility. There are a couple of rather odd-looking glass tanks set into the wall either side of it. There's also a space that might have been used for administration—a desk, chairs, power sockets, that sort of thing. Oh, and there are several sheer-sided metal pits sunk into the floor, covered with thick gratings. Mr. Shima is examining those."

"Alright. This is obviously the place. We need to start looking for some sort of onward lead."

"Agreed. If you'll check the lockers upstairs, we'll search down here."

"Fine." Theo headed toward the nearer row of lockers, which ended at the same point as the lower level, and started opening them up, checking the floor, walls, door and even ceiling of each for some scrap of information. It was dispiriting work. They all seemed empty, and he found himself imagining what it would be like to be locked into one of them, paralyzed, confined and unsure. He tried to guess at the faces that had grimaced out at the doors. Young or old? Unearthly, bestial or plain? He shook his head, trying to clear it so he could focus on the job at hand.

He was almost at the end of the first row, back up by the doors, when a wisp of sound snatched at his attention. Had there been a click, outside? He stepped back warily, drawing his knife just in case. A moment later, the door swung outward soundlessly, and a tall, powerful figure slipped inside, red slit eyes gleaming in the darkness.

The man caught sight of Theo and froze, instantly wary. In the dim light, Theo could see that the newcomer was around the same height and build as he was, with a short, prickly beard and long red hair hanging down his back from the fringes of a receded scalp. Rings, studs and hoops glittered out of the man's ears and nose. He was dressed in black, leather by the way it gleamed.

The man moved slightly, and the shadowed face resolved into a fiercely proud set of features that Theo had not really expected to see again. Certainly not here.

"Xaviar." The word was barely a whisper.

His head whirled at the implications. Xaviar, the former justicar of Clan Gangrel, had taken his entire clan out of the Camarilla several years before. Theo had gone some way to pushing him to do it, even. Had the Gangrel decided to take revenge?

"Bell. I might have known I'd find *you* here." Xaviar spoke quietly, but his voice sounded like the howl of a storm.

"Much good it will do you." Theo drew his knife slowly, taking a step backwards.

"I have not forgotten your betrayal. Your punishment is long overdue," Xaviar said with a snarl. He leapt at Theo like a rocket, red hair billowing out behind him.

Theo dropped, and the world exploded. Power ripped through him as the blood seemed to detonate inside him. His muscles screamed, swelling desperately to contain the rush of force and speed that his relentless will demanded. Xaviar hurtled toward him. Theo fell to the ground, already coiling, and kicked savagely at Xaviar's hip as he tore through the space Theo had just vacated.

Xaviar overbalanced as he landed, crashing heavily against several cupboard doors, which bent like paper under the impact of his massive frame. He pushed himself upright as Theo got to his feet, danced forward a step or two, and kicked savagely at Theo's head. Theo managed to catch the blow before it took his jaw off, and his knife clattered to the ground. He grabbed Xaviar's boot and twisted. The man leapt and spun as he did so, his other foot smashing into the side of Theo's skull like a pile driver. Theo's teeth rattled, and his eyesight blurred.

Theo stumbled back a pace or two, staggering badly. Xaviar advanced, a ferocious sneer on his face.

"Stop." The word was like an avalanche of rage. Theo looked around in surprise and saw Kristine standing at the top of the steps, her arms held high. She seemed twenty feet tall, her aura flaming with power. Theo fell back before her, only just aware that Xaviar had halted in his tracks.

Kristine stared at them both, sublime in her fury. Her eyes were like knives, transfixing him. "Are you working for these slavers?"

The accusation stung to his very core. "No," he shouted, furious, hearing his enraged denial blending with Xaviar's.

"Then...." The word thundered out. She dropped her arms, and suddenly she was just Kristine again. "Then, gentlemen, why the hell are you fighting?"

He stared at her and then turned to look cautiously at Xaviar. Suddenly the note's comment about woodsy types made sense. They must have been preying on Gangrel, using the clan's new isolation from the Camarilla to help keep their activities hidden. Sympathy welled up in him, but he was careful to keep it from showing.

Xaviar scowled. "This faithless dog has shown his true colors before. I have heard of his banishment. Why should I not believe this abomination to be where his true loyalties lie?"

Theo gritted his teeth. "You know me better than that, I hope. I know I disappointed you back in Baltimore, but I didn't have any damn choice. I believed you—I still do—but there was nothing I could do. What would you have done in my place?"

"I would have spat in Paschek's face," Xaviar said, but the fury was lessening.

"If more of us had seen what you had seen, if the Sabbat had not been such a pressing problem…."

Xaviar stiffened. "Enough. The chance is past, and we will all pay for the Camarilla's cowardice in the nights to come. Why are you here, Bell?" He turned to glare at Kristine. "And who are you?"

She drew herself up haughtily and matched Xaviar's stare, the effort slightly undermined by a small tremble in her arms. "I am Kristine Gayton, childe of Thomas Godley of London."

Xaviar looked at her for a moment. "You know who I am." It was not a question. Kristine nodded, looking slightly offended. He held her stare for a moment more, then turned back to Theo. "Well?"

Theo fought down a growl. "I am going to find the motherfuckers behind this operation, exterminate them all, and get this bullshit blood hunt off my back. That is a fucking promise."

There was a long silence and then Xaviar sagged a little, the last vestiges of anger leeching out of him. "It appears we have something to talk about," he said at last.

Chapter Eight

Control Issues

The table in the lower section of the room was only big enough to allow Theo and Xaviar to actually sit at it. The others stood around on the sidelines. Kristine stayed up at ground level, on one of the gantries overlooking the administration area. She claimed that she was keeping an eye on the door, but privately, Theo thought she was just glad for an excuse to get away from the Gangrel. The twins were visibly awed by him too, but Delphine seemed determined not to let that get in the way, and they were sitting together on the floor, next to Itio, who merely looked amused by it all.

As a peace offering, Theo gave Xaviar his information first—a thumbnail sketch, but leaving nothing important out. After he'd finished, Xaviar gazed through him impassively, saying nothing. Theo resisted the temptation to ask any questions, determined to allow the Gangrel free rein to share what he chose. The man's temper was notoriously short, and he had some very strong convictions about privacy and status.

After about a minute, Xaviar shook himself back to the here and now, his face troubled. "I hope you are wrong about Cerro, but I fear that you are not. Too many of our people have fallen, Bell. Far too many. I will tell you what I knew when I stepped through the door above. Synthesis can wait until afterwards."

Theo nodded.

"When we removed ourselves from the Camarilla, my clansmen and I found an unexpected freedom for a time. In the sect, the demands of the blue bloods were never adequately repaid. We knew the need for stealth and secrecy, but the other clans used us as foot soldiers, ordering us to give up our existences in their defense. In return, we got only restriction. You should take your people out too, Bell. You have no need for those weaklings."

Theo grunted noncommittally, and waved for Xaviar to continue.

"Well. A year or so ago, rumors started to spread. Faces missing from gathers. Simple duties going unfilled. Our numbers started to shrink, and now and again, a tale would be passed of well-equipped mortal abductors, non-lethal attacks and narrow escapes. Some regions were stripped bare between one meeting and the next. I was asked to speak at a gather in Maine five months ago, yet I was the only one to attend. The only one, Bell. Fourteen or more, I was expecting." Xaviar shook his head sadly.

Theo started to ask a question, but Xaviar shook his head, cutting him off.

"No, Bell. There was no mistake. I stayed in the area then, and investigated. I knew the towns that some hunted in. Three months ago, word reached me of a kidnapper caught. When I got to the woman who had caught him, the man was long dead. She spoke to me of dark things, of things they called the 'Chain' and 'Way Station.' She said that our clan was being targeted because we would not be missed. The man had given her a name and a place. I followed both to a half-dead village in Kentucky, and found nothing but old dust and a forwarding address. That led me to a woman, who gave me this location before she died. The next link. I will find the perpetrators of this abomination, and I will free those of mine who remain in captivity."

He trailed off, staring at the table, then looked back up at Theo fiercely. "What you have told me chills me, Bell. The synthesis is inescapable: Your slavers and my abductors are the same. Their purpose is clear. Blood, for the end—either for themselves or to curry favor with. The Chain that Mary mentioned is a food chain. Last time I asked for your help in the interests of all, you spurned me. I will forget that now, if you will join me this time, and help free my people. What do you say?"

Theo sighed heavily. It had to be the same group. Xaviar was right about that at least. "If you will help me destroy these bastards and their organization, I'll help free your Gangrel, and anyone else they have stashed."

Xaviar nodded fiercely. "They will go to dust, screaming."

"It's a deal then," Theo said. "Your people will be freed. My word on it."

Xaviar grinned, displaying an impressive mouthful of teeth. "Mine too."

Itio nodded calmly toward the table. "I am pleased that we stand side by side, Xaviar. The pattern draws strength from our association. Do you have any information that can help us move beyond this site?"

Xaviar looked at him flatly. "I have followed the trail to this place. There must be a new scent to track."

"Ah," Itio said delicately.

Theo suppressed a groan. "No sign of anything useful, Itio?"

"Nothing, alas."

"Not all tracks are out in the open," Delphine said thoughtfully. Everyone turned to stare at her, and she glowered back at them defiantly. "There's nothing here, but that doesn't mean that there aren't trails we can follow."

"Speak plainly, girl." Xaviar sounded impatient.

"Someone has to own this place," she said, matching his glare.

"A holding company or some similar blind," he said, dismissively. "A dead end in the mazes of society."

"No such thing," said Nathalie, spiritedly.

"She's right," Delphine said. "Everything has a paper trail somewhere. There will be records, logs, notes…. Something will trace back to a lead we can use. It's the only shot we have."

Nathalie's brow furrowed. "Besides which, how do you think a holding company would ever have found this place? Someone had to do the groundwork and deal with the locals, if only to keep a low profile. If mysterious faceless companies bought a crappy old barn in butt-fuck nowhere, it might get noticed. Jealous neighbors are the biggest spies ever. More likely there's someone near here who knows something."

Xaviar shot a doubtful glance at Theo. "How do you expect to find this person?"

"Oh, the usual," Nathalie said breezily.

"Greed," Delphine explained. "With maybe a bit of envy and sloth thrown in for good measure." She grinned evilly at her sister. "Lucie Simich."

"Candy from a baby," Nathalie agreed. "Leave it to us, gentlemen."

Xaviar frowned at the pair of them, then turned to Theo. "You seem to allow childer greater latitude than I would expect, Bell."

Theo arched an eyebrow, ignoring the twins' scowls. "They've proved themselves resourceful—more so than some established Kindred I've known. Besides which, it hardly costs us any time if Nathalie looks into things tomorrow."

"Excuse us for a moment," Delphine said pertly. She got up, helped Nat to her feet, and went up to the ground level.

Xaviar shrugged. "Do as you see fit, Bell. I intend to search this emplacement thoroughly."

Itio smiled mildly. "We shall of course be happy to assist should you require it."

———

Half an hour later, they had pretty much dismantled the entire place. Xaviar had certainly been thorough, checking inside equipment, under pieces of furniture, behind benches and shelves, and anywhere else he could think of. They had even pulled out some of the lockers to see if there was anything they could use. They were just in the process of pulling the dissection table apart—just in case—when Del and Nat appeared on the gantry above, looking slightly damp.

"There's a small town called Fair Bluff about ten miles away," Delphine announced.

Theo looked at her, vaguely irritated.

She grinned at him, and poked her tongue out. "Brooks Realty on Scott Street is the declared official agent for two houses and one barn on this road. They're the only real estate agent mentioned on any of the buildings here. There's a sign at the back of this building that looks like it might once have been a Brooks Realty banner. If you gentlemen haven't found anything better—and I have to say, by the looks of it, my hopes aren't high—then why don't we go spend the day in Fair Bluff and see what Nat can winkle out of Brooks?"

Theo looked at her doubtfully. "Such as what?"

"The name and address of the building's owner, for starters. If it's someone local, we can go look into what sort of possibilities that presents. Otherwise, a distant individual may well be at least in the right geographical area for the next link in the chain, and there should be some way to trace on up. A company has to have owners—even a corporate shell-game will leave a paper trail. This place is seriously obscure. I'd more or less expect whoever set it up to rely on that side of things for security, more than going through convoluted double-blinds. If there's a local owner, he's probably the local overseer for the place."

Itio nodded thoughtfully. "You may have a point, pretty lady. The alarm I disabled on the door had remote reporting functions. Such reports usually go to an individual who is able to either double-check on them in person, or to send someone local to investigate. Either way, there needs to be an individual or firm in the immediate area."

"You wouldn't trust it to a company," Theo said flatly. "Too high a risk of attracting interest, if it's a measure that none of your neighbors take. No mileage in standing out."

Xaviar stood up from the wreckage of the dissection table, a low growl rumbling in the back of his throat. "Enough. This speculation is pointless. Go play at investigator if you wish, childe." He spat disgustedly on the trash surrounding him. "It cannot yield any less information than we currently have."

"Great, thanks," Delphine said brightly. Her eyes were glittering with irritation, though. "We'd better line up somewhere to crash in Fair Bluff, Theo."

He sighed, and nodded. "I suppose so."

Kristine came over from the door to stand with Delphine. "It's my turn to take care of that," she said. "I assume you'll be making your own arrangements, Justicar?"

Xaviar looked up at her sharply, searching for any hint of mockery. After a moment, he grunted. "I will continue searching for tangible information, and rest near here. You may do as you need, however. Just ensure that you are back in good time tomorrow evening, for I will not wait long."

Kristine satisfied herself with a perfunctory nod, relaxing slightly when Delphine stepped in close to her.

"If I might make a suggestion, Xaviar?" Itio sounded diffident.

The Gangrel waved a hand magnanimously.

"There are certain devices and wires that might trigger remote alarms if damaged. It would be safer to avoid harm to them. I can show you which quickly, if you so wish."

Xaviar agreed reluctantly, and Itio started pointing features out. While they were absorbed, Delphine looked at Theo and rolled her eyes theatrically. Theo winked at her, and then went to find out if the Gangrel had a cell phone.

Fair Bluff looked like something out of the forties. It was a pretty little riverside community that could probably scrape together a couple thousand residents on a good day. The church was a tall, white building with an elegant air, and many of the houses were similarly attractive. The main street was decked out with sidewalks and street lighting that had either been perfectly preserved for the last sixty years, or had just been installed fresh as a retro gesture. The place was a very welcome break after the oppressive decay of Marietta.

Kristine drove through the main part of town muttering to herself quietly. The business park outside town seemed to be more to her tastes. There were a couple of large industrial units that had clearly been recently closed, which perked her up. She nodded to herself in satisfaction, and a minute or so later, she was winding her way around a residential area just beside the business park. The houses here were cheaper than the ones downtown, and a couple of streets showed clear signs of disrepair. Eventually she found somewhere that she liked the look of, the end of a slightly shabby row that faced out over the back of a small commercial unit.

She pulled up, letting the engine idle quietly. "These three are all empty. There's a garage there we should be able to get the car into. If we're discreet, we won't attract any attention. People tend to ignore empty houses."

"Fine," Theo said. "We'd better check it out first though, to make sure."

"Please, allow me," Itio said pleasantly.

"My thanks, Mr. Shima," said Kristine. Delphine stifled a small giggle, which she ignored.

Itio slipped out of the car and vanished. He was back three or four minutes later. "The building is indeed untenanted. There are a couple of rooms that should serve us well enough, and the garage is empty. I have opened the door to it, so you may drive straight in."

Kristine smiled. "Thanks again."

It only took a few minutes to settle into the house. Nathalie didn't like being led around in the dark, and bitched a bit about Kristine's choice of place, but Theo did his best to block it out. There wasn't much for any of them to do until Nat had tried tracking down the barn's owner, and after a while, the girls picked a room and retired to it, Kristine in tow. Theo bustled around for a bit making sure that the closet he and Itio were going to use was suitably lightproof—he sealed a few possible cracks with plastic from one of the garden sacks—and prepared a few traps downstairs.

After a while though, he was forced to admit to himself that he was just killing time. The town was too small to risk feeding in—Delphine had been suitably warned—and wandering around outside would have been a pointless indulgence. Itio seemed perfectly happy to drift off into some sort of trance or other, occasionally muttering to himself quietly. Eventually, Theo made do with settling down to wait for the dawn, idly wondering whether Xaviar had ripped the Way Station to little shreds or not.

Nat woke up slowly, her whole body aching. The sun was streaming in through a side-window, and she had to fight down panic for a moment or two before reminding herself that Del had kicked her out just before dawn. She sat up, and tried to rub some warmth back into her legs. No one had thought about the fact that the fucking place was almost unfurnished, oh no. She sighed grumpily, stood up, and began a short stretching routine to work the kinks out.

When she was feeling a little less snarled, she went out to the car. Her dirties were in a big trash sack. She stared at it balefully, but it didn't get any smaller. Laundromat time—she wouldn't be able to do much for Del if she was a stinking mess. She grabbed it, along with her last change of clothes and a sack of groceries. Theo had left one of his toys in the kitchen, but it was easy enough to thread around it. There weren't any knives around, so she had to make do with ripping a tomato apart, tearing some roughs strips of cheese to go with it, and then just wrapping a hunk of loaf around it all. It looked like shit, but hell, fuel was fuel.

Once she'd wolfed down the sandwich, and followed it with a Snickers and a disgustingly warm Coke, the morning didn't seem quite so unpleasant. She stripped out of her clothes with a faint shudder, dumping them all straight into the laundry bag, and after a long, wistful moment daydreaming about power showers, climbed into the fresh stuff. There was no mirror, so after she'd fought her hair back into shape, she made do with a dusting of eye-shadow and some lip gloss. Human again. Well, sort of.

Outside, the car in the garage was a serious temptation. It would be lovely just to go for a cruise around, maybe even blow this little shit-hole and find what passed for a decent town. Del was depending on her, though—and the sedan would hardly be low-profile in a rural armpit like this. She shouldered the laundry with resignation, and cut through the scrub across the road to head down past the butt end of whatever cruddy little company the house looked out on.

It took ten pain in the ass minutes to find out that there was a bus between downtown and the business park, and twenty more to wait for the next one. There were a few people around—subdued, ground down even. None of them seemed able to rouse themselves out of their apathy long enough to be interested in her, which suited her just fine. They all looked neat enough, but the fabrics they wore were cheap, and their eyes were kind of flat. No sparkle. It took all she had not to burst out laughing at them. If only they knew… Little people, leading little lives. Getting old and ugly, and whiling away the days until death by working shitty jobs they hated that only just kept them in television, beer and hair-cuts. That was no way to live.

On the bus finally, she found herself sharing the small passenger space with a weather-beaten old woman who looked like she was on the verge of senility. The old crone eyed Nat's crop top with obvious disapproval, so Nat dredged up a bright smile, and asked her about Laundromats. That floored the old woman, who seemed to find a streak of sympathy from somewhere. Directions to a dry cleaner with a laundry service on Main Street somehow turned into a rambling discussion about how the Watermelon Festival just wasn't the same any more since the boys died. Nat managed to hide her amusement. A fucking watermelon festival? The highlight of the year, apparently. Well, she could believe that.

The old woman was clearly disappointed when Nat's stop came up. Out on the street, Nat heaved a sigh of relief, and went to ditch the laundry. After she was rid of it, she popped into a clothes store to check her appearance. She was surprised to see that she was looking a little thin, but her hair was none the worse for the night's abuses. It was a little too cold out for the short skirt she was wearing, but everything else was being washed. She didn't exactly look corporate, but revealing would work just as well for her purposes. She tugged her neckline down a little more, grinned at herself, and took off seconds before the irritated clerk finally got up the nerve to ask if she wanted to look at any clothes.

She decided to wait until the afternoon had settled in before checking out the realty place. No point going there while the boss was out to lunch. Remembering her reflection, she decided to while away an hour in the House of Pizza across the road from the clothes store. It wasn't exactly a hot spot of activity, but the food was surprisingly good, and it was nice to eat something hot for a change. At one point, she was sure she could feel eyes boring into the back of her neck, and she looked up. A knot of boys over in one corner were checking her out, big time. She fought her grin down and shot them a cool look, then went back to the pizza, just flashing a quick glance from time to time to check they were still interested. All in all, it was a good lunchtime, and by the time she left the restaurant, she felt as if she was warming to the town a little.

Mr. Brookes of Brookes Realty ended that trend. He was a fussy little man with stupid John Lennon glasses, tidy gray hair and an over-clipped mustache. He'd been disapproving right from the start, and he definitely didn't want to play ball.

"I am aware of the specific property that you describe, Miss Austin. I can only confirm however that the owner is not currently soliciting offers. There are several other similar items on our books, and I find your preference for this particular one whimsical, to say the least."

Nat fought down a wave of anger and tried again, keeping her voice as secretarial as possible. "My employer..."

"Ah, yes," Brookes said, interrupting her. "Your employer. Sentimental value. Generous offers. If you genuinely have an employer, which I doubt, he is probably breaking child labor laws by employing you—and he is certainly demonstrating poor judgment."

Nat growled, stood up, and leant over Brookes' desk, too pissed off to care. "Listen to me, Brookes—"

"No," he said, cutting her off *again*. "I have work to do, little girl. Go play somewhere else."

She gritted her teeth, and battled the urge to rip his smug little head off. "My employer will not be happy about this."

"Then please tell him that he is welcome to discuss it with me in person before seven thirty, Monday to Friday. I'm sure the owner would be happy to drop by himself, in the event that there was some sort of *credible* inquiry. In the meantime, I have real business to take care of. Please close the door on your way out, Miss Austin."

Nat stared at him furiously for a long moment, then stormed out, deliberately leaving the door open. The girl working the front desk shot her a contemptuous look, and Nat fought down a fresh wave of fury so strong that it made her head swim.

She still had half an hour to kill before she could get her laundry, so she clomped irritably across Main Street and on behind the shops and houses, down to the river. They'd erected a high walk above the bank and out over the water, and she marched up there, still furious that she'd failed Del. She allowed herself a small amount of comfort in the fact that Brookes had revealed that there was a local owner, but it didn't stop her wanting to tear something to shreds. She picked at the wooden balustrade furiously and gazed into the murky depths of the river beneath her.

"Hello." A guy's voice, unfamiliar.

She looked up. It was one of the boys from the pizza place—a tall, pleasant looking guy somewhere around twenty. He was dressed in black, with boots, jeans, a scruffy leather jacket and some rock-band T-shirt or other. He was smiling openly, obviously trying to be friendly.

Nat glared at him, strangely glad to have a target for her irritation. "What do you want?"

"Your name would be cool," he said.

"Tough."

His smile slipped a bit. "Hey, there's no need to be like that. I'm only trying to be friendly."

She sneered. "Is that so? I wonder why."

"Because you're one of the most beautiful girls I've ever seen and I'd have hated myself if I didn't at least say hello," he said sincerely.

She frowned, suddenly cross that he was being too nice to be angry with. "So was it worth it?"

He nodded. "Yeah."

She shook her head irritably.

He smiled at her again. "I don't reckon you're really like this. That expression doesn't fit your face."

She stared at him, then the fury erupted. "Who the hell are you to tell me who I am or not?"

He held up his hands, trying to pacify her. "Hey, I didn't mean anything by it. I just meant that you look really nice."

"Nice?" She spat the word, advancing on him. "What do you fucking know, farmer boy? Nothing, that's what." She poked him in the chest and he stumbled back a step or two, a dumb look of hurt and surprise on his face. "Do you think I'm like you?" She grabbed him by the collar of his jacket, and pushed him back so that he fell. "Do you think maybe I'd make you a good wife?" The image flashed past her, and the mix of boredom and longing it evoked was so unexpectedly fierce that it brought tears welling up in her eyes. "Do you think I'm normal?" He flailed at her uselessly, his eyes bugging at her. She realized with a savage shock that she was twisting his jacket so hard that she was throttling him.

She brought her face very close to his, filled with a wild need to get her own back, and grinned slowly and nastily at him. "Still think it was worth it?" She twisted harder, holding him down easily. He was trying to splutter now, his face reddening. His legs were drumming hard against the walk as he tried to kick free, but she held him down easily. He looked at her, his eyes full of horror, and then he went limp, her fury draining away with his strength.

A minute or two later, once she was absolutely certain that he was dead, Nat released her hold, and lay down, draping herself over him. Then she turned his sightless head round to face her, and kissed him slowly and deeply. "I'm Nathalie," she said, and giggled. She kissed him again, then stood up. She thought for a moment, and then pulled the body upright, propping it against the balustrade.

"It's for the best," she told him seriously, looking around to make sure that there was still no sign of anyone else around. "You'd have had a really boring, stupid little life. You'd have hated it. You'll thank me in the end." Then she giggled again, kissed him one last time, and heaved him over the side into the water. There was a dull splash, and he floated there face down for a moment, before the increasing weight of his clothes and the lack of air in his lungs pulled him under.

She grinned, and checked her watch. Time to go get the laundry.

―――――

Theo awoke to voices chattering away loudly. The twins sounded like they were in a good mood, which had to be a start. He rose smoothly, and went out into the next room, which had presumably been a lounge at some point. Delphine and Nathalie grinned up at him happily.

"Nat's found out that the barn has a local owner," Delphine said. "The realtor wouldn't give her the guy's name, but he's in the office for another forty-five minutes or so. I was thinking of dropping back over there and seeing if turning on the charm helps at all."

"It would be quicker if Kristine or I did it," Theo said.

"No," said Nathalie firmly.

Theo stared at her.

"What she means," Delphine said quickly, "is that they've already seen her. It makes sense to keep exposure minimum. I can pretend to be Nat from earlier. It's a small place. Better if you keep out of sight."

Nat didn't look much more convinced at Delphine's explanation than Theo himself felt, but it did make a certain amount of sense. "Alright. But if you have problems, then it's my turn."

"Mine first, Archon," Kristine said.

Theo shrugged "Whatever. Let's get on with it though, shall we?"

Ten minutes later, they were all packed up and had assembled at the car. If Itio felt in the least bit irritated by being hurried up and out, he was hiding it exquisitely. Operating on the basis that they would not be staying in the same location, Theo hung around to close the garage after Kristine drove the car out, and made sure that everything looked undisturbed.

Nathalie guided them back to Main Street and into a discreet parking lot that she'd seen earlier, and then she and Delphine got out. Kristine tried to join them, but Nathalie shot her such a ferocious glare that she actually backed off, and left them to it. She watched them head off round the corner, a slightly mournful expression on her face.

Theo looked at her curiously. "What was that about?"

She shrugged. "Maybe Nat wants a private word with Del en route. They don't get much time on their own, after all."

"Everything is a matter of life and death when you are young," Itio said calmly.

"Perhaps," Theo said.

Kristine smiled at him. "Don't worry about me, Archon. I'm not concerned by a child's temper."

Theo thought back to Nathalie wildly attacking the men in the service station, and said nothing.

A few minutes later, the twins were back, beaming in stereo.

"We've got the fucker," Delphine said proudly. "Here." She passed forward a piece of paper with a name, and an address just outside town.

Theo took it, glanced at it, and passed it on to Kristine. "How sure are you?"

"Absolutely certain. He would have given me his life savings if I'd wanted them."

Theo nodded. "Good work, girls. Thank you. Bear with me a moment while I phone Xaviar." He dialed the number he'd obtained the night before.

After a couple of rings, Xaviar answered. "Bell?"

"Good evening, Xaviar. Any luck?"

There was a pause. "No direct leads, no. You?"

"The girls came up aces. We have the owner's name and address. He's local."

"Really? That *is* interesting. What is your plan?"

Theo snorted. "Grabbing the guy and extracting information sounds like a good standby."

"That works for me," Xaviar said.

Itio tapped Theo on the shoulder. "Your pardon, Theophilus."

He looked round and nodded. "One moment, Xaviar. Go ahead, Itio."

"If you recall, the driver of the car we stopped in Minneapolis was so heavily conditioned that I had to shatter his mind completely to circumvent it, and we found getting answers difficult. What do you think our mark is likely to do if the barn alarms go off, or he hears that you are in town?"

"He'll probably panic and report me in," Theo said.

"Exactly," Itio said, beaming.

"By phone," Delphine said, a slow grin spreading across her face.

Itio nodded. "Very good, pretty lady. Yes. And if I am standing there beside him, I can observe the number he dials, and the location of his contact information, and he will be none the wiser."

"Which means his boss won't know he's been compromised," Delphine finished. "Just that you're investigating this area."

Theo nodded. "Ok, I'm sold. Xaviar, did you get that?"

"No." The Gangrel sounded a little put out.

"Alright. The plan now is to spook the guy into reporting up the chain, while Itio watches in."

"I see," Xaviar said. "So be it. We can always question the man afterwards, if necessary. You will want me to set the alarms off here?"

"Yeah. I'll text you when we're ready."

"Very well."

"See you later." He hung up, and turned to the others. "Right. Let's get to work."

The guy's name was Ray Vasey, and he lived on one of the large, colonial-style houses that overlooked the winding river. It was set in a generous parcel of land, including a well-kept garden area. Vasey was obviously prosperous, and his grounds gave him a fair amount of privacy.

They parked up a block along the road, and Itio got out of the car. "Ten minutes will allow me plenty of time to join our host. After that period Theophilus, may I suggest that you cause enough disturbance to warrant police attention, and then ask Xaviar to set the barn alarms off?"

Theo grinned at him. "It will be a pleasure."

"Excellent. After you have put the cat among the pigeons, return here, and I will either have the details we require, or the man himself."

Theo nodded. "Good luck, Itio."

"My thanks, Theophilus. You too."

Kristine took the car back round to the lot they had parked in earlier. When it had been ten minutes, Theo looked round at the others with a grim smile.

"I want you three to wait here. I'm going to go cause enough trouble to bring the cops out, and then I'm going to drop out of sight. At that point, I'll make my way back here and then we can go find Itio. I'll stay out of sight as much as possible, so it would be best if someone else took the front passenger seat. I know it's dull, but just wait in the car for me, okay? I don't want any complications."

"Don't worry," said Delphine acidly. "I think we can manage to sit still and do nothing for ten minutes."

"I hope so," Theo said. "I'm going to go give these farmers something to talk about for the next decade."

"Watermelons," Nathalie said.

Theo looked at her, wondering if it was some odd comment that Delphine understood. She seemed as lost as he was, though.

Nathalie grinned, but didn't explain further.

Theo shrugged and left the girls waiting. He threaded his way through a couple of narrow alleys and out onto the main street. He considered his options for a moment, and then sighed. He had to make this plausible, or the local contact might catch wind, and the only plausible excuse for breaking cover would be to simulate frenzy—without ripping the Masquerade to shreds, if possible. He shook his head wearily, and looked up and down the street. There was a quiet-looking bar a couple of blocks away, so he made for it.

Up close, the bar proved to be a little busier than he would have liked—and a little more pleasant, too—but there was no help for it. He spent a moment composing a short text message for Xaviar on his cell phone, but held off sending it. Then he went into the bar.

It was a reasonably nice-looking place, given the area. The fittings were due for a change—probably had been for a while, in fact—but everything was clean, the bar stools were nicely upholstered, and the patrons looked like decent enough country folk. He went to the bar, aware that he was the focus of attention, and deliberately twisted his face into a vicious scowl. The girl behind the counter looked at him with a certain amount of nervousness.

He glared at her. "Give me a beer."

She nodded uncertainly, picked up a glass, and poured him a cold one. Then she set it down in front of him, her hand trembling slightly at his expression. "That'll be a buck-eighty please, sir."

Theo fished around in his pocket, and brought out a fifty. At least she'd have a little something to make up for it. He stared at the note, trying to look as if he barely recognized it, and then he flung it at her. "Fucking keep it, bitch."

"Hey fella," protested one of the men at the bar. "Politeness don't cost nothing."

Theo growled, a low, savage sound that started deep down in his chest, and turned to stare at the man who had spoken, his face like thunder. The guy recoiled. Theo shrugged to himself and roared furiously, feeling self-conscious, then picked up the stool next to him and smashed it down onto the surface of the bar. The stool shattered, the bar cracked, and people started diving for cover. The waitress shrieked and vanished.

Theo started roaring like a wounded bear and lashed out randomly at furniture, fittings, stools, tables, and anything else within range. Several people dived out the front door and made a dash for it, while the others, who he was blocking off, retreated back as far as they could. After kicking a sizeable hole in the bar itself, he picked up several heavy glass ashtrays and threw them into the bottles of spirits behind the bar. They shattered spectacularly, showering the area with drink and broken glass. He turned to a nearby table and punched it into splinters, then roared again. He grinned savagely, enjoying himself now. People were gathering outside, so he grabbed a large armchair and hefted it at the plate glass window, which smashed impressively. The bystanders scattered, and he followed the chair, out of the bar via the broken window, and into the street. People screamed and ran.

In the distance somewhere, a siren was audible, quickly getting louder. Theo turned to a public bench on the sidewalk, ripped it up out of the paving, and swung it round his head like a club several times before flinging it through the window of the beauty salon next to the bar. Then he dashed into the middle of the road and roared again, feeling immensely foolish. A car across the road made a good target, so he dashed over to it, punched the windshield out, and kicked a six-inch dent into the driver's door.

A police car screamed round a corner, and slid to a halt. Finally. Theo turned to face it and screamed wordlessly. The doors opened, and he could see a couple of cops getting down behind the door. Then a loudspeaker crackled over the siren. "Lay down on the ground with your arms by your sides at once or we will open fire."

Cringing slightly with embarrassment, Theo forced his voice full of mindless anger, and yelled "No one shoots Theo Bell!" Then he dived behind the car he'd just been ripping up, and slid round it so that it hid him from everyone. He immediately stilled himself, blocked the noise of the outside world away, and filled his mind with dark sidewalk and old brick. He calmed down gradually, his aura settling, and slowly the world edged away. He stood up then cautiously, and looked around.

The cops were heading toward the car uncertainly, guns out and ready. They looked shit-scared, but resolute, and Theo felt a momentary pang of shame. He hadn't hurt anyone, at least. They split up around the car, timing it so that they both swung round to stare straight past him at the same time.

The older one shook his head. "Where the hell did he go?"

His partner shrugged. "Maybe he slipped down Bardin."

"Yeah. Call it in."

The young one nodded, and grabbed a mike. "Jess? This is Ted. The suspect has made a run for it. Black male, thirties, maybe six five, powerful build, wearing some kinda baggy tan pants and a tight white top. He said his name was Theo Bell. Run that and get Roger to head down Swamp Fox Highway, will you? Over."

The radio crackled something in reply.

Ted nodded to it unnecessarily. "Will do. Out."

The cops started jogging off toward a side road maybe fifty yards away. Theo watched them go with a certain amount of satisfaction, then checked his phone, thumped the button to send Xaviar his message, and headed back to the car, keeping his thoughts firmly on the dusty road around him.

Quarter of an hour later, the sedan was parked back where they had let Itio out. The center of town had been kicked into a light bustle, but the activity had not made it out much past Main Street, and everything was quiet.

Delphine was enjoying herself poking fun. "I had no idea you'd seen Godzilla, Theo. You pulled off a pretty mean imitation. I'm impressed." She grinned at him.

He looked at her blankly. "Would you rather I'd started tearing limbs off?"

"Hell yeah," Nathalie said enthusiastically, then grinned impishly at their expressions.

Theo sighed. "Just let it rest, childe."

The car door opened, and Itio got in. "I see you, ladies, Theophilus."

At last. "I see you too, Itio. Any luck?"

Itio's face burst into a broad smile. "The group's coordinator is known as Control, and she is in Jacksonville, Florida."

Chapter Nine

Bagman

The sedan was slightly cramped with Xaviar coming along for the ride as well, but Itio and the girls were slim, so Theo piled in the back with them. Nathalie, squashed between him and Delphine, didn't seem to mind. The girls were still more than a little frightened of the newcomer and the aura of quiet anger that rolled off him, and no one spoke much. It made rather a pleasant change from the usual stream of chatter.

The journey took a little over six hours, including half an hour at a generic service station in South Carolina for gas and food. Nathalie looked a little brighter when she finally made her way out of the self-service restaurant. Itio seemed uncomfortable however, and spent most of the rest of the journey muttering to himself queasily.

Jacksonville International Airport was some way outside the city, and it boasted several relatively cheap hotels, all well used to people keeping odd hours between flights. Nathalie took it upon herself to organize a family room for the group, although Xaviar made it perfectly clear that he had absolutely no intention of joining them. Some Gangrel had mastered the art of melding their bodies tracelessly into the bare earth during the day—a very secure practice—and as Xaviar had traveled more in the last century than any other justicar, Theo was pretty certain he'd be looking for a patch of unobtrusive ground somewhere.

Xaviar did not indulge in much conversation with the others during the trip, but he was far from idle. He had a steady stream of contacts calling him on his cell phone. He spoke mainly to acknowledge calls and, presumably, reports, but nothing he said gave anything away. Theo could see Itio twitching with curiosity each time another call came in, but the man was clearly unable to make out any more than Theo was. It was an amusing change of pace to see Itio fidgeting around, clearly out of sorts.

When they finally got to the hotel, Xaviar headed off to take care of business. Nathalie checked the rest of them in, and they headed up to the room. After a quick examination to make sure it was going to be suitable—very few hotels had bathrooms with outside windows, wanting to maximize light in the bedrooms—they settled down. Nathalie was tired from the drive, and quickly dozed off. Delphine went to lie with her.

Theo turned to Itio and Kristine, and beckoned them in for a quiet conversation so as to not disturb the twins. "Do you have any thoughts on tomorrow night?"

"It's difficult without some sort of knowledge of what to expect," Kristine said. "We don't know whether the place is a home, an office, a fortress or all three."

"I agree, beautiful lady. Surveillance would seem to be the first order of business."

"Sure," Theo said, slightly irritated by the way that they were just stating the obvious. "That's not really what I'm talking about though. I was thinking more of the subtlety versus direct action issue. This Control woman is sure to be cautious now that she knows we were mucking around in North Carolina, but there's no way she'll expect us on her doorstep tonight. If we can get what we need from her without her realizing it, we might be able to get a lead on the fuckers behind it all."

Itio nodded. "That would certainly be ideal, if possible. I am sure we can concoct a suitable diversion when the time comes. Police, perhaps."

Theo looked at him curiously.

"A pair of police officers requesting entry as part of a door-to-door sweep often causes a disproportionate amount of consternation, in my experience, particularly when there is something to hide. It is easy enough to arrange."

"Ah," Theo said, grinning. "Yes, that sounds like it could be fun."

———

Sunny Acres was a tidy, quiet little district some distance out of the center of Jacksonville, focused around a small park, community center and a children's play ground. It overlooked the creek, and seemed to attract mostly exasperated young parents and elderly dodderers, if the folks out and about were representative of the population. The air was noticeably warm, even compared to North Carolina, and Nat in particular looked like she was having some problems with the heat. According to the map, the district was located right between Craig Municipal Airport—a domestic air field—and the Blount Island Marine Terminal. That seemed to make sense, at least.

Broad Water Drive itself was a winding street that curled pleasantly down toward the creek. The houses were large and well spaced—most of them sprawling, white and blue bungalows set in manicured gardens or ornamental yards. Shingles, palms and bleached bits of driftwood were recurrent decorative elements. It looked like the sort of street which housed aging committee secretaries, club treasurers and well to do drug dealers. Theo was prepared to bet that most of them would have small dogs, and far too much clothing designed to look good at the yacht club.

Their destination was toward the end of the road, and there was little to distinguish it from any of the other units. The house certainly went back a reasonable distance, but there was no sign of any unusual attempt at privacy or security. They drove past, and Theo eyed the place doubtfully. It just didn't seem right.

He leant round and looked at Itio, suddenly uncertain. "Is this the place?" Xaviar was frowning, too.

Itio nodded calmly. "That is the location, Theophilus."

Xaviar looked faintly disgusted. "It will not take long to discover the truth of the matter."

"I dunno," Delphine said, staring back at the place as Kristine came to the end of the road and started turning around.

Xaviar craned round to stare at her in disbelief, his face darkening.

Theo shot him a warning glance. "What is it, Delphine?"

"Well, it's just that if that place is the right one, it's got to be a smoke screen. You know, like the people who hid Jews in Nazi Germany and shit. I mean look at it. It's so normal. It just screams that its got a couple inside, going about all their usual daily stuff, all that pointless shit that these people get up to. Walking the fucking dog. Face it, this is the sort of neighborhood where everyone watches everyone else through the curtains, all day long."

Nat looked interested. "Weiss?"

"Exactly," Delphine said. "If I was going to hole up there, I'd do just that—hole up. Have a loft or a cellar or something that was isolated, even the entrance hidden, and at the first sign of any sort of trouble, I'd just pull back inside the shell and hide."

"Shells crack," Xaviar said, but his voice was thoughtful.

Delphine grinned. "Yeah? If you went in there and started tearing the place up, how long do you think you'd have before a pair of squad cars showed up? Three minutes? With a dozen more just five minutes away?"

Theo's heart sank. "Shit. You're right. Any decoys would be conditioned to the hilt, too. You'd never get anywhere near them. We punch our way in, the woman goes turtle. We cause trouble, she goes turtle. We do anything even slightly odd, she goes turtle. How are we going to get in there without fucking things up royally?"

Delphine shrugged. "Fucked if I know."

Itio grinned. "If I may make a suggestion...?"

———

It felt decidedly strange following Itio up the path to the house. Theo was flanked by Kris and Xaviar, who looked just as uncomfortable as he felt. The isolation of Itio's cloaking was almost stifling, like being mentally wrapped in too many layers of thick canvas, but even so Theo felt decidedly overexposed just marching up to the front door. When he was in position by the doorbell, Itio gestured for the others to stand against the outside of the porch wall, out of the way. It hardly qualified as real cover, but all three of them were able to deflect casual attention at least a little.

Theo jumped as he suddenly felt as if a gigantic searchlight were spearing him, picking him out. Itio's cloaking had dropped away. He flinched, half-expecting guards to start shouting at him in bad German or something, then pulled himself together. He relaxed his mind, walling off his concerns, and concentrated on imagining the bare wall behind him, the shingle underfoot. He felt the world grudgingly pull back a half-step, noting as he did so that he appeared to be truly alone now.

The doorbell rang.

A few moments later, there were some footsteps, and the door opened.

"May I help you?" The voice was politely curious, and sounded like a middle-aged woman.

"I may be able to help you actually," Itio said pleasantly.

"I'm afraid we…"

Itio cut smoothly over the woman's protests. "Have you thought about death?" His voice deepened, withdrawing to become little more than a cavernous whisper. "Darkness. Pure, cold, eternal darkness. It has currents, the darkness, just like the deepest ocean. What do you think swims those currents? Bloated sacs of teeth, lit by the lantern of souls, fuelled by the hunger to consume. Life is a tiny speck of warmth, covered either side by a titanic abyss. Time is a mistake. Your time is a mistake. Do you know how to swim the lightless eternity? Do you think your lawyer and manicurist will help when there is nothing left of the world but the icy black, and the *things* that endure within it?"

He paused a moment, and Theo shuddered, trying to block out the horrible images that Itio's ramble had conjured.

"Do you hear me, woman?" Itio's voice was back to normal.

"Uh-huh." The woman sounded like she was utterly stunned, her voice absent.

An unfamiliar male voice called from deeper in the house. "Honey, who is it?"

"Um, yeah," the woman replied, half-heartedly.

There was further movement from inside as the man, presumably the woman's husband, came up to the door. "What's going on here?"

"Ah," Itio said, his voice already thinning out spectrally. "They are everywhere, you know."

Theo made a special effort to block Itio's words out. He had absolutely no wish to hear whatever the next set of crazed revelations were going to be. He threw himself entirely into visualizing the walls around him, keeping out of sight. He was aware that Itio was speaking, but he refused to let the words register.

After a minute or so, the murmuring stopped, and Itio crunched round the side of the porch, smiling pleasantly. "Lady, gentlemen, I see you. Please, this way." He turned around, and headed back. Theo waited a few seconds, and then followed.

The entrance hall was conservatively neat, prosperous without being showy. Itio, Xaviar and Kristine were standing around watching a couple in their forties. The woman had light brown hair, and probably had been pretty once. She was playing with the switch of a small table lamp, flicking the light on and off dreamily. The man was absentmindedly dusting the wall with a pocket handkerchief, grimacing occasionally.

Itio beamed at them fondly. "They'll be no trouble to us now. Come, let us investigate this residence. I suggest that we head in different directions, being cautious not to try locked doors, and then meet back here in five minutes to discuss our findings." He kept his voice to a whisper.

The others nodded their agreement. As they were about to set out, Theo caught Itio's arm, and gestured at the couple now wandering around the hallway in a daze. "How long will they be like that?"

"Fear not, Theophilus. They will be distracted long enough for our purposes," Itio said, smiling. "Probably not more than a month."

Theo fought down a shiver. "Does it…" He couldn't bring himself to ask.

Itio nodded, just the faintest ghost of a grin on his face. "Yes, Theophilus. It does. But it is less certain on the Kindred. Living minds are so… preoccupied."

"Oh."

They all split up. Without any clear idea of who was supposed to be looking where, Theo decided that the safest bet was to give the whole place a quick look over. Despite Itio's assurances, he spent a moment stilling his mind and aura, and filled his head with the rooms around himself, just in case he stumbled across someone unexpected.

The house itself was exactly as anyone would have expected. Everything was tidy, but it was the sort of order that came through domestic care and attention to detail, rather than the more usual sterility found in lairs that were never lived in. The refrigerator held plenty of fresh food (and no sacks of blood), there was a bowl of authentic fruit on the dining room table, and the bathroom sink clearly showed that the man of the house had shaved that morning. There wasn't anything out of place at all. It was becoming harder and harder to imagine that anything unusual had ever happened there before Itio had fried the owners' minds.

There were several closed doors around the house—one in the kitchen, one in the master bedroom, one in a hallway, and two more in what was probably a study. None of them were in lightproof spaces, and there didn't appear to be any unusual security around any of them. Theo didn't try to open any of them, just in case. When the five minutes were up, he made his way back to the hallway, dropping his concentration and allowing himself to come back into normal view.

The others had already assembled. Itio looked serene, as usual.

"Well, what's the verdict?" Theo kept his voice low.

"I was about to ask you the same thing, Theophilus." Itio smiled pleasantly.

"It all seems pretty normal to me. Kris? Xaviar?"

Kristine shook her head.

Xaviar's eyes narrowed. "I am surprised by your inattention, Bell. The door to the cellar is guarded by a sorcerous ward."

Theo blinked, ignoring Itio's broad grin. "Which one is the cellar?"

"The one in the kitchen," Xaviar said. "It is pointing toward a wall across the yard where a bricked-up ground-level entrance is still visible, and the structure of the lobby behind the warded door means that there is no space for a room behind it."

"I guess that's got to be it. We'll need to find out how to get in from your space-heads, Itio."

"They may be able to facilitate the process for us," Itio said. "Theophilus, will you come with me? Lady, gentleman, we will only be a moment."

Itio led Theo into the next room, where the woman was wandering around staring at a small row of little commemorative trophies and plaques. Itio took her by the hand and pulled gently. She looked up, startled, and then let herself be led along. He tugged her to the kitchen, and stood back a little, pulling Theo with him so that they were out of a direct line of sight of the door.

Theo allowed Itio to position him, and looked carefully at the door. Remembering one of his sire's old lessons on the nature of wards, he brought the door into the focus of his mind, shutting out everything else. He tried to push past the mere surface-level visual of the door, and thought about its essential nature, its relationship to the wood that had created it. He moved deeper, visualizing the sun and rain those trees must have fed on and the life-force residual in their growth that still lingered in the wood. Ever so slowly, a faint impression of a sparkling circle formed within the door, almost as if it was buried under the paint and shining through. The ward. It could well be the case that it was under the paint, actually; wards were usually drawn in the casting thaumaturge's blood.

Itio was talking quietly to the woman, who was nodding dreamily. Then he gave her a small push toward the door, and stepped back. He looked around, and then a vicious jolt of unreality lurched straight through Theo, shaking him. The room looked the same, but felt entirely different—fake, somehow. Or, even worse, perhaps he was the fake, the intruder into what was correct. It made his head swim. Itio looked up at Theo and smiled apologetically, and Theo realized it had to be Itio's cloaking. He shook his head wryly.

Miming carefully, Itio indicated that they should enter the door once it opened. Theo nodded curtly, still feeling decidedly odd.

The woman was standing in front of the door, looking uncertain. Finally, after a long moment, she knocked on the door. The pattern of knocks was simple enough—two staccato, followed by a pause, and then three more—but Theo noticed that every knock was placed right in the center of the sparkling ward.

"Yes, Janet? What is it?" The unfamiliar female voice was curt, and seemed to come out of the floor.

"Hello Lady," said the woman.

"Well?" The voice sounded impatient.

"Need..." The woman trailed off.

There was a pause. "Need what? Are you quite well?"

"Oh, yes, Lady. Yes. I... Deep."

The pause was longer this time, and when the woman spoke again, she sounded resigned. "I can't hear you properly. Come down."

The door clicked, and swung outward slightly.

Itio made an urgently sweeping gesture that he'd probably seen on a bad police show or something. Theo stifled a grin, and followed him.

The woman, Janet, pulled the door open unsteadily and started tottering down the stairs in front of her. Itio and Theo followed close behind, keeping as low and treading as softly as they could.

The stairs opened out onto a large basement that looked like something out of *Dr. Strangelove*. One wall was dominated by large maps of the various continents, with particular attention to the United States. Most of the maps had pins of various colors tacked into them, and there were occasional photos up amongst the maps as well. The opposite wall was stacked high with filing material. A long, low desk ran the length of the room. It held at least twenty telephones and a number of computer terminals. Despite the sheer volume of material, it all looked well organized.

A slim, dark-skinned and quite beautiful woman was sitting toward the center of the long desk, looking mildly irritated. "What is it, Janet?" It was the same voice.

Janet stumbled down the last steps and out onto the carpet. "Don't want to die. Scared. Make it go away, Lady. Please?" Itio was moving past her, fumbling around with a deep pocket in his pants.

The woman looked at Janet, perplexed. "Have you been drinking? What..."

She broke off, alarmed by some sixth sense as Itio moved swiftly toward her, pulling a wooden stake from the pocket he'd been fiddling with. She took a step back swiftly, looking around uncertainly. Itio lunged forward like a snake—the movement made Theo feel like he'd been suddenly dunked into scalding water—and hammered the stake through her chest. The woman froze, Janet collapsed to the floor weeping, and Itio smiled happily.

"There, Theophilus. If you would go and fetch the others, I believe we can begin the next stage of our investigations."

Theo grinned back at him, and headed up the stairs, relief washing over him. They were finally going to get somewhere. He bounded into the kitchen, turned the corner toward the front of the house, and his face erupted in white-hot pain. He stumbled backwards into a table, blinking furiously, slowly becoming aware that the door from the kitchen to the yard was open. A towering shape filled his vision, all wild hair, black leather and sunglasses.

The man spat. "Prick." The voice was instantly familiar, and utterly shocking, as surprising as if Hardestadt himself, founder of the Camarilla, had turned up to smack him around.

Theo braced himself on the table and kicked out hard with both feet, keeping the blow low so that it drove into the man's knees. "Karsh?" The man stumbled back a little, giving Theo time to stand up and back off a bit himself.

"I don't know how the hell you found this place, Bell, but I'm glad you did. Time to follow your sire." Karsh patted his stomach and smirked evilly.

Theo's head whirled, and red clouds slammed at him, buffeting him with their fury. He refused to let the rage in, desperate to keep control. "You…" It was the best he could manage.

Karsh's form blurred and vanished, and a truck smashed into Theo's chest. He went flying back into the refrigerator, bones splintering, and he crumpled onto the floor in sheer agony. Karsh looked down at him in mocking disapproval, shaking his head. "You can do better than that." The blood in Theo's chest started to seethe, the splintered bones tugging agonizingly as it pulled them back into line. Karsh was just standing there, waiting patiently.

Theo pulled himself up slowly, concentrating inwards. The blood seemed to catch fire in his veins, filling him with its heat. It piled into his muscles, wave upon wave of it powering into him. He could almost feel his arms and legs writhing as the moment stretched out. While he stood up, Theo casually caught hold of his knife in his left hand, using his rising to hide the fact.

When his legs were underneath him, he shot up straight, bringing his left arm up with his body in a tight arc. He forced the arm upwards, the fist with the knife at the very summit of his movement. He was moving so fast that he could almost feel the air parting around him. Just as the blow landed, his spine came straight and his hips locked, the entire force of his body's explosive motion channeled into the tip of the blade. The knife sank into Karsh's chin, the power of the blow so great that it snapped the warlord's broad head back. The man's feet came up off the ground, and he actually partly somersaulted backwards, landing in a crumpled heap.

Then, incredibly, he unfolded.

Karsh stood up, tugged the knife out of his jaw, and smiled, a peculiarly avuncular expression. The small cut was already sealing over, and Theo's heart sank. "Good, Bell. Very good, actually. That would have decapitated an ox." He stretched his hands languorously, long claws springing out of his fingers. "You've earned yourself a clean destruction."

Suddenly he folded again, backwards this time. Theo had just a moment to register the surprise on Karsh's face before he was flipping round in a confused jumble.

"Traitor!" The roar was Xaviar's, but it cut short as Karsh dropped into a crouch and lashed out, catching Xaviar viciously in the stomach. The blow made the former justicar stagger, and Kristine darted past him smoothly, a long knife in each hand. Karsh darted back a couple of steps toward the open door, just a blur against the darkness outside, and glanced round quickly.

"How many more have you got hiding in there, Bell? Ah, no matter. Until next time." Karsh span round, looking like nothing so much as a whirlwind, and vanished, just a streak of black against the darkness.

Xaviar bellowed furiously, pulled himself upright, and shot into the yard. Theo and Kristine shared a long glance, and then Xaviar returned, looking furious. He pushed the door closed.

"Fuck me, he's fast," Theo said, slightly awed. "He was about to tear me a new asshole. Thank you. Both of you."

"You're welcome, Archon." Kristine smiled.

"That disgusting scum is a traitor to his clan, his society and his kind. He has damned us all to a vile destruction." Xaviar's eyes burned, tinges of red showing. "I am not surprised to find that he is involved with this abomination. No treachery is beneath him. And yes, as it pains me to say it, he is fast. Faster than you, Bell. Faster than me, even. Strong too. His skin is like granite." He spat on the floor. "It won't fucking save him. I'm going to eat his fucking heart."

Theo nodded. "I'll help. In the meantime..." He raised his voice. "Itio! We've got to get out of here now!"

"Very well, Theophilus." He sounded a little put out. "If you would all be so good as to come down here to lend a hand?"

Theo and Xaviar headed down, while Kristine made a quick call on her telephone. Xaviar's eyes bulged a little as he saw the room, and he darted over to inspect one of the maps, growling a little. Itio had assembled a big pile of folders and documents, along with a chunky-looking portable computer, and a plastic shopping bag full of other stuff.

"We should kill this servant," Xaviar declared, looking at Janet, who started sobbing in terror at his feet. "Does anyone want her blood?"

Theo stepped forward without thinking, but the words caught in his throat. Killing her in the heat of battle was one thing, but just... His thoughts trailed off and he shrugged. He didn't owe her anything, and she *was* working for the slavers. "I will, If you're going to kill her anyway."

Xaviar hauled the wailing woman up off the floor and flung her over to Theo. He shrugged to himself, then bit her throat out and started draining her, replenishing the blood he'd burnt trying to make an impact on Xaviar. When her corpse was more or less dry, he let her drop. Kristine was already heading up the stairs with a big stack of documents. Xaviar had the computer and some more papers, and Itio was hefting the bag.

"I regret leaving the remaining material," Itio said sadly. "If there is no time however, then I suggest we set a fire in this room. We have the material we need."

"Karsh might be back at any moment, with reinforcements," Theo said. "Come on. I'll bring the woman."

By the time he had got the frozen woman up the stairs, Kristine was already back. "The sedan is out front. Get the statue in the back. I'll finish up here."

Theo nodded, tucked the staked vampire under one arm, and made his way out to the car.

Chapter Ten

Enemy Mine

No one spoke as they headed away from Broad Water Drive. Kristine was back in the driving seat, Xaviar next to her. The rest of them were piled in the back again, which was further complicated by the paralyzed woman , who they'd had to dump in the seat well. After a brief hesitation, Nathalie pointedly rested her feet on the woman's head, grinning a little when no one called her on it. Itio was off in a little world of his own, mumbling and nodding to himself occasionally.

Finally, Kris broke the thoughtful silence. "This car must have been compromised. We need to change vehicles, and then get the fuck out of this city quickly."

"It's too obvious," Theo said. "There's a whole bunch of us now, and we've got a load of baggage."

"So I stash you all somewhere, go swap cars a few times, and then come back again."

"Alright," Theo said. "I guess that makes sense."

"Let us not be hasty," Itio said. "I have found somewhere that we may go."

Theo looked at him. "What sort of place are you talking about?"

"Somewhere secure." The customary calm smile slid back into place. "There is nothing to concern yourself with, Theophilus. We may stay there for several days, if necessary."

Up front, Xaviar shrugged curtly.

"Alright," Theo said cautiously. "Let's give it a try. Can you provide directions?"

"Of course."

Itio proceeded to guide Kristine out from the center of the city in the direction of Atlantic Beach. After a few miles, he directed her into an underpass junction that cut beneath a bustling shopping district. Rather than taking them back out however, he directed the car into a series of what looked like access roads, including one that was clearly marked as one way in the other direction. That fed them onto a down ramp, and out into a small underground parking deck. Itio confidently led them to a pair of closed doors that looked like they led into someone's office, then hopped out of the car with an admonition to be patient. He went over to the doors, fiddled about for a bit, and then threw them wide expectantly.

The doors opened on to a pitch-black tunnel that looked as if it had been unused for the last forty years. The floor was covered with a thick layer of dust and spotted here and there with old papers and other bits of crap. No one spoke, and after a moment, Kristine headed in nervously. Once the car was inside, Itio held his hand up for her to wait, then came inside, shutting the entrance up behind himself, and wrestled a large metal bar into place across the doors. He then got back into the car, and motioned for Kristine to resume driving.

After a few hundred yards, the tunnel opened up into a large concrete room that could have been a store room at one point. It was a lot less dusty than the tunnel had been. It was fairly Spartan, but it did have a table and chairs to one side, framed by a small circle of standing lamps, and, off in one corner, a random assortment of climbing bars appeared to have been built into the wall.

Theo looked around, unsure whether to be impressed or worried. "What is this place, Itio?"

"A home away from home." Itio smiled.

"One of yours?"

"No, but do not let that concern you."

Theo frowned. "Are we safe here?"

"Absolutely, Theophilus. No one knows that you are here."

Kristine looked uncertain too. "What if someone else drops by to stay?"

"That is impossible, lovely lady."

"Enough," Xaviar said irritably. "It will serve. I want to examine this information we have retrieved."

"Of course," said Itio, unruffled.

Theo sighed, and gave them a hand carrying the material over to the table. They also dragged the woman out of the car, and left her lying in a corner. While Itio turned his attentions to the computer, the others started going through the paperwork.

It was obvious within seconds that they were onto something huge. The folders were organized by city or area, and each was full of detailed information on organizational structure, key players, political leanings, and even degrees and type of leverage that the group had with specific individuals. Another section of the material seemed to correspond to particular operations. These were generally written up as notes—someone's mental shorthand rather than a deliberate code—but they were still fairly obscure.

Kristine passed one sheaf of papers to Theo, her expression unreadable. It was titled simply BELL. He looked through it with mounting disbelief. They had information on just about everything, from his history with Angus through to his family members. On one page, they had done a diagram that seemed to represent his personal network of connections—professional, family, personal, everything. Most of the lines leading away from him had been struck through. He felt a tide of anger rising within him, and fought to keep it down. Once he had himself back under control, he folded the paper up and slipped it into the pocket of his pants.

Delphine and Nathalie were poring over something themselves, huddling together and looking tearful. Kristine's eyes were gleaming, however. She looked up to meet Theo's gaze, and grinned triumphantly at him, then turned back to the documents.

"Bitch." Xaviar was the first to break the silence, his voice thick with pain and anger, and he slammed a fist down onto the table furiously, making it rattle. "Tonight. It stops tonight. Let me out, Bell. I have work to do."

"I crave your indulgence for just a few moments more, Xaviar." Itio's voice was unusually urgent.

Xaviar looked at him closely. "Very well."

"My thanks," said Itio. "I have located two items on this machine that you may wish to examine. One is a set of receipts for shipping crated cargo from the Jacksonville Marine Authority to an address near the city of São Paulo in Brazil."

A loud growl cut Itio off. Theo was astonished to discover that it was coming from his chest. Xaviar looked at him approvingly, and clapped him on the shoulder. "Soon, Bell."

"Indeed," said Itio. "The other item is a list of persons who are in the direct employ of the organization, organized into three lists: Camarilla, Sabbat and Independent."

"Give me that," Xaviar snapped. He whipped the laptop round, and glared at the screen. After a moment, he flinched, and started paging down rapidly. A few seconds later, he straightened up, passed the computer back to Itio, and sighed, massaging the bridge of his nose. "My apologies for my rudeness, Mr. Shima. You have done Clan Gangrel a great service, and I am in your debt. All of you." He reached down and ruffled Nathalie's hair.

Delphine and Nathalie stared back at him in utter astonishment, identical mirrors of surprise. Then they broke into sunny grins.

Xaviar winked at them, and then looked back at Theo. "We are going to fetch my people and destroy these scum, yes?"

"Yes," Theo said flatly. "That's exactly what we're going to do."

"Good. First, I have to cleanse my own clan of this vile infestation. Within two nights, all those Gangrel who still know the old ways will be pure. I swear it. I also intend to enlist some assistance for the next phase. I will return two nights from now."

"Good luck," Theo said.

Itio smiled pleasantly. "Can I offer you a lift back above ground?"

Xaviar nodded. "My thanks, yes."

Kristine passed Itio the keys, and he and Xaviar bustled off to the car. A moment later, they were heading off out of the bunker.

Theo suppressed a weary sigh, and pulled the computer round so that he and Kristine could have a look at the file. It was basically a long list of names and locations. Most of them were utterly meaningless to Theo, although every now and again there was one he thought he recognized, and a very few of them were utterly shocking.

They read through the list several times, Theo's heart sinking. He looked up at Kristine. "There's too many. What the fuck are we going to do? It's not as if we've got Xaviar's level of influence over his people."

She frowned. "We're going to have to take this to the council of justicars."

"Are you nuts? They think we're both grade-A wackos. Actually, they think *I'm* crazy. You are supposed to be long-since destroyed. Without cast-iron evidence, they'd never believe a word of any of this. Shit. Not one of them would even listen long enough to hear what we've found."

Delphine looked up. "Hey Theo, how about your boss?"

Theo blinked. "Oh yeah, great idea. If anyone's going to hack me into chunks, it's Paschek."

Delphine rolled her eyes at him. "Duh. So he knows you're not going to get in touch unless you really have something to say. Plus he must know you pretty well by now, so isn't he going to be the least likely to believe the bullshit?"

He thought about it for a while, then finally shrugged uncomfortably. "I suppose it's as good a place to start as any, but he'll have to be eased into my involvement later, I figure. Kristine, you're going to have to call him. There's a phrase that will let him know that it's a critical emergency. It should make him take what you say extremely seriously—none of us use it frivolously. See if you can get him to come down here. We need him to see this stuff."

"Okay. What's the phrase?"

Given the fact that Kristine was blood-bound to Delphine and so would tell her anything without question, there didn't seem much point trying to keep the phrase secret from the twins. "It's 'in return for that time in Pittsburgh.' Misuse of it is punishable by final death."

Delphine grinned. "That's not much of a code phrase. What about 'The Rabbit flies South' or something?"

Theo sighed. "The idea is to sound inconspicuous, childe, not stupid." He gave Kristine the number. "Delphine, Nathalie, stay quiet."

They nodded, and Kristine dialed Paschek on her cell phone. She waited for the call to be picked up, looking slightly nervous. There was a faint bleep from the cell phone.

Kristine waited a moment before speaking. "Justicar Paschek. Good evening. I need you to listen to me for a moment, in return for that time in Pittsburgh."

There was a pause, and she looked at Theo warily. "My name is…"

Theo hissed at her, cutting her off. Then he bent over to her other ear and whispered "Daisy," so quietly he himself could barely hear it.

"Daisy," Kristine said dutifully.

There was another pause.

"Justicar Paschek, I have been given a list of traitors in your organization to pass on to you. Both, actually. I do. Come to meet me, and I will give you the list, along with the evidence."

She flicked a glance at Theo again.

"The lobby of the Sunbird hotel at Jacksonville International Airport, in Florida. Ten o'clock tomorrow evening."

She arched an eyebrow.

"I know. Yes, I know. Please listen to me, Justicar. It is vitally important for your personal safety that you avoid mentioning any of this matter to anyone—even your destination tomorrow. Your personal organization is compromised, and these people would not hesitate to strike you down if they even heard the word Jacksonville. Yes. Very well, Justicar. I understand. Thank you."

She hung up, looking weary. "He sounds suspicious as all hell, but he'll be there."

The next evening, Itio drove them back to the airport in an SUV he'd acquired somewhere. Delphine had flatly refused to come along, which really wasn't all that surprising. She and Nathalie decided to remain in the city, and Itio dropped them somewhere lively but fairly discreet. Kristine was clearly reluctant to leave them, but Delphine agreed with Theo that she was necessary at the meeting.

The meeting. Theo sighed. He had thought over a whole range of possible approaches. Paschek was going to be mightily pissed, there was no way round that. The best policy seemed to be to avoid deceiving him any more than necessary. They got to the hotel early, and went straight to the lobby, settling down into a nest of armchairs surrounding a low coffee table. Theo had selected half a dozen files and a handful of documents, which combined nicely with the laptop to make it look as if the three of them were conducting some business. The woman—"Control"—was in the trunk, covered loosely with some trash sacks.

A vacantly pretty waitress pestered them into ordering a round of coffees, which they promptly ignored. They had deliberately left all their significant weapons behind, although Theo for one still had his knife. The three of them watched the lobby carefully from behind folders and documents, keeping close watch for any signs of a trap—either from Karsh or Paschek.

At three minutes to ten, Jaroslav Paschek walked through the hotel entrance, seemingly alone. He was a slender man, slight even, barely five feet tall, with light hair and delicate features. He was wearing a slightly old-fashioned navy suit with a somber tie and a white orchid in the buttonhole. He looked around the lobby, then turned and started heading toward the three of them, his face carefully neutral.

He sat down smoothly. "Daisy, I assume. Mr. Bell, too. What an expected surprise. I trust that you recall the penalty for misuse and revelation of the emergency designator?" His voice was cold but composed.

Theo stifled a groan. Like that, eh? "Good evening, Justicar. Thank you for coming to Jacksonville. Yes, I remember the penalty. Please hear me out, and then I think you will agree with me that there has been no misuse."

Paschek arched one eyebrow. "If I had been even a whisker more certain that you were behind this ridiculous cloak and dagger summons, I would have sent a hit squad in my place. What makes you think I'm going to put up with your inane ravings for a moment longer than I have to?" He was getting steadily more icy.

Theo ground his teeth together, and forced his anger down. "I know we don't see eye to eye. I've worked faithfully for you for years, though. Does that not count for anything?"

"A rabid dog is fit only to be put down, regardless of his prior value. I hear rumors that you consort with demons now, Bell. If that is true—and I shall find out, believe me—then, in God's name, I shall burn the corruption out of you myself, one flaming mote at a time."

"How dare..." began Theo, furious.

"*Who are you to question what I dare?*" Paschek's shriek of rage cut Theo cold. A number of people turned to stare, and the man visibly calmed himself. "You disgust me, Bell." He turned his gaze on Itio and Kristine. "I have no idea who you two are, and I do not care. You are part of this infection."

"Justicar, examine these documents. There are diabolists and traitors in..."

"Enough." Paschek stood up. "The next time I set eyes on you Bell, you will be destroyed." He turned to go.

Itio smiled slowly, a sinister gesture with little humor in it, and reached out to take Paschek's arm. "Jaroslav, listen." His voice was laced with peculiar significance. "God picks strange messengers."

Paschek froze for several seconds, then shot a long, questioning look at Itio before sitting back down. "Very well, Bell."

Theo stared at the justicar in amazement, then pulled himself together rapidly. "A corrupt group based in São Paulo is organizing the large-scale abduction of vampires and mortals. They are extremely influential in Kindred society, and some or all of them are diabolists. I have inadvertently made myself a threat to them, and they tried to destroy me and everything close to me. They destroyed Don Cerro a few nights ago. With the aid of…" He hesitated. Xaviar was not exactly a high-credibility source in the eyes of the Camarilla. "With the aid of my companions tonight, I have obtained details of their personnel."

"Do you have even a shred of evidence?" The fury had ebbed, and Paschek sounded slightly bored.

Theo thought about it for a long moment. "The Aurora primogen. I was there, a week or so ago. They were destroyed because I spoke to them."

"Just your word. Besides, it could easily be one demonist meeting with another," Paschek countered. He didn't sound convinced though.

"You know better than that," Theo said mildly. "You've met Michael Aldridge. He was absolutely straight. However, there is also the Rockton massacre, which the group attempted to frame me for."

"Ah yes, I heard about that. Surely that is just evidence of your own debauchery."

Theo let the expected insult slide. "There is also the paperwork I have with me, justicar."

"That is the least of all, the easiest to forge."

"I know. But please humor me and have a look at it. Here. You are still in New England, aren't you?"

Theo picked up the folder that dealt with the area, and passed it over. Paschek glanced at it dully, then took a second look, his curiosity growing. He opened the file up, and started flicking through the contents. Then he started a little, turned back to the beginning, and began reading more slowly, totally absorbed.

After several minutes, Paschek put the folder down. "How in the name of God did you get that information, Bell? Is this a threat?"

Theo shook his head wearily. "It's no threat, Justicar. There's no way I could know that much information about your private affairs. I don't have the resources. There's only one group that does. I retrieved similar dossiers for more than eighty cities and regions across the United States and Western Europe."

Paschek looked at him, an expression of horror growing on his face. "Who are these conspirators?"

"We retrieved this computer from their base of operations." Theo gestured to Itio to open the computer. "It contains, amongst other things, a list of the people who are willing collaborators. Traitors, in other words."

Paschek peered at the screen, and the few shreds of color he possessed drained out of him. "Preposterous." The word was a whisper, though. He kept reading, his hand trembling just slightly as he reached out to scroll down. When he'd read the list, he looked up again. "Do you realize...? How can I possibly...?"

Theo had been hoping for the question. "Run a test. Right now. They're desperate to kill me."

"Who?" Paschek seemed shaken.

"Anna Petrova," said Theo dully. The Russian woman had been an archon of Paschek's for several years now, and the justicar had held her up as a loyal example to Theo on several occasions. She was also on the list of traitors. "She's one of ours. Where is she at the moment?"

"Denver," Paschek said quietly.

"Tell her I'm coming into the city with important evidence. Tell her I'm coming by limo from the airport to the Elysium, so that I can report to the prince there. Order her to protect me at all costs."

Paschek thought about it. "Yes." His voice got stronger. "Yes. We can disprove this here and now, settle your ridiculous persecution fantasies. Your document doesn't mean anything for certain." He opened his jacket and Theo tensed, but he only pulled out a mobile phone. Even the phone looked huge in his dainty fingers, though.

Paschek dialed a number. "Good evening, Archon Petrova. I have an urgent task for you." He paused for a moment. "Theo Bell is flying in to Denver International. He claims to be in possession of vital information. He is going to get a blacked out limousine from the airport to Elysium. I want you to meet him at Elysium, and make absolutely certain that he remains safe while he reports to the prince. Do you understand?" He paused again. "Good. Expect him within the hour. Do not fail me in this. Good evening."

Paschek killed the call, then dialed again. "Mary. I need a limousine with blacked-out windows to drive from Denver International Airport to the city's main Elysium. As soon as possible. No, use a commercial firm. Monitor progress, and report as soon as it arrives. No. Do not discuss this externally. Good." He snapped the phone shut with a flourish. "Now we wait."

The next forty-five minutes passed in stony silence. Theo was perfectly happy to let Paschek sit there and stew in his own juices; he was relieved just that the man had decided to wait. He wasn't going to do anything to risk aggravating Paschek further. Eventually, Paschek's phone rang. The justicar shot Theo an inscrutable look, and then answered the call.

"Paschek. I see. No. Thank you, Mary." He hung up, and slipped his phone back inside his suit pocket.

There was a long pause, which seemed to stretch on an on. Theo tensed, ready make a break for it.

Paschek turned to look at him, absent-mindedly adjusting the orchid in his suit lapel. "It would seem that we have a serious problem, Archon Bell."

Theo paused, uncertain. *Archon*? "The car..."

"Destroyed," Paschek confirmed. "Before it even made it off the interstate. A traffic accident that nudged the vehicle over a modest edge, where it subsequently exploded."

Theo let out a long, ragged breath. "So you believe me."

Paschek nodded, slowly and thoughtfully. "I do not see that I have any choice. It would be easier to swallow if there was more to go on."

A thought hit Theo, and he suddenly grinned. "Actually, there is."

Paschek eyed him disapprovingly. "Pray tell, Archon. What is so amusing?"

"We have the organization's regional controller staked out in the trunk of our vehicle."

"Ahh." Paschek's eyes lit up. "You have questioned him?"

"Her," Theo said. "No. There didn't seem much point. She is bound to be recalcitrant, conditioned even."

"Oh my, yes." Paschek was actually smiling. "She is. Are you prepared to hand her over?"

Theo grinned evilly. "Justicar Paschek, none knows—or respects—your talent for obtaining confession better than I. It would be an honor to deliver her to you."

"Perfect, Archon Bell," Paschek murmured happily. "You've done well, and you may even find yourself adding to your impressive tally of accolades. My congratulations to you and your team. I assume that the events leading up to the blood hunt lodged against you were the result of this organization's actions?"

Theo nodded. "Yeah. The Minneapolis council were being strong-armed into it, though. Their file is on the table as well."

"Very well. Leave the matter with me. I will have the hunt annulled just as soon as I have moved against the traitors in your list. I would not want to startle them into flight. It will be difficult to round them all up quietly as it is. I will need to speak with certain of my colleagues, I think."

Itio handed Paschek a floppy disk. "This is a copy of the list, Justicar."

Paschek took the disk with a certain satisfaction. "My thanks. Come now, Archon Bell. Let us transfer your prisoner, and start cleaning out this nest of vipers."

In Denver, Anna Petrova was waiting dutifully with the Elysium doorkeeper, so that she could provide escort for a guest whom she knew would not be coming. She'd been there for almost two hours, but she was perfectly happy to hang around all night—as long as it took for Paschek to call and inquire about Bell's arrival. A small commotion caught her attention, and she looked round to see the prince and her second in command approaching, dressed for venturing out. A couple of flunkies were trailing along, getting last minute orders or something.

The gatekeeper opened the door deferentially, and the prince went over to stand in it, enjoying the view out over the city. Then she stuck her head back inside, and smiled at Anna. "Come look, Archon. There's something I'd like to show you."

Anna nodded obediently, and joined the prince in the doorway. The woman pointed across the city, approximately toward a towering building that was silhouetted against the rising moon. "Do you see?"

A sharp pain blossomed under her left shoulder, and she felt her body seize. Horror washed over her, but she couldn't so much as twitch an eyeball, let alone scream in panic. The prince caught her by the shoulder, supporting her. "Justicar Paschek asked me to ensure that you knew where you'll be seeing the sun rise from in the morning, my dear."

Anna tried to scream, to protest her innocence, to flee, even to give in to the panic and lose herself in frenzy, but there was absolutely nothing she could do except watch, in terror, as they propped her in a small courtyard outside and the sky began to lighten.

In a small room in upstate Virginia early the next evening, Jaroslav Paschek was waiting impatiently for a critically important visitor. After what seemed an age, one of the establishment's staff came to announce his guest's arrival. Paschek composed himself, pushing his irritability aside with pleasant memories of his success with the Lucy woman that Bell had given him.

The door opened and a slight young woman dressed in somewhat outdated formal clothing came in, her hair pulled back tightly into a severe bun. She didn't look particularly pleased to be there.

Paschek rose to his feet, and took her hand, pressing it to his lips gracefully. "Maris. Thank you for meeting me at such short notice. We have a problem. There's a traitor on the council." There was a faint whisper of air, and the Justicar of Clan Malkavian trembled slightly. "You." Her expression became pained, and then her head toppled forward, puffing into dust as her body crumbled away.

A gangling scarecrow of a man loomed behind the pile of dirt that had been Maris Streck. He looked like he'd been assembled awkwardly out of sticks, and topped off with a distorted, bird-like face. Paschek nodded to him, grimly satisfied. "My thanks, Robin. Your gadget is most impressive."

The man bobbed a nod back, his tiny mouth twisting in what might have been a smile. "Pleazur." His voice was a piping whistle. He gestured down at the ash and grimaced. "Tidy?"

Paschek shook his head. "Leave it. We both have more work to take care of tonight."

In Pittsburgh, the sheriff of the city was dismayed to arrive for his scheduled appointment with the prince to discover just a dusty pile of clothes and a rather rude note about inappropriate loyalties.

In Cleveland, Ohio, Archon Julian Dean of Clan Ventrue was investigating a rather spectacular attack on the city's telecommunications infrastructure when several bursts of gunfire from a nearby bus shelter ended his duties, both official and unofficial.

They fell in New York, in Chicago, in London and in a score of other locations. They fell unaware, or fighting, or screaming for mercy. They fell from exalted heights, hidden depths, and every place in between.

And on it went.

Chapter Eleven

Journeyman

In the end, it took Xaviar three full nights to get back to Jacksonville. They met him in a small, deserted diner on the outer edges of the city's suburbs. He did not seem inclined to explain why he'd picked that particular establishment—it could have been any one of ten thousand identical places across the country—but Theo was perfectly happy to let the matter lie. Nathalie ordered more than enough food to justify the group's presence at the table, and once the waitress had served them, they got down to business.

"I am pleased to say that my house-cleaning is well under way," Xaviar said. He actually sounded cheerful, which was a first in Theo's experience.

"As is ours," Theo said. "Paschek took some convincing, but once he realized we were telling the truth, it was all we could do to keep him around long enough to give him that woman we captured."

Xaviar grinned nastily at that. "He has a reputation for being a viciously sadistic inquisitor."

"Yes," Theo agreed pleasantly. "It's well deserved, too."

"Good. As for his actions, I've heard whispers of people being purged," Xaviar said. "Some at the very highest levels of the Camarilla."

"Yes, so Itio and Kristine have been saying. I'm glad its being taken care of."

"What about the Sabbat?" Xaviar's look was intent.

Delphine's ears pricked up, and Theo groaned. "What about them? It's not as if I have contacts there."

"You should let them know," Xaviar said mercilessly.

Theo sagged. "Yes. I know. I want to, genuinely. I've already sent word to the very few sane anarch leaders I know. Paschek would flay me—literally, not metaphorically—but I want these bastards cleaned out of everywhere. I don't see any way to progress getting information to the Sabbat, though."

Xaviar turned to Itio and Kristine. "How about you?"

Itio smiled benignly. "I have taken steps to pass on information to those of my brothers and sisters who will listen, regardless of their political viewpoints. Whether they will truly hear or not... Who can say?"

Kristine looked at Itio doubtfully, and then shrugged. "The Sabbat situation beats me. I don't have any contacts there. Sure, I don't have any love for the fuckers, but then I could say the same about the Camarilla too."

Xaviar nodded, satisfied. "Good. Wait here." He got up, and strode out of the diner.

Theo watched him, puzzled, and exchanged an uncertain glance with Kristine.

A moment later, Xaviar returned. He was accompanied by a tall, bony man with a young, mournful face and a shock of snow-white hair. The newcomer was wearing a beautifully cut charcoal suit, and he stretched out a slender hand with an unusually long fourth finger for Kristine to shake.

"My name is Talley," the man said. He had a politely formal British accent.

"Kristine Gayton," Kris said, clearly puzzled.

The name clicked into place, and Theo felt his eyebrows arching toward his hairline. "The Hound."

The man turned toward him and nodded lugubriously. "So they call me." The name certainly suited him, with his long face and sad eyes. "It is interesting to meet you at last, Archon Bell."

Theo shook his offered hand, his mind whirling. Talley the Hound was a Sabbat templar, the enemy equivalent of an archon. He had a fearsome reputation, and had last been spotted in North America during the summer of 1999. He was said to be as dangerous as they came. "Likewise. The twins are Delphine and Nathalie, and this is Itio Shima. You know Xaviar?"

Talley nodded. "It is my pleasure to meet you all. Yes, Archon. I have had dealings with Xaviar before."

"I assume he's filled you in on the situation."

"He has. I know him to be a man of probity, and your reputation speaks highly of you as well. If you attest that the information you have identifies a members of a tainted cabal undermining our organizations, then that is a matter that concerns me greatly."

Theo looked Talley in the eyes. "Believe it."

Talley hung his head glumly. "I do."

"Then you are welcome to a copy of the master list. These fuckers must be stopped."

"I appreciate your generosity," Talley said. "Given the situation, I am both impressed and heartened. When the ancients arise, perhaps this cooperation can bear fruit—if decent men and women on both sides can find ways to work together."

Theo stifled a groan. The Sabbat were firm believers in the End Times, when the stories said that the most ancient of all vampires would rise and consume all their younger descendants. The Sabbat claimed to be dedicated to opposing these mythical ancients—which was a nice way to justify their own brand of power-mongering. Theo contented himself with nodding politely. "If the final nights ever come, rest assured I won't be worrying about politics."

Talley looked amused. "I would expect nothing less from a man of your reputation, Archon. Xaviar has told me of your expedition to the south. If you are willing, I would like to offer my assistance."

Theo couldn't help himself. He burst out laughing, slowly pulling himself back under control when he saw how offended Talley looked. "Sorry, Sir Talley. I wasn't laughing at your offer. Your help will be very welcome, and definitely nothing to belittle. It was the image of the combined force that we will be fielding and, in particular, the expression that my boss would be wearing if he ever found out about it."

Talley's face lightened, and the corner of his mouth even twitched a little. "It is rather unprecedented."

Theo looked around the table. The twins looked fairly baffled, Delphine slightly sulky about the fact. Kristine and Itio were both grinning broadly however, and Xaviar looked extremely satisfied.

Talley's next words rather dampened the general spirit of amusement, however. He looked at Theo sternly. "Is there a plan?"

"Um. Sort of. We were thinking along the lines of 'Get to São Paulo, scout the place, go in.'"

Surprisingly, Talley didn't look too put out. "Without better information, I suppose the absence of a rigid approach may be wise. I can be in São Paulo in ten nights." He turned to look at Xaviar. "Is that acceptable?"

Xaviar nodded. "It's going to take my people another week or more to get assembled."

"Very well," Talley said. "I will meet you outside the Museu de Arte de São Paulo at twenty-two hundred hours, local time, in ten nights' time. If there are delays, then I will try for three nights afterwards before assuming that an evil has befallen you."

"Sounds good," Theo said. "We'll be there."

"Ladies, Gentlemen, fare well." Talley nodded to the group, and left.

"OK," Delphine said grumpily. "What the fuck was all that?"

Theo grimaced, and tried to keep it simple. "Talley the Hound is one of the Sabbat's most notoriously efficient agents. He doesn't exactly do things for the same sort of reason that I do—they aren't organized that way—but he is something of an opposite number. Just the news that we sat down at the same table would be enough to have reactionary old fools on both sides condemn us both to destruction. Actually cooperating together..." He tried to dredge up some sort of example that might make sense to them. "It's like agents from the CIA, the KGB and, uh, Mossad agreeing to work together."

Delphine shook her head. "You're forty years late old man, but I see where you're coming from. So he's Sabbat, is he? He didn't seem all that monstrous."

"He was kinda cute actually," Nat said grinning. "He looks like he needs a big hug."

Theo looked at them both wearily, then turned to Kris to take over.

She shot him an amused glance. "Daughter, none of us are exactly model citizens by mortal standards. The Sabbat are, in general, more open about their cruelty and savagery, and thus they tend to get more of a taste for it. Sabbat-controlled cities therefore tend to be somewhat more violent and unpleasant than Camarilla cities. There are always exceptions, though."

"Is that it?" Delphine looked incredulous.

"More or less," Kristine said with a shrug. "They believe that we should rise up, embrace our savagery, and take control of society openly. The Camarilla prefer to do so from the shadows, retaining a convenient mask of humanity. There are other differences—they believe that we are being manipulated in turn by long-hidden ancients, for instance, while they resist them—but they're mostly cosmetic, matters of faith and religion."

Delphine shook her head. "So what you're saying is that you're trying to wipe each other out because they're messier."

"It is a simple struggle for power," Itio said. "The reasons and differences are, like all such struggles, merely excuses. Mortal society is no better—look at the wars that they get involved in. Religion has always been a convenient excuse."

"I suppose so," Delphine said. "So it's just people being people, then."

"Dead people being dead people, please," Nathalie said primly.

"Lifeist."

The pair of them started giggling.

Theo left them to it, and turned to Itio, a thought surfacing. "You said something the other night about a file of shipping receipts to São Paulo."

Itio nodded. "Indeed. It seems to have been their main transmission route."

"Any patterns?"

"Very much so, Theophilus. The same shipping agent, the same company, even the same scheduled sailing on the same day of the week."

"Is it a freight line?"

Itio shook his head. "Passenger, it seems."

"Perfect," Theo said. "The woman here must have an arrangement in place with some of the customs officials. I take it you can find enough information to make a consignment appear to be one of her regular shipments?"

"Easily," Itio said. "She was rather obsessive about documenting costs and companies."

"Then if Nathalie will do the honors, perhaps we can take a little cruise down to Brazil."

Kristine smiled. "It certainly beats having to drive."

Theo woke abruptly, uncertain for no reason he could put his finger on. His instinctive concern faded rapidly as he realized that he felt none of the crushing lethargy associated with being woken during the day. He still appeared wrapped inside the garden sacks that he'd got into the night before. Confident that the sun had set, he tore the bags open and sat up.

As expected, he was on the floor of a metal container, lit by a small battery-powered lamp. The others were around him, fighting their way out of the bags as he had. There was a strong smell of sweat and urine in the air, and he looked around carefully, puzzled.

Xaviar sat up, and Theo realized that there were a couple more figures behind him, writhing slightly. Xaviar followed Theo's gaze, then looked back round grinning. "Breakfast."

Theo stood up for a look. A pair of dark-haired young women were lying at the back of the container, tightly bound and gagged. They both looked absolutely terrified, and at least one had pissed herself. One had a note pinned to the front of her T-shirt that read, *See you on deck. Nat.*

He sighed unhappily.

"Oh my god." Delphine was staring at the girls, looking horrified. "What the fuck was she thinking?" She took a step toward them. "Come on, let's help..."

Theo grabbed her by the shoulder, stopping both her movement and words. "I'm sorry, Delphine. We can't."

She looked up at him, appalled. "But you can do that memory thing to them, and it'll all be cool."

He shook his head gently. "Not without knowing exactly what happened, where they came from, how they might be here… It's impossible. I'm sorry."

Xaviar looked at the pair of them curiously. "Surely she's not squeamish."

A tear trickled down Delphine's cheek, and Kristine came up to take the girl in her arms. Delphine buried her face in Kris' neck, small shakes betraying her silent sobs.

"Childer." Xaviar shrugged. "I can't manage them both myself, and their deaths are senseless if the blood goes to waste."

Kristine shot him a rueful and slightly regretful smile over Delphine's head, looked down at her childe, and rolled her eyes. Xaviar nodded, and knelt by one, hammering his teeth into the soft flesh of her neck. She stiffened, and made a small sighing noise in the back of her throat, her face suddenly transcendent. Itio and Theo descended on the other, taking a wrist each. It was over quickly. Once they'd finished, they bundled the corpses into some of the garden sacks. If either Xaviar or Itio noticed that both girls bore a more than passing resemblance to Kristine, they kept it to themselves. Somehow, Theo didn't think he'd need to ask Delphine to have words with Nat about the situation.

There was a handle on the inside of the container that opened the doors smoothly. It turned out that they were actually within a second box, just a little larger that the first. Theo nodded approvingly to himself. With the door open, he could hear the deep, rhythmic throbbing of huge engines deep under his feet. Everything else was quiet. He opened the outer door, revealing a dimly lit cargo hold. There were several long, evenly spaced rows of identical metal shipping containers, stickered with various logos and identifiers. A good ways overhead, the large metal shutters that ran the length of the compartment were clearly retractable. He nodded for the others to come along, and set out trying to find his way above decks.

The ship was huge, something like a floating shopping mall and hotel rolled into one. The lower decks were a dark maze of tiny, cramped corridors, unhelpfully color-coded into meaningless regions of red, blue, green, yellow and gray. One stretch of corridor was almost entirely indistinguishable from another, even when the carpet and wall tiles had been taken into account. Theo decided to give himself plenty of time to find his way back down to the cargo area before dawn.

Further up, the maze gave way to several floors of glittering bars, restaurants, shops and other facilities. According to the signs, they had casinos, a cinema, gaming zones, and even a sauna center. The shopping levels were thronging with people who seemed unaware that the whole area was designed to extract money from them. Most of the passengers were white and aging, although there was a smattering of scruffy youngsters. He shot Xaviar a rueful glance—the two of them were especially out of place. Itio noticed the look and smiled in a way that made Theo decidedly nervous.

Further up still, the frantic shopping gave way to a large, glass-walled lounge bar, the decks clearly visible. Theo headed on out, unsurprised to notice that there seemed to be several levels of accessible decking. The sea stretched out black and cold beneath him, and he shivered a little. It would be a horrific tomb.

They finally found Nathalie on the top deck, lounging comfortably in a big chair beside a sparkling swimming pool. There was a bright, lively open bar behind her, which was where she'd obviously obtained the unlikely looking multi-colored drink she was sipping. She smiled at them as they approached and waved cheerfully. Her grin faltered as she caught sight of her sister's expression. As they got to the table, Delphine turned to the others.

"Excuse us a moment. I need a word with my sister. Theo, could you tag along please?" Her face was like granite.

Nathalie arched an eyebrow, but she got up and followed Delphine over to a quiet patch of rail. Theo sighed and followed. He took the spot next to Nathalie, and turned to look out over the barren sea.

"I know what you're going to say, Del." Nat's voice was still fairly light. "Relax, will you? Don't be so uptight. Okay, maybe you can't have a drink, but you should kick back and chill." She shot Theo a quick glance, coloring slightly, and her voice took on a defiant tone. "You've definitely got to try screwing, too. An older guy. It's *incredible*."

Delphine was fighting to keep calm. Theo could see it in the lines of her back. He started thinking maybe he'd made a mistake picking Nathalie to stand next to. "You killed those girls, Nat. There was no need. We don't have to hurt people— not unless they're serious witnesses to shit. You fucking made us *murder* them. That's fucking sick."

Nathalie shrugged. "Do you actually care?"

Delphine stared at her in disbelief. "What? They could be anyone. They could have mothers and fathers and sisters..." she broke off for a moment, her voice thick with emotion. "They could be you. Or me. It's horrible."

Nathalie glared at her, suddenly furious. "Fuck them." Her voice was thankfully low, a hiss of anger. "That's what *we* should have been, sis. Your pet bitch fucking ripped that from us. All the things we should be doing. School work. Boys. Having a fucking *life*. All we have now is dust and ashes and darkness. All I can do is to try to make you happy."

Delphine flinched, her eyes full of horror. She looked to Theo, desperate for support, but for once he couldn't think of anything to say.

The movement just seemed to make Nathalie angrier. "They took it so much for fucking granted, the silly sluts. Now they've lost it, just like you did. Just like I did. Boo fucking hoo. Yeah, alright, I killed them. Know what? I *enjoyed* it. I've been thinking about them all day, lying there shitting themselves in the dark, just to have you guys wake up and rip them to pieces." There was a terrible, hungry pain in her voice. "It got me really hot. I had to go ball some forty-something to relieve the pressure. He thought it was Christmas, but it was those little whores tied up down there that got me off."

Bloody tears were trickling down Delphine's cheeks. She looked as if she'd been shot in the stomach. "You can't go around killing people because of what we've been through." Her voice was a thin, hollow little whisper.

"Yeah? They're not the first, *sis*. All those fuckers, with their safe little lives. They've got no fucking idea of the darkness and torture waiting for them. I want to rip them all to shreds. I want to drown the world in their blood. I want..." The anger faltered, and suddenly she was crying—low, insistent, racking sobs to match Delphine's. "I want it to be like it was. Oh god. Oh god. What am I?"

Theo sighed as a tide of sympathy washed through him. They were so young. He moved round behind the girls, and put an arm round each of them. They collapsed into him, arms round each other, weeping desperately. He just stood there, holding them gently, looking out at the desolate waves.

The twins were noticeably subdued over the following nights, even failing to make any jokes about the garish holiday wear that Itio had presented to Theo and Xaviar on the second evening. Kristine was concerned and spent a lot of her time watching over them at a discreet distance as they sat quietly together. Itio seemed unusually interested in their wellbeing, too. Theo got a little tired of it all, and took to spending much of his time on a quiet rear deck which had no facilities, little light, and consequently next to no people. Looking out from the stern, the oppressive expanse of water was at least partly broken by the wash of the engines.

Theo glared out at it for hours, resenting its emptiness, his mind a million miles away. There were plenty of other vessels following similar routes, from liners like the one they were on all the way down to small fishing boats and private yachts. When he needed a break from the water, he spent time idly whittling the table leg he'd taken from Don Cerro's house, which was now a very creditable wooden poignard-cum-stake.

On the penultimate night of the voyage, he was idly watching a small boat that appeared to be playing chicken with their liner when Xaviar appeared at the rail beside him, wearing one of Itio's gift shirts, a horrible short-sleeved affair with a palm-tree print. The former justicar had been even less sociable than Theo himself, so he was slightly surprised to see the man. He turned to him and nodded pleasantly.

"Hello Xaviar."

"Bell. I've been thinking about our arrival tomorrow night. There must be a danger that they have figured out we are coming by boat. They may even be anticipating this particular arrival, given that it is their regular shipping chain. We should be cautious."

"Yeah, it's always worth being careful," Theo said. "I'm not all that worried, though. There are a lot of people on this damn thing, and they'd have a hell of a time trying to find us disembarking in the crowds, particularly with Itio helping out. It's not as if we have to stay in that container, which they might have traced."

Xaviar nodded. "Very well. I have heard from most of my people. They will be in position within forty eight hours. I do not know what numbers Talley is bringing, but I will have up to a score, all capable. Your pair seem highly competent. I think we should be equal to the task ahead."

Theo smiled grimly. "We'll get the bastards, one way or another."

"You know why this is happening, don't you." The man's voice was distant.

Theo kept his voice studiously neutral. "I don't really care why. I'm more interested in stopping it."

"The Final Nights are here, Bell."

"Then we'd better make the time we have count," Theo said carefully.

Xaviar sighed. "It's too late for that."

"It's never too late to fight."

"A good sentiment, that." The voice was cold and harsh, and came from behind them. They both spun around and Karsh was standing at the corner of the deck, looking oddly out of place with his wild hair and long, dusty coat. Theo immediately reached for his knife.

Xaviar growled furiously, and a red light kindled in his eyes as his fingernails slammed out into long, wicked-looking talons. "Traitor."

Karsh arched an eyebrow. "Fool. You put your faith in the hopeless."

Xaviar spat on the deck. "You've doomed us all, you stupid, arrogant bastard. You won't be there to see the results of your betrayal, though. I won't allow you the satisfaction."

Karsh grinned nastily. "Give it your best." He started walking across the deck toward the pair of them steadily, his eyes fixed on them.

Theo and Xaviar moved in opposite directions, each circling warily. Karsh advanced to the mid-point between them, clearly relaxed, his clawed hands loose by his sides. Theo stared at him for a long moment, finding it difficult to believe the warlord's arrogance. Hot rage started to boil up inside him, sweeping away any traces of doubt. The blood sang within him, intoxicating him with its power. He concentrated, and it surged inside him, scalding him with its fury as it slammed through his body. His muscles tightened and hardened, screaming their protest at the force they were being asked to contain. The world seemed to stammer, the relentless waves freezing in place.

Xaviar was rocketing toward Karsh, his outline little more than a smear against the darkness. Theo threw himself at the back of Karsh's legs, sweeping out to try to stagger the man. He flashed across the deck, and smashed into the back of... nothing. Karsh seemed to almost fade from between them, reappearing a few feet away. Theo barely had time to register that the warlord had moved before he was sliding underneath Xaviar's wild leap.

Karsh brought his fist down on Xaviar's back, and pounded the former justicar straight down onto Theo in a painful tangle of limbs. Xaviar was up in an instant, Theo just a fraction of a second behind him. Karsh took a few steps back from the pair of them until he was up against the railings. He looked amused.

Theo and Xaviar shared a quick look, and moved in for the attack again while their opponent was boxing himself in. Theo switched his knife from palm to palm rapidly as he went in. The deck seemed to blur beneath his feet. Xaviar slashed in with his claws, a long, sweeping attack, while Theo drove his knife out in a long, powerful lunge. Karsh didn't even attempt to evade either blow. Theo felt a moment of uncertainty, and then his knife sank straight through Karsh's thigh.

There was no resistance whatsoever. It was like cutting through air. Theo's hand followed the knife, and then he smacked into the railings like a wrecking ball. The metal creaked, and a section tore out, floating gently out to start its glacial descent to the waters below. Theo grabbed the railings wildly with his left hand, trying to steady himself before he went the same way. His momentum was too much, though, and he pivoted out over the edge of the boat, flailing wildly with his knife hand. There was an explosive crunch from somewhere behind him.

Theo managed to get a toehold around the railings with his right foot, and held on for all he was worth. His body swung out over the drop, and the railings he was barely clinging to creaked horribly, then he started to sway backwards again. His knife was long gone, joining the railing in the slow descent to the waves. He threw his arm back, clutching desperately for another hold. His fingers caught slippery metal, and he grabbed at it, pulling himself backwards as hard as he could. A moment later, he fell back onto the deck, shaking.

Xaviar was in a bad way. He was lying all the way over the other side of the deck, one leg bent out in an impossible direction, his chest sunken and drenched in blood. Karsh was walking toward him comfortably. Theo struggled to his feet. Xaviar saw Theo's movement, looked him in the eye momentarily and howled in agony, a low, intense sound. He tried panting a few words in between moans, nonsense noises. Karsh paused, then moved forward more swiftly, apparently interested. Theo grinned at Xaviar's quick thinking and charged, trying to keep his footsteps light as he raced across the deck.

Xaviar screamed again, and as Karsh bent down to look at him, Theo drew his fist back, ready to deliver a crushing blow. The instant he was in range, he lashed out, driving a devastating punch square into the center of the man's spine.

Theo's hand erupted in agony as the bones inside it crushed together and splintered. Karsh felt like a solid wall. He whipped around then and lashed out, swifter than a cobra. He grabbed Theo's jaw in an iron grip, and actually lifted him off the ground a few inches, bringing their faces level. Theo tried to say something, but his jaw was held firm. He grabbed Karsh's arm with his good left hand. Blood flooded into the other one, twisting the wrecked bones back into shape agonizingly.

Karsh grinned. "A fair try, Bell, but stealth is not your forte. I'm impressed you avoided falling." He started walking away from Xaviar comfortably, Theo still dangling from his outstretched arm. "I find that I like the thought of you on the ocean floor, however."

Theo started writhing desperately, trying to worm his way out of Karsh's grip. The writhing agony in his other hand started subsiding, and he tucked it into his pocket, fumbling painfully. Karsh tightened his grip still further, stabbing his claws through Theo's cheek. They were like bars of fire, and he howled in agony. Karsh shook him, amused, and Theo finally found what his hand had been looking for. He forced his screaming fingers to close around it, gritting out the pain. Xaviar yelled something—the roaring in Theo's ears was too furious to make the comment out—and Karsh turned his head for a moment to call back tauntingly. Theo took advantage of the distraction to lunge at Karsh with his free hand.

It was a comparatively weak blow, with no leverage or power, just the raw strength of Theo's arm. Karsh saw it coming, and confidently ignored it. The stake, almost needle-sharp, sank into his chest like a knife into butter. He realized his mistake at the last moment, and threw Theo away desperately, toward the gap in the railings, but it was too late. The tip pierced Karsh's heart, and he froze, suddenly as immobile as the granite his flesh felt like. Theo skidded along the floor, his face burning from Karsh's claws.

He stood up, watching as Karsh toppled over with a meaty thud. Somewhere down below, there was a loud splash as the section of railing hit the water.

Xaviar was sitting up, looking sickly, his chest pulsating horribly. "Bring him to me, Bell."

Theo shook his head. "No."

"*What?*"

Theo grinned nastily. "I find that I like the thought of Karsh on the ocean floor."

Xaviar laughed weakly. "Yes. So do I. But I need some of his blood, at least."

"Some, I can do." Theo dragged Karsh's immobile form over to where Xaviar was lying. "I'll straighten that leg for you first."

Xaviar nodded. "Thank you. On three."

Theo took a firm grip on the ankle. "One." He wrenched the leg back into position with a savage jerk, pulling the joint further out than necessary so that the splinters of bone slid back beneath the skin. "Two, three."

"Ouch," Xaviar said, wincing. Then he leant down over Karsh's neck, and started drinking.

Between them, it only took a minute or two to drain Karsh right to the edge of destruction. Then they hauled his stiff body over to the gap in the railings. Theo held up a hand for Xaviar to wait for a moment, and then took a firm grip on the stake and pushed it further in, so that the tip was almost through to his back. "We wouldn't want that coming loose now, would we?"

Xaviar grinned. "Wouldn't we?"

Theo thought about it, and shrugged. "Better safe than sorry." He tried to remember Itio's words. "Have you thought about death, Karsh? Darkness. Cold, eternal darkness with currents in it. Have you thought about the things that swim in there, all teeth and hunger, nibbling your soul away?" He pushed the warlord hard in the center of the back, and watched as he fell toward the water. There was a splash, and he grinned savagely. "It was something like that, anyway."

Xaviar put a companionable arm round Theo's shoulders and smiled. "I can see why you like it up here, Bell. It's a beautiful night."

Chapter Twelve

The Chain

São Paulo was a chaotic sprawl. The city was gigantic, home to nearly twenty million people, and everything seemed to be in overdrive. It seemed to flicker, not just visually but at some deeper level—as familiar as Manhattan or Capitol Hill one instant, as confusing as a desert bazaar the next. The people were all rushing around, intent on getting from one place to another as swiftly as possible, and with as little consideration for each other as they could get away with. It felt as if everything was a little more urgent down here. A lot of the city was painfully new, the edges still raw enough to grate. Other chunks of it were decaying into filth. Cars jammed every possible square inch, braying and roaring to each other, and undoubtedly contributing to the vile-tasting smog that seemed to permeate everything.

After the grotesque emptiness of the sea, it was like being readmitted to heaven—even after being gouged on the exchange rate. Del and Nat seemed overawed by it all, although they still hadn't really recovered from the boat. They were both on edge, and Kristine looked especially worn. Itio appeared content enough however, and had relaxed from his compulsive vigilance over the pair of them. When Theo asked him about it, he merely made some reference to patterns holding, and smiled mysteriously.

They spent the first day holed up in a cheap hostel on the edge of the city's central district. The place looked like most of its visitors had backpacks rather than suitcases, but the room was sturdy enough, and so dingy that Theo would almost have taken his chances out in the main dormitory if necessary. Nathalie seemed happier the next night, having been out and about during the day, which lightened Delphine's mood too. The pair of them rushed off so that Nat could show her sister some set of sights or other, Kristine tagging along as bodyguard.

That left Itio and Xaviar to accompany Theo to the Museu de Arte. According to the rather overblown pamphlet that he picked up in the roach-filled hotel lobby, it was one of the most important museums in South America. When the taxi finally dropped them off at the place, it was difficult to imagine that was the case. The building was a large modernist affair, all glass and red girders, bulging out uncomfortably from its base. There were plenty of people hanging around however, which made Theo feel a little more secure.

Talley turned up at precisely ten o'clock, wearing a crisply pressed cotton suit and somehow making it look as if it were a suit of armor. Theo bit back a groan when he realized what he must look like in the knee-length shorts and Bermuda top he was wearing. With Xaviar and Itio dressed similarly, Talley probably thought the three of them were pretending to be vacationing gangsters. If the image occurred to him however, he was far too polite to let it show.

He nodded to them formally, a crisp gesture which only just stopped short of being a bow. "Good evening, gentlemen. I trust your journey went well."

"Sublime, Sir Talley." Xaviar still had a big grin plastered across his face.

"Yeah, it turned out pretty well actually," Theo said. "We met up with an old friend, and... uh... gave him some diving lessons."

"Ah. One of the opposition?"

"Very much so," Xaviar said smugly.

"Excellent," Talley said. "I have enlisted the assistance of a small handful of seasoned colleagues. We are staged just outside the city proper."

Xaviar nodded approvingly. "Excellent. Sixteen of my people have made it so far. One fell en route, but the last two will arrive tonight."

"I have asked the locals for assistance," Itio said. "I am not sure how many will respond, but I think all understand the gravity of the situation."

Theo looked at him uncertainly. "I thought you didn't know anyone in Brazil."

Itio nodded mildly. "That is correct, Theophilus."

Theo glanced at Xaviar and rolled his eyes quickly. "Oh. Well, we'll see what happens I guess. Thanks Itio. It sounds as if we have a sizeable force assembled, gentlemen. All we have to do now is to gather the intelligence to use it."

Xavier smiled toothily. "I sent some of my people on a scouting mission last night. They report at midnight. Would any of you care to join me?"

—————

One of Xaviar's people had apparently obtained a battered jeep from somewhere. Xaviar drove them out of the city with a certain relish, heading for a place that he described as a staging post. After about forty-five minutes, they arrived at a large suburban park on the edge of the city, in a bustling, underprivileged neighborhood. The park was far from deserted, even at nearly eleven o'clock, and there were several patches of public seating, most of them looking out across the city—the place was obviously on a slight rise.

Xaviar led them to one particular picnic area, and sat down comfortably on a bench, looking out at the view. Theo followed suit, impressed despite himself. São Paulo stretched out across the plain like a crazy sea of glittering stars. It lacked the regularity and patterning common to most North American cities—high-rises were not confined to a central district, but seemed scattered around at random. The streets cut the buildings into a crazy patchwork of odd shapes, rather than into neat squares. Hills across the plateau gave the city a bumpy texture too, like gopher holes in a yard.

A small knot of figures approaching drew Theo away from his contemplation of the city. A small, dusky-skinned woman dressed in several layers of colorful shawls and skirts with a knot of trinkets around her neck could have perhaps been a local, if it hadn't been for the power beating off her in almost tangible waves. The other two however were clearly Kindred. Theo knew Mark Decker, the Prince of Milwaukee, fairly well from his investigations into that strangeness in Wisconsin earlier in the year. A tall, haggard man with jet black hair, Mark always seemed to be exhausted. He was escorting a small, wiry-looking guy with a big grin and a shock of bright red hair. Mark spotted Theo, and raised a hand in greeting.

Xaviar stood as the newcomers arrived, nodding to them respectfully.

The woman took a step forward, proudly erect. "I am Inyanga, childe of Seneca. I walk on four paws, and know secrets that even ghosts are scared of." Her reputation was impressive.

Mark hesitated a moment, then nodded. "I am Mark Decker, childe of Lucian. The lupines run in fear from my approach." Despite his brave words, he sounded more weary than proud, and mouthed the greeting as if he were reading from a card, his voice flat and disinterested.

Talley, who had risen as the group approached, bowed formally to the pair of them. "I am Talley, although you may know of me as the Hound. I have the honor of serving the Sabbat as Templar." If his declaration was news to any of them, they hid it very well.

Theo shrugged to himself. "I am Archon Theo Bell, representing Justicar Jaroslav Paschek for Clan Brujah. They call me Killa-B, sometimes. I kick ass as required."

Itio stayed seated, smiling amiably at everyone. "Good evening, my friends. My name is Itio Shima. If you are interested in what I do, I usually spend my time acquiring antiquities and legends. Over the centuries, I have garnered some small skill at making my way unnoticed into guarded buildings."

Xaviar glanced down at him, and then looked at the little red-haired guy. "I am Xaviar. I serve my clan."

"Well, I'm just very grateful," the little guy said, looking a little startled at the company he found himself in. "My name is Simon Crabb, and Mr. Decker here saved my ass from the sun last night."

"Inyanga deserves the credit," Mark said modestly. "She was the one who found Mr. Crabb. All I did was pull the stake."

Xaviar brushed the comment aside. "Come, sit with us. What have you discovered?"

They all took seats around the rough wooden table. Mark glanced at Inyanga, who gestured at him to continue.

"We found the location easily enough, keeping to a safe distance. Ramona, Calvin and I worked our way up to a handy vantage point, and examined the place and the surrounding terrain with binoculars. It's a villa in the hills above the city, off a small, quiet road that winds it way up toward some of the high villages. The area is lightly wooded, and the villa has a very commanding view down to the city. The road is clearly visible for something like ten miles, and traffic was light while we were there. Any approaching vehicles are going to be pretty obvious. The villa itself is about quarter of a mile off the road, up a dedicated small road which is screaming out for security devices."

Inyanga shook her head briskly, looking disgusted. "The road is not monitored, it is tainted with the vile stench of the infernal."

Mark accepted the correction gracefully. "My thanks. Anyway, the place is pretty large. The building itself looks to be a couple of hundred feet long, maybe eighty or ninety wide. There are extensive balconies and patios, an ornamental garden, a car lot, and so on. The official land probably covers a couple of acres. Ramona insisted she could see the entrance to an underground parking lot, but it could easily have been a small storehouse wing too. There's a fair amount of apparent activity, but we couldn't get details. There appeared to be a guy out on a balcony at one point, but we didn't get a clear look. While we were snooping, Inyanga got in closer."

The woman nodded crisply, and then shot a cautious glance at Talley. "The building is wrapped in suffering and cruelty, swathed in a blanket of demonic interest. It stinks of it. There are many inside, both willing and unwilling. The ground mutters with their actions and imprisonment. I saw little to suggest mechanical observation, but there were sentries with automatic weapons in the grounds near the building. I found this one staked to await the dawn."

"The only other thing to add is that Ramona said the place looked 'wrong,' but she wouldn't go in to any details." Mark looked slightly apologetic.

Xaviar looked thoughtful. "Thank you, both of you. What is your role in this, Mr. Crabb?"

Simon shrugged unhappily. "I'm from Chicago. The prince had me tracking down any reports of strangeness—we've had our share of shit storms over the years, believe me. Anyway, I caught wind of some horrendous satanic stuff down in Aurora, and went down for a look. I decided to see out the day in a downtown hotel, and woke up staked in a cage. They shifted me around for god knows how long, and somewhere along the line the stake must have jolted loose. I managed to help a couple of others, and when they started unloading us here, we played dead, then made a dash for it."

"They caught you," Xaviar said flatly.

"Yeah. They caught us. Put the other two back with the rest, and decided to make an example out of me."

"Did you see anything of the villa?"

"Not much, unfortunately. There's some sort of underground complex, and they've got a stack of guards and so on. As far as I could tell, the ones in charge just go by 'The Lord' and 'The Lady,' respectively. That's about it, though. I managed to get into the grounds, but they caught up with me, slammed me in a pen, and then hung me out to dry. I know it's not much, and I wish I could tell you more."

Xaviar nodded tersely. "More would have been good, but we should not be greedy. Can you fight?"

"A little," Simon admitted. "I can shoot."

"No disrespect," Theo said, "but frankly, I'd rather keep you out of it. An amateur in a battle line is a weak link."

Talley looked at Xaviar and Theo. "For security reasons, we cannot let this man go tonight."

Xaviar nodded reluctantly, ignoring Simon's startled expression.

Mark sighed, stepped forward, and hammered a stake through Simon's back, catching the guy before he fell. "Sorry, Simon. We'll let you out tomorrow, once we've taken care of business. It's this or we have to destroy you. I'm sure you understand."

"That was a little harsh," Theo said mildly. "We could have just locked him up."

"Expedience is not always kind," Talley said.

"Enough." Xaviar sounded slightly impatient. "We have to agree on an approach."

"Diversionary frontal assault," Talley said flatly.

Theo nodded "It's the only approach that makes sense."

Xaviar sighed. "It will be expected."

"Yeah, I know. But they still have to answer an attack. Three groups. One for the main assault, one to take out the primaries, and one to release the prisoners."

Xaviar frowned. "Four. One backup for primaries and prisoners. I mean no insult Sir Talley, but it seems safer to keep my people and yours separated. There may be history."

Talley didn't seem put out. "Reasonable caution is no bad thing."

"Good," Xaviar said, satisfied. "The bulk of my people will engage in the frontal attack. Mark, I'd like you to direct that. I'll take the scouting team and release the prisoners. Is that acceptable?"

To Theo's mild surprise, it was Inyanga who nodded. "It is acceptable."

Xaviar smiled his thanks. "Talley, how good are your people?"

"We are comfortable against competent foes, Xaviar. Have no fear."

"Excellent. I'd like you to take the lead against the primaries."

"It will be a pleasure," Talley said. "They expect nothing less, Vincent in particular."

"That leaves me in backup," Theo said, slightly disgruntled.

"Partly," Xaviar admitted. "Don't make the mistake of thinking you're in a support role, though. I'd like your team to cause as much chaos as possible from the inside. If there are two primaries, as Simon's intelligence suggests, then they may split up. Go after them, but if you get a chance to free people, seize it."

"Alright," Theo said. "Itio's best cut loose, though." Itio smiled at that. "That leaves just me and Kris. Can you spare me a second front-liner?"

Xaviar pursed his lips thoughtfully. "I'm not sure who could keep up with you. Graham, perhaps… It would weaken the frontal assault a little, though."

"I can lend you one of my men, Archon" said Talley.

"Thank you," Theo said. "That would be great."

"You are welcome. I have just the man. His manners are a little rough, but he is highly competent, and I know that he holds your reputation in some esteem. His name is Lavenant."

"I look forward to meeting him," Theo said.

Xaviar slapped his hand down on the bench firmly. "So we're agreed then?"

Theo and Talley nodded, and Xaviar smiled tightly. "Good. I'll get people in position tonight if possible. Bell, Talley, if you travel by car, I suggest running without lights. Mark, I want you to start the frontal attack at eight o'clock. Make plenty of noise. The rest of us will wade in once you are engaged. No major exposure, remember. You just have to draw the guards off, not wipe them out entirely."

A thought crossed Theo's mind. "Itio, how likely are you to have some assistance?"

Itio smiled pleasantly. "I would expect a few gatecrashers. Fear not, Theophilus. Those that arrive will aid me in contributing some confusion. Think of us as a fifth column."

"Perfect," Theo said, carefully not looking at Xaviar's rather strangled expression.

Itio glanced at Xaviar with a sly grin. "May I suggest an identifying mark?"

"What did you have in mind, Itio?"

Itio grinned. "A spot of blood, in the center of the forehead. Obvious, easy to put in place, and potentially misleading."

"Very well," Xaviar said. "I suppose it is for the best." He extended his right hand. "To tomorrow, my friends."

Talley clasped it swiftly, with Theo, Mark and Itio following suit a moment later. "Tomorrow," they said in unison.

Back at the hotel, Theo was going through some last minute preparations—checking over the clothes and knife Itio had got him for the operation, and trimming down and overhauling the shotgun he'd picked up in Hagerstown—when Delphine came up to him, looking concerned. She took hold of his hand and wordlessly pulled him out of the room they shared into the hallway, where there was a small smoking area, deserted this early in the morning. She sat him down, but seemed unable to settle herself, pacing back and forth.

"What is it childe?" Theo kept his voice gentle.

"I... That is... Uh, well, there's Nat for starters. She's been going through these swings, all normal and happy one moment, then like suicidal if she thinks I'm not watching or something. I'm really worried about her."

Theo sighed unhappily. "Delphine, what you've done is reversible at this stage. She won't like it—our blood is addictive—but you can stop feeding her. At that point, the darkness should ease. But you have to accept that her behavior might have to do with the way she was tortured, too. It's got to have fucked her up, and all the stuff that's happened to her since... Many people would snap, even without a diet of

Kindred blood. If you take her off the blood now, you might destroy her mind completely."

Delphine's eyes welled up with bloody tears, and Theo put an arm around her waist, pulling her in against his shoulder.

"You also ought to know that the blood is helping her cope with what you have become, too. Your body is a corpse, and that is hard to disguise, even when you are awake. I know she was okay at first, but Itio may have had a hand in that. I don't know for sure how she'll react. On the other hand, if you keep feeding her, then she will acclimatize slowly to her new nature. She'll come to enjoy the way it twists her, eventually."

"Oh God," moaned Delphine softly, her voice full of pain. "What would you do in my position?"

I wouldn't be in your position, Theo though. He didn't say it, though. "I don't know. Help her to be herself and come to terms with her new existence, to accept what she's been through and where it's taken her. Help her to forget what might have been. Regret is a useless waste of time. You have to direct her, though. She'll obey orders from you. If those orders are directed at helping her be herself and cope with it all, you can make her happier."

"Is there no way to go back, no way to…?" She trailed off.

"Not really, kid. I'm sorry."

A tear rolled down her cheek in a bloody streak. She sniffled, and audibly made an effort to hold herself together. "That's not all. On the boat, Xaviar kept talking about the… the end of the world. For us. Maybe for everyone. He said these were the 'Final Nights.' That we had months left, maybe." Her voice was ragged.

Theo shrugged uncomfortably. "It's an old myth with a load of hokey signs which some people think are coming true. Xaviar has seen some very weird shit, and he genuinely believes it. He's not the only one. I think maybe Itio does too, and I'm pretty certain these assholes we're taking on tomorrow are banking on it."

"What about you, Theo?"

"I think it's a bunch of horse-shit, to be honest. I don't have much time for fairy tales. If I'm wrong, well, then there's a load of fuckers that need some serious payback for lying to us all for centuries, and I'll make sure they get it while I can still deal it out."

"I see. It's just legends then, is it?" Her voice was hopeful.

"I reckon. We've all got to go some time, though. The trick is to make the most of the time you have."

"I suppose." Suddenly she was bending down to hug him fiercely. "I've got a really bad feeling about tomorrow, Theo. Be careful, okay? You've been a good friend, for an asshole." She had to be crying again—he could feel the wetness against his cheek.

"I'll be fine, kiddo. Keep out of the way, and we'll come get you later."

"What if…"

He made a conscious effort to keep his voice stern as he replied. "Then you'll cope, Delphine. You'll meet the future head-on with a grin. You're Brujah, girl. That means you fight. Not just to win—never make that mistake. You fight, because the alternative is to curl up and die. You'll do us proud, I know it."

"Thanks." Her voice was a whisper, but the pain had receded, for the moment at least. "I forgot."

Theo stood up, pulled her into a big bear hug, then started walking with her back to the room. "It's okay, kid. I forget too, from time to time. Sometimes it's good to have someone who needs reminding."

She leant up and kissed him on the cheek. "Good luck."

He smiled at her sympathetically. "You too."

Henri Lavenant was something of a surprise. Tall and chunky with rumpled brown hair and several days' stubble, he looked like he'd just rolled out of bed after sleeping in his clothes. For a week. It was the first time that Theo had ever seen someone manage to make mission-friendly black clothing look shabby. Lavenant was loud, crude, chain-smoked foul-smelling cigarettes, and Theo liked him immediately. He picked them up from the arranged meeting point—a downtown square—in a battered old station wagon, swinging lazily into a free parking space and sticking his head out of the window to bellow at them.

"Bell, yes?" His voice was rough with smoke and abuse.

Kristine winced at the volume, but Theo grinned, and made his way over to the car. "You must be Monsieur Lavenant."

"You must call me Henri, and I will call you Theo," Lavenant said cheerfully. "Please, your chariot awaits."

Theo got into the car, the others a few moments behind him. It stank of tar and stale nicotine.

"Itio, Kristine, this is Henri Lavenant," Theo said. "Henri, meet Itio Shima and Kristine Gayton."

Henri watched Kristine getting into the car with undisguised admiration. Then he grinned crookedly, and elbowed Theo in the ribs. "Ah, Theo, I can see why you keep that one around. Such breasts!" He made absolutely no attempt to keep his voice down.

Kristine, just settling down, stared at him in amazement.

Henri glanced at her in the rear view mirror, still smiling. "Magnificent. A beautiful woman is good for a man's soul. Particularly when she is built like that. It is my pleasure to meet you all."

Itio looked thoroughly amused, and, after a moment or two of indecision, so did Kristine. She started fiddling with the catches on her case, and pulled her sword out a moment later. If possible, Henri looked even more impressed.

Lavenant coughed the car into reverse, stuck his head out of the window to yell quick obscenities at the hapless driver behind him, and then lurched off into the traffic. "Now, let us away from this polluted hole. I think we shall drive past the villa, yes? Once we are safely clear of their damned view, we can park up and sneak back in, quiet like little mice. Then we will creep up behind them and grab them by the nuts, my friends, and squeeze until they pop."

Mark Decker had positioned his force out beyond the perimeter of the villa's grounds, spread out along the side furthest from the road, and in along the top and bottom for some distance too. At precisely eight o'clock, the line started advancing cautiously. The perimeter was walled off with a steel mesh fence. He came up close to it, grabbed a handful, and then lashed out with the claws on his other hand, slicing through the links as if they were paper.

He wormed through the gap, confident that the villa's security personnel would be rushing around in response to the alarms that they had just set off. Senses extended to the limit, he unholstered the semiautomatic pistol he'd brought along for the occasion, and started picking his way through the trees. At the far end of the line, Xaviar and his team would be peeling off to circle round to the other end of the villa's grounds.

A few moments later, the sound of chattering gunfire off to the left announced clearly that hostilities had been opened. He grinned and continued advancing. Up ahead, a hint of movement in the trees made him pause. There was someone ahead, trying to be cautious. The guard was looking the wrong way. Mark picked his way toward him silently, moving like a ghost. The man took another step, exposing his back. Mark darted forwards and buried the claws of his free hand into the small of the man's back and through into his gut. The guard screamed, shockingly loud in the silent night. Mark slowly pulled his hand upwards, sawing through the man's torso. The shriek got even louder, and then cut off as the guard sagged, and then crumbled into ash. Mark smiled grimly, and continued ghosting toward the villa.

The orchard erupted around him.

The agonized howl cut off suddenly, and Claudia nodded, satisfied. "It has begun."

Rodrigo nodded. There was no need for further comment. He got up, and as Claudia made her way to the stairs down to the food cellar, he started heading toward the laboratory, already rehearsing the ritual in his mind.

By the time Theo and the others made it to the parking lot at the end of the long driveway, the far side of the villa sounded like a war zone. Guns were chattering constantly, a savage underline to the barrage of shouts and screams. Wrapped in Itio's concealment, the battle felt muted, somehow less urgent and threatening. There was a large set of double doors mounted in the villa wall at the edge of the parking lot. Theo made directly for them.

The doors were locked. Theo shifted his shotgun to a secure hold and took a step back to kick the doors open, but Itio put a restraining hand on his shoulder, and bent over the lock. A few moments later, he straightened up and tugged the door open smoothly with a big smile. The doors opened onto a broad set of stairs leading down beneath the villa. Theo started down them without hesitating, aware that the others were following.

The walls shook, and there was a loud rumble from up above somewhere. The lights cut out, and were replaced after a second or so by small red emergency lamps set at ground level.

"Some madman has grenades," Henri muttered. "It is not Talley."

"I don't remember Xaviar mentioning explosives either," Theo said.

Itio grinned. "Shall we continue?"

Theo looked at him suspiciously. "Alright." They headed on down into the bowels of the villa.

The room was cavernous, almost the same size as the villa above. A forest of tall wooden poles bristled out in front of Xaviar, a hundred of them or more. Well over half were occupied, with a motionless figures lashed upright to them. Each of the unfortunates was staked. His head swam.

"Free them," he growled.

Calvin and Ramona darted forward, their faces bleak. Ramona was carrying a large knife. Inyanga held back, her eyes darting everywhere. It made Xaviar pause. When the witch was cautious, there was a good reason for it.

"There is something foul here," she declared.

Xaviar growled. "All the more reason to hurry."

Ramona was the first to cut a victim free, a young woman with long ash-blond hair wearing a punkish outfit. She wrenched the stake out, and threw it across the room as if it were venomous. The girl shuddered. "Y'alright," Ramona said gently, holding her upright. "I'm Ramona."

The girl launched herself at Ramona furiously, a blur of teeth and fists. A couple of blows landed hard, and Ramona staggered back amazed, barely able to fend the woman off. Calvin looked over, shocked. The man he'd just released smiled, grabbed him by the throat, and lifted him smoothly off the ground.

Xaviar cursed and darted forward, even as Inyanga fell back muttering formulae or curses or something. Suddenly a woman was standing calmly right in front of him, a beautiful vision with alabaster skin and a silk dress the color of blood. She lashed out lazily, and Xavier went flying backwards to the room's entrance. As he scrambled to his feet, the woman advanced toward him slowly, utterly composed. He looked past her to where Inyanga was helping Ramona, then fell back a step. He had to draw this creature away to give the others a chance. He took another step back, and the woman glided smoothly after him, smiling gently.

It was all he could do not to bolt running.

Chapter Thirteen

Rear Guard

The area beneath the villa made Theo think of some kind of government facility. It seemed to consist of stretches of tiled corridor, seemingly blood-red in the dim emergency lighting. Many of the corridors had large metallic pipes running along the ceiling, some sort of ducting or air conditioning. There weren't many doors, but those that they did find were solid steel, without handles or keyholes, and wouldn't budge.

They were walking down a short stretch of corridor when Itio suddenly stopped dead in his tracks. Theo looked at him curiously, and was about to ask him if everything was alright when he blinked, looked round at the others, and bowed. "Forgive me. I must take my leave for a short while. I will return as soon as I can."

He turned around, started walking back the way they had come, and vanished into thin air.

Kristine looked at Theo. He just shrugged.

Henri flicked his current cigarette butt in the direction that Itio had departed in. "Fuck it. Maybe there are important things for him to do for us. So. It is just the three of us now. You are not going to run away as well, I hope."

"I'm with you," Theo said.

"Good. I am not scared, but I do not like to be played for a peasant either. Come, my friends." He fished out another cigarette from the pack tucked inside his holster, lighting it with a small electric lighter. "Let us find some ass to chew."

They had only taken a few steps more when there was a loud click that seemed to echo through the entire area, reverberating strangely through the corridors.

Henri paused for a moment, looking oddly thoughtful. "Did you hear the way that fucker echoed? It is my thought that it came from many places." He set off at a brisk pace. "Perhaps your little friend has done us a favor."

Theo exchanged a blank look with Kristine. Henri led them swiftly to the end of the corridor, where a door stood at the other side of a cross passage. He went straight to it, and pushed. It swung open easily. He turned round and grinned at them. "Locks."

They went in cautiously. Inside, they found some sort of maintenance room. A whole nest of metal pipes thrashed their way across the ceiling, leading to several different large pieces of machinery. Henri was immediately fascinated, and wandered over to one particular steel tank that looked like some sort of boiler.

"Let me guess," Theo said. "We can cut off their hot water from here, right?"

"We could indeed," Henri admitted. "But look, do you see this tap here?" He gestured at a small red valve, then dropped his reeking cigarette and ground it out carefully. "A quick wrench, so..." He took hold of it, and rather than turning the handle, he pulled the whole thing down sharply. There was a cracking noise, and the valve shifted in its socket. A hissing noise started. "There. Now here, in this pipe above..." He reached up, and jabbed his thumb through the steel ducting of a junction. "Good. Now we have gas going into the air, and air going into the gas. So." He clenched his hands together, then suddenly ripped them apart. "*Boom!*" Theo started a little at his sudden shout, clutching his shotgun to keep it in place. "Maybe. It is worth a try, yes?"

Theo grinned. "You're a resourceful man, Henri."

"Do not tell me, friend Theo. Tell the incredible Kristine beside you." Henri winked at her.

Kristine shook her head, amused. "I'll bear it in mind, Monsieur Lavenant."

They continued exploring cautiously. For the most part, the rooms seemed to be functional—either for the maintenance of the villa, or storage space. One room looked as if it might be a temporary dorm, with several small packs that could have been bedrolls were laid along the walls. Another was a small dressing room of some sort, and held long robes and gowns in several different colors.

As they were coming out of the chamber, Theo caught a hint of sulfur on the air. It was more powerful off to the left. He turned to the other two. "Do you smell that?"

Henri laughed. "With these cigarettes, I smell almost nothing my friend. A cat's asshole is as fresh as a rose for me."

"That explains a lot," Kristine murmured.

"It's stronger this way," Theo said. "Come on."

He led them down a corridor, through a small room that looked like some sort of telephone exchange, and across another junction. The stench of sulfur was getting steadily more powerful.

The corridor opened out into a broad, marble-paved area. A thick carpet ran in a wide strip up to a large pair of ornate doors that looked as if they were bleeding in the sickly red light.

Henri grunted in satisfaction. "Now I think we are getting somewhere, eh?"

Theo nodded. The stench was emanating from behind the doors. "Let's see what smells so bad."

He walked up to the doors, got his shotgun ready, and pulled on the ornate handles. They swung open easily, and for a wild moment he wished they'd stayed locked.

The room inside had an earthen floor, and was lined with cases and shelves on all the walls. A large circle of sigils was drawn onto the ground, rendered in what looked like paint or chalk. Flaming braziers stood evenly spaced around the circle, casting a flickering light. There was a fire in the center of the circle too, and a very dead-looking naked woman lay beside it, an ornate dagger hilt protruding bloodily from her chest. A tall, dark-haired man in a jet-black robe was standing outside the circle, looking round at Theo and the others, his face impassive. The stink of sulfur was overpowering.

"Bell. I've been expecting you." The man's voice was ice-cold, and resonated with power. There was something strange about his intonation, too. A small shiver ran down Theo's spine.

Rather than waste time answering, Theo raised his shotgun smoothly and fired. He barely had an instant to see a flicker of disgust cross the strangely smooth face, and then the man was standing immediately in front of Theo. He reached out and plucked the gun from Theo's hands, letting it fall, then he grabbed Theo's shoulders in a savage lock, fingers digging into the bone painfully, and rolled backwards.

Theo felt a wave of nausea at the man's touch, and then he was flung into the smoky room. He crashed into one of the braziers, which went flying, scattering burning coals in an arc across the room. The metal was scalding, and for a moment, all Theo could think of was backing away from the hungry flames. Then the man was beside him again, looking irritated. He hauled Theo up off the ground easily, pushing him back against a bookcase.

Back across the room, at the door, Kristine and Henri were standing as if in a daze. Then they suddenly gathered themselves, and started approaching carefully.

The man shook his head wearily "Is this what we have we been reduced to? Thugs? You disgrace the legacy of Troile."

Don Cerro and Theo had spent altogether too much time going over the legendary history of Clan Brujah when Theo was younger. The age-old murder of the clan's founder by his childe Troile—and the supposed curse of rage that resulted—was, they'd agreed, almost certainly just one more piece of bullshit used to keep their kinsmen in line. Theo wouldn't take it from a stuck-up prince, and he certainly won't take it from this piece of shit sorcerer.

Theo gathered his strength while the man was talking, and as the others approached, he drove his fist into the man's side. His muscles writhed as blood flooded into them, filling him with fresh strength.

"Fuck the legacy of Troile," Theo said from between gritted teeth. "I'm not the one putting Kindred and kine in chains, asshole!" He smashed another blow into the sorcerer's face.

The man took a half-step back, looking slightly put out. "Such ignorant bravado. I'll enjoy seeing your horror when I feed you and yours to the elders, Bell." Then he reached out and ground Theo's shoulder into the shelving. The bone cracked like eggshell, and Theo screamed as agony washed over him. His arm dangled uselessly.

Kristine darted forward suddenly, so fast that she looked like a dim streak. The man dropped Theo casually, sending a fresh jolt of pain through his ruined shoulder, and idly swayed aside, somehow avoiding her dizzy flurry of slashes. Then he took a step back onto one of Theo's ankles and ground his heel into the joint. Fresh agony blazed through Bell's body. He howled again, unable to stop the sound, and forced himself to concentrate on pushing the blood to his shoulder and ankle. The pain swelled in both joints, seeming to bubble upwards.

A fountain of darkness gushed up from the bookcase and crashed down onto the man. He staggered, suddenly encumbered by long ropes of twisting, writhing blackness. Kristine made the most of the moment and moved in, cutting savagely into the man's torso. He groaned in pain, and tried to move, but he was held back by the shadows constricting and crushing at him. Kristine slashed at him again, cutting along one arm. The fire in Theo's joints gradually receded as the blood inside him hauled his bones back into alignment, giving up its vitality to reconstitute the shoulder and ankle.

The man turned to face Henri with a baleful stare. Flame seemed to burn deep inside his eyes and he spoke a long string of syllables in a forgotten tongue. Though Theo couldn't understand a word of it, the man's voice was damnation itself, hell's gates clanging shut. Henri screamed once, a piercing sound that trailed off into a whimper, and then he collapsed. The shadows imprisoning the man vanished. He immediately ducked under a blow from Kristine and struck her savagely in the chest, smashing her across the room and into the circle of sigils. Theo clearly heard bones cracking.

"Pathetic," the man murmured. "Your lackeys aren't even worth saving for the great feast to come." He bent over Theo's prone body, and held a hand out. Fire immediately burst out along it, rippling in sickly sheets along each finger. He could feel the heat from where he lay, could imagine the hot, hungry tongues licking at his flesh. The flame filled his mind, and he tried to scrabble back into the cold earth to escape it. It took him a moment to realize that he was the source of the pathetic whimpering he heard.

"That's it," the sorcerer said. "Beg and plead like the slave you are, Bell. You see it now, don't you? That your pathetic ideas of honor and freedom are just so much self-delusion?" He brought his flaming hand closer to Theo. "The Final Nights are here, Bell, and the only question is who will feed on whom."

"Theo!" He looked up to see Kris half-raise herself from the corpse she'd slammed into and throw something along the ground toward him. The man turned round, irritated, and flicked his hand at her. The fistful of balefire shot from him. She tried to duck, but it struck her right between the shoulder blades, and immediately ignited her clothes and hair. She screamed, a mindless noise full of terror, and started rolling around on the floor weakly, trying to quench the flame.

Theo reached out, and grabbed the object she'd thrown. It was the dagger he had seen buried in the girl's chest. It felt truly vile to the touch, as if it were somehow made of slime and hatred. Still, it was better than nothing. As the man turned back round to face him, Theo lunged out with the dagger, burying it deep in the man's gut. For a dazed instant, Theo was sure he could hear a dark, distant voice emit a soft moan of pleasure.

The reaction was shocking. The man screamed, in horror rather than pain, and staggered back a step. Incredibly the stench of sulfur bloomed still further, until it was as if the whole world was consumed by it. Then suddenly the man was melting, the flesh bubbling on his bones. He sank to his knees, already skeletal, then continued collapsing, folding in on himself until he was nothing but a small heap of stinking bones and a gleaming white skull. A loud, satisfied chuckle rang out of thin air—an evil, gurgling noise full of malice and unholy glee. Then the skeleton was crumbling to ashes, all the fires went out, and the stink of sulfur vanished.

Theo blinked several times. His shoulder and ankle still hurt, but he tried standing up, and found he could manage it. He went over to Kristine first. She was still rolling around, panicked, although the flame was long since gone. He leant over painfully and shook her. "Kris. Kris, can you hear me. Kris, it's Theo."

"Theo?" She stopped flailing around. Her voice was weak, but lucid.

"It's okay," he said. "Can you stand?"

She nodded, and rose slowly, looking like an old woman. "I fucking ache, though. I think that fucker broke all my ribs. What happened?"

Theo thought about telling her what he had just seen, and decided it would just make him sound like Itio. "He's finished. It was your dagger that did it. Thanks."

She smiled, leaning on him for a little support. "A pleasure."

Henri was not in as good a state. "I can hardly move a muscle," he said weakly. "That shit-fucker. I am as weak as a puppy. It will not heal."

Theo grimaced sympathetically. "Are you going to be able to walk?"

"I think so, in a minute. Just."

"Get out of here, then. Get clear if you can. We'll go on."

"My apologies, Bell."

Instead of answering, Theo reached an arm down. Henri took it, and Theo pulled him to his feet. He stood there swaying for a long moment, bracing himself against a wall, before he could find the strength to talk further.

"Good luck. I will see you later, if the devil decides not to piss upon us further."

"You too, Henri." Staggering painfully, Theo and Kristine made their way out of the room. The marble-lined corridor continued to either side of the ritual chamber, and rather than go back, they followed it around the room, which turned out to stand entirely separate from the rest of the villa. The corridor continued on at the back of the room, leading away. After a short distance, it opened out into a large, luxurious hallway with three separate corridors leading off it, and a sweeping flight of stairs at the far end. The floor was still marbled, and accented with lush carpeting. A faint scuffing noise from the staircase warned Theo that someone was approaching. He and Kristine sprinted quietly over to a corridor leading off the hallway and pressed up against the wall nearest the stairs, so as to keep out of sight as much as possible. He'd lost his shotgun in the fight with the sorcerer, so he had to settle with drawing his cruelly ridged hunting knife. Kristine had retrieved her sword, and was also standing ready.

Another tiny hint of a footstep warned Theo that the newcomer was just about to draw level. He leaped out with a savage bellow and lashed out with his knife, hoping he was roughly on target.

Talley was in front of him, momentarily frozen in surprise. Theo desperately tried to rein the blow in, and the blade sliced a thin line down Talley's forehead, rather than sinking through the top of his skull.

Theo leaped back as Talley did the same, looking startled. Theo immediately held his hands up wide. "Shit. Sorry Talley. I didn't realize…"

Talley mournfully wiped off a bead of blood that was trickling down his nose. "No matter, Archon. I should have been more cautious." He looked up the corridor, and saw just Kristine. His face fell further. "What news?"

"We have destroyed one, an infernalist. It looked like he was in the middle of a ritual—human sacrifices, sulfur, the works. He did something to Henri, drained him of all his strength, but I think he'll survive. He's making his way out. Itio is off on some mission somewhere. I feel like shit, but I'm still standing. How about you?"

"We came upon a knot of guards with assault rifles in the villa, in a kitchen area. I was separated from Lin and Vincent. I hope they are well. I have been upstairs, but there is no sign of anyone important there, so I decided to come down here. It sounds like chaos out on the grounds. I do not know how Xaviar's men are fairing, and I have seen nothing of his rescue party either."

"Me neither," Theo said. "All we've found up to now— apart from that fucking devil-worshipper—have been store rooms and shit like that. If they've got all these damn prisoners of Xaviar's, they have to be around somewhere."

A hoarse scream echoed from one of the tunnels across the hallway. It was full of agony, desperation and hopeless rage. The three of them shared a look, and then sprinted as best they could in the direction it had come from. They entered the new corridor, still marble-lined with carpeting, and another scream rang out, more terrible than the last.

They ran round the corner, and slid to a stop. An opulent room was in front of them, elegantly furnished with what looked like regency-period antiques. It appeared to be a combination of stateroom and office. There was a door open on the other side of the room, leading out onto another luxuriously appointed corridor. Xaviar was slumped in the far doorway, drenched in blood, his skin a dreadful gray color. A large patch of his scalp had been ripped away to dangle loosely from his head, exposing bloody bone. His legs were clearly shattered—he could barely sit upright—and it took Theo a moment to notice that all ten of his fingers had been torn from their sockets.

A woman was standing over him, dressed in a stunning red dress. Her face was painfully beautiful, a perfect and terrible symmetry. Her eyes blazed. She was supporting Xaviar with one hand, and further tearing open his scalp with the other. She noticed Theo and the others across the room, and smiled. Then she reached round under Xaviar's chin and lifted his head up so he could see them. His eyes were utterly hopeless, his expression begging for forgiveness. She slowly raised her other hand, perfect ruby nails glittering in the half-light, and sank it slowly through Xaviar's shoulder and on down into his chest. He screamed again, the despair wrenched from the pit of his soul.

The woman jerked her arm, and pulled her hand out clutching a withered black ball. Xaviar slumped. She bit into it, smiling, and blood gushed down her chin. Then Xaviar was folding in on himself, crumbling to dust, and the heart in her hand was just ashes.

Theo groaned, filled with disgust and loathing. He called to the blood inside him, forcing it to concentrate in his muscles. Force washed over him in a wave of pounding, his whole body seeming to stretch and writhe as the blood lent him fresh strength and resilience. The woman watched him for several seconds, amusement playing over her face. She lounged against the doorframe indolently, and smiled. Then somehow she was halfway across the room, sitting in one of the ornate chairs. There was a whisper, and then she was in front of them, her face a bare inch from Theo's.

She spun on her heel and punched Kristine smoothly in the nose. There was a vile crack and Kris flew back, her face a mask of blood. It looked as if her cheekbones had sunk in upon themselves.

The blood whirled within Theo, boiling up inside him in a ferocious rage. It exploded into a maelstrom of energy, hammering into him so strongly that for a moment he felt sure his skin would split. The world stuttered. Kristine, flying across the corridor, seemed to suddenly be caught in molasses, the drops of blood spattering glacially from her face. Talley's expression of surprise and distaste froze, and his step backward was so slow it might not have been happening at all.

Theo seized the opportunity and slashed viciously with his knife, dropping low as he did so. The blade ripped through the cloth and the skin beneath. He cut again and again, hacking the woman's dress to ribbons, slicing through the flesh and bone beneath as if it were water. Power blazed through him, dizzying. He cut across and deep with one final blow, burying the knife blade in her gut in a savage hack that would have sliced most people into two chunks. He dropped low to put his weight behind the cut.

A hammer pounded into his forehead, cracking his skull and crushing him to the floor. White fire blazed between his eyes. His weakened ankle snapped beneath him as his leg was forced down awkwardly by the weight of the blow. He looked up, and saw that the woman had slapped him down contemptuously with her open palm. The rag that her dress had been reduced to clearly showed her abdomen—smoothly untouched, as if his blows had never happened.

Theo felt the meager blood inside him fighting its way to his ankle and forehead, giving up the last of its vitality to force his bones back into shape. Fresh agony blazed as his joints ground together, and he screamed, desperate to allow the pain some way out of his system. A pool of shadow was spinning around Talley, welling out of him as if it were oozing from the pores of his skin.

The woman was suddenly across the hall, beside Kristine. Even as slow as the world seemed to Theo at his heightened speed, there was nothing to suggest that the woman had moved—she was just somewhere different. Kristine groaned and tried to lash out, but the woman plucked the sword out of her hand, raised it, and smoothly drove it down through the top of Kristine's head, burying it up to the hilt. Kris stiffened, and then she was sloughing out, nothing more than a cloud of ash. Theo closed his eyes for a moment, then tried to stand. His head swam with pain, and his stomach burned with empty hunger. He sank back down to his knees.

The shadows around Talley had coalesced into a nightmare form, an ever-shifting figure of claws and teeth that flew across the hall toward the woman. She eyed it coolly, hefted Kristine's sword, and threw it like a spear—not at the approaching beast, but at Talley. The man flinched back, but it was not enough to stop the blade from sinking into his neck. Blood gushed from his throat and he collapsed, a puppet with severed strings. The shadow-beast vanished in a wisp of foul smoke.

Theo tried to summon the strength to move, and managed to struggle to his feet. It was useless, though. He was so hungry he could hardly think—Talley's blood spilling across the floor was like a burning summons. He could walk, but he had no strength left for much else. He forced himself erect, determined to go down fighting. The woman watched him struggling with a calm smile on her face, then strode toward him.

Then, she stopped, her head cocked, clearly hearing something. She looked around, and then shot a glance over her shoulder, looking irritated. There didn't appear to be anything there. She looked around again, slightly confused. Then something else seemed to catch her attention. She whipped round again, her face suddenly contorted with fury. There was nothing there, and she screamed, a howl of rage and frustration. Theo stared at her, perplexed, as she seemed to spot something in the corner of her vision, and span round to hammer her fists into the wall a few yards from him. The stones cracked, and she shrieked again. Her forearms sank through the marble-work and into the wall behind it.

Theo threw himself toward her. Rather than try to launch a blow, he sank his fangs deep into the back of her neck. The woman screamed in rage and shock as a firestorm of blood blasted into him, filling him with wild surges of power. He clamped his teeth together, cutting through the top of her spine. He sucked at her blood greedily, feeling it hammer through his body, blasting his aches and discomforts away. She flailed her head, but her body was paralyzed, and would not obey her. Theo could feel the bone regrowing beneath his teeth, and kept chewing it away as he drank.

She screamed again, more quietly this time, a note of regret in her voice. The blood ran dry, and her head dropped. A sudden memory flashed through him, the blast of power as he had consumed Carnell, a wave of ecstasy like nothing he had ever known... She was his to absorb, to add her power to his.

The desire to drink her soul was overpowering, and after her another and another until he had drained them all—

He shuddered, and released his hold, and she collapsed to the ground, exploding in a mess of ash.

He stood up, momentarily regretful at the wasted opportunity, simultaneously horrified with himself for his regret. He was utterly unsurprised to see Itio helping Talley to his feet. The templar looked fit to drop, but Itio was his usual unruffled self.

Chapter Fourteen

Last Words

Theo, Itio and Talley made it out of the villa to find a huge group of bemused Kindred standing around. Theo shook his head, slightly awed at the size of the gathering. Talley, beside him, looked thoughtful.

"Do you believe now, Bell? That these were agents of the ancients, I mean."

"These fuckers dealt with devils and ran a slave-service across continents, worming themselves through both our sects, Talley. I'm sure they thought they were Caine and Lilith sitting down for tea in the Land of Nod."

Talley allowed himself a smirk. "Perhaps, but some very aged Cainites apparently thought their operation worth protecting. If not to feed the rising elders, why would they want a global network of captive blood?"

Theo didn't say anything for a full minute. "That's a good question, Templar, but I'm not sure as how it changes much. Either these fuckers were out for their own jollies or they were making plans for the End Times. Either way, we took 'em down for good."

"And if the ancients are rising? If these are the Final Nights?"

"Then I'll go down fighting the fuckers, and do right by my own," Theo said. "Same as it ever was."

Talley smiled fully now. "I'd expect no less, Archon. I think my contribution here is done. I have house-cleaning to do elsewhere."

Theo smiled at him. "Yeah. Thanks for everything. It's been a pleasure."

"That it has. I may see you again, Theo Bell. I pray that it will be on our own terms. As free Cainites."

"Me too," Theo said sincerely.

"I have to find Lavenant, and see if Lin and Vincent made it out. Until next time."

"Goodbye, Talley." The man headed off away from the main body of confused vampires. Theo waved to him, then spotted Mark talking to a group, and made for him. Mark saw him coming, and came forward to meet him.

"Theo, what happened?"

"Xaviar is gone, along with the controllers of this sick little scheme." Suddenly he felt exhausted, despite the exhilaration of the blood singing inside him. "Are these your people?"

Mark nodded, clearly upset. "Yeah. More than just ours, too. We were expecting that, though."

"How did it go?"

"Better than I feared at one point, actually. We got a bunch of unexpected reinforcements. Ramona tells me that the clan lost nine of the assault team in total—eleven if you count Xaviar and Calvin."

Theo sighed. "Can you take care of this lot from here?"

"Yeah, don't worry. It was part of the plan."

"Oh. Good."

"Look, get out of here Theo. If there's anything I need your help with, I have your number."

"Thanks, Mark. Good luck." Theo collected Itio, and the pair of them started walking back to where Henri had left the station wagon.

"Thanks for distracting that bitch, Itio."

Itio grinned. "A pleasure."

A strange suspicion hit Theo, and he decided to run with it. "Did you find what you were looking for?"

"Yes, Theophilus. This time I did. I can finally go to work. Your help has been invaluable, as always."

"How long..." began Theo, suspiciously.

Itio chuckled, and shook his head. "Come, Theophilus. You know better than to ask questions when you are not prepared to hear the answers. We have the twins to collect still."

Theo grinned, and followed Itio up the drive.

Back at the hotel, Delphine saw the pair of them walk into the room, peered round past them, and her face fell. "Is...?"

Theo nodded. "I'm sorry."

A bloody tear trickled down her cheek. Beside her, Nathalie turned her head away, not quite hiding a nasty grin.

Delphine sniffed. "What now?"

Itio bowed to her flamboyantly. "Now, beautiful lady, I follow up on the promise I made you some weeks ago, and take you to an immensely lavish party in your honor. I have the last piece I need right here." He held a bronze coin up, before putting back in his pocket with a flourish. "I need your help in playing a little prank upon some Austrian friends of mine. A Passion Play, in the grand biblical tradition. If you perform your parts well, and we convince them that there is just the one miss Decourt, I can say in all honesty that you will absolutely blow them away."

"It sounds like fun," Nathalie said. "Del?"

"Yeah," Delphine said, still sounding sad. "Sure. A party would be good right now."

"Do you wish to come along, Theophilus?"

Theo shook his head. "I'll come with you as far as the states, but I've got to get back to work. Which reminds me. I have to phone Paschek."

He moved aside a bit, leaving Itio and the girls talking with increasing animation. He fished out his telephone, and dialed his boss. The call was answered immediately.

"Paschek."

"Justicar Paschek, this is Theo Bell. I wanted to inform you that the principles behind the slave operation have been eliminated."

"Excellent. Please accept my congratulations on your new promotion, Praetor Bell. I hope you are ready to return to your duties?"

"Yes, sir," Theo said, his head whirling. Praetor! That put him above all standard archons, in theory at least.

"Good. I will arrange transport to Europe where you will receive further instructions and details regarding your target."

"Europe? Who's the target?"

"A troublesome Gangrel named Beckett."

About the Author

Well, what can I tell you? I've been writing professionally for over ten years now, and I'm approaching eighty published works, including twenty or more pieces of fiction. A lot of the early stuff was written under one or other of my rather odd pen names. In addition to the **Clan Brujah Trilogy**—which has been one heck of a lot of fun—I've also been lucky enough to get to write **Hunter: Apocrypha** and **Tribe Novel: Glass Walkers**, along with bits and pieces for the **Orpheus**, **Hunter: The Reckoning** and **EverQuest RPG** game lines.

In addition to my work for White Wolf, I've done stories and reference material for several other games systems—*SLA Industries*, *Feng Shui*, *Unknown Armies*, *Magic: The Gathering*—and I've also done a whole range of non-fiction work, which is a lot less fun. The non-fic ranges from computer reference works to books on organized crime, jokes, good sex, magick, health and fantasy. I frequently manage to disturb my friends, one way or another. Titles like "The Complete Guide to a Good Abdomen in Just Five Minutes A Day," under the name of Richard Steel, help make sure I never, ever get in danger of taking myself seriously. I feel a bit like Troy McClure sometimes.

I currently live in Prague, which is one of the most beautiful and fascinating cities I've had the pleasure to stumble into. I recommend the place without reservation. If you ever find yourself in the area and fancy a pint, drop me an email.

Should you fancy digging a little deeper, I've got a website up for the trilogy at http://www.benzo8.org/brujah—yeah, it's moved from earlier in the year. It's got some notes, bios, useful writers' resources and other bits and pieces up on it. I'd love to know what you thought, good or bad, so please do drop by and say hi. I reply to all email sooner or later—and that's a promise.

I owe thanks to a load of people, but none more so than the excellent Philippe Boulle, the Managing Editor of White Wolf Fiction. I've tried his patience in just about every conceivable way during this trilogy, and I can honestly say that he rocks. These books wouldn't have been anything like as good without him. I'm also especially grateful to Liz Sharma for her unswerving love and support, to my brother and father for everything, to John and Gail, and also (in random order) to Jared, Dave & Angus, James Wallis, Trev & Angie, Jorge, Joe & Joe, Sophie, Tom & Ed, Lucie, Billy, Gez & Rad, Ali, Alexandra, James & Andy, Paddy, Jon, Said, David S and everyone else who's done so much to keep me sane and fed over the last year or so. Special hellos go to Dan Blakeman, John Dodd, Katie Feidt, Peter Lennox, Rodrigo Gonzales, Robert Sachs, Adam Schaller, Bill Sorensen, James Terbrack, Abi Tinkler, Sue Wilson, 'Zak', and Phillip Zarick.

Curious about other Crossroad Press books? Stop by our website: http://crossroadpress.com
We offer quality writing
in digital, audio, and print formats.

Subscribe to our newsletter on the website homepage and receive a free eBook.